DANGEROUSLY
HOT

A *HOSTILE OPERATIONS TEAM* Novel

USA TODAY BESTSELLING AUTHOR
LYNN RAYE
HARRIS

Copyright ©2014 by Lynn Raye Harris
Cover Design Copyright © 2014 Croco Designs
Interior Design by JT Formatting

www.**lynnrayeharris**.com

Printed in the United States of America

First Edition: April 2014
Library of Congress Cataloging-in-Publication Data

Harris, Lynn Raye
    Dangerously Hot / Lynn Raye Harris. – 1st ed

    ISBN-13: 978-0-9894512-5-3

    1. Dangerously Hot—Fiction. 2. Fiction—Romance
    3. Fiction—Contemporary Romance

OTHER BOOKS IN
THE *HOSTILE OPERATIONS TEAM* SERIES

ONE

"FUCK ME," KEVIN "BIG MAC" MacDonald said on an exhaled breath.

He was the only one who'd spoken, but the expression on the other guys' faces echoed the sentiment. Colonel John Mendez stood before the team, hands on hips, face grave. Mendez was a throwback Army officer, the kind who ate nails for breakfast and took no prisoners. Not one man in this room had ever dared to disobey an order from him.

Well, maybe one. Matt "Richie Rich" Girard had done it, but he'd nearly lost his career in the process.

"That's right, son," Mendez said, giving Kev a hard look. "Al Ahmad ain't dead."

Matt swore. Kev could only clench his fists in his lap and pray he didn't break something. HOT went after terrorists. It's what they did, what they lived for. Al Ahmad was a terrorist. A low-life fucking evil bastard who liked

1

to hurt people.

He was supposed to be dead. It hadn't been more than a few months ago now that they'd gone after his second in command, Jassar ibn-Rashad. That mission had gotten fucked up six ways to Sunday, and they'd lost two good men in the process.

Kev swallowed. God, he still missed Marco. Marco San Ramos had been his best friend, the guy he'd gone through boot camp with. Kev wouldn't have made it this far if not for Marco.

Thoughts of Marco inevitably led to Marco's wife. Lucky. Kev squeezed his fists tighter, trying to keep himself from going down that mental road.

It was no good. He always thought of Lucky. Always felt the guilt and regret roiling away in his gut. Goddamn he was an asshole, thinking of his best friend's wife.

Widow.

Yeah. Wife, widow, what the fuck. He wasn't allowed to think of Lucky, not like that, but he hadn't ever been able to turn it off. Not since the first moment he'd seen her, before she ever belonged to Marco.

"If I don't get out of here, take care of Lucky. Promise."

"You're getting out. We're both fucking getting out."

"Promise anyway."

"Yeah, fine. I promise."

Some promise. Lucky hadn't spoken to him since they'd shipped Marco back in a casket. She'd left the military, taken Marco's military life insurance, and gone to Hawaii.

"We're going after him," Mendez was saying. "This time, we're getting that bastard."

2

"Yes, sir," Matt said for them all. "What's the plan, sir?"

Mendez eyed them very deliberately. He was a wily bastard, but Kev knew there wasn't a better soldier in the whole damn Army. "We need someone who can ID him, someone who can get close enough to do so."

Kev's blood ran cold. He told himself there was no reason for it, no way Mendez would want to bring in an outsider. But Al Ahmad was a tricky bastard. Unlike other terrorists, he didn't like to make videos and broadcast them to the world. Because of that, few knew what he looked like. There were sketches, always sketches, based on intel they'd collected here and there.

And then there was Lucky's debrief. The only person who'd gotten close enough to see his face and survived.

Mendez's eyes were cool and penetrating as he swung his gaze toward Kev. "We need someone who got close once before. We need Lucky San Ramos."

Kev felt like he'd been sucker punched. Matt looked at him, and he knew the horror was written on his face. Goddamn.

The two new guys—Sam "Knight Rider" McKnight and Garrett "Iceman" Spencer—looked confused. The others glanced at each other, faces grim. Kev's gut twisted into knots. He'd been the one who'd gotten Lucky out the last time. The one who knew what that evil bastard had done to her.

He'd lost Lucky, thanks to Al Ahmad. Given her to Marco and walked away. Because he knew he couldn't be what she needed then, and Marco could. Because Marco loved her, and Kev owed Marco too much to let one woman stand between them.

3

Coward.

Kev sat immoveable, like a block of granite. How was it cowardly to let a woman go because you couldn't be what she deserved? Because all you wanted was to have sex with her until it burned you up and you could move on to someone else?

Because a man like him didn't do forever and happy ever after and all that bullshit. It didn't exist. Not in his world. He might have been tempted to think so once, when he was much younger and far more naïve, but he'd learned in the hell of his childhood that love—or what passed for love in his family—was often a brutal thing.

"She's out now," Kev said, focusing on the problem at hand instead of the nightmare of his past. "And it's been two years since she's seen Al Ahmad. How do we know he hasn't changed his face? Hell, how do we even know it *is* Al Ahmad? What if someone in his organization is trying to make us think he's alive? Ibn-Rashad might be yanking our chain."

Mendez's expression didn't change. Which, come to think of it, wasn't necessarily a good sign. "Good questions, Sergeant. But trust me, if we didn't have confirmation at the highest levels, we wouldn't be here now. Do you think HOT goes out in the field for nothing, son? You've been here long enough to know better."

He leaned forward then, two broad hands on the desk in front of him. "We need Lucky, and we're getting her back. One way or the other. We can do it nice, or we can do it hard. But since my mama always said you get more flies with honey, I'm sending you after her, son. Go to Hawaii and convince her to come back. Or I'll make her come back."

Acid roiled in Kev's stomach. He wanted to stand up and wrap his fists in the man's perfectly starched collar. But he wouldn't do it. Not if he wanted to keep his ass *and* his job. Not if he wanted to remain a part of HOT—which he did because he damn sure couldn't imagine a different life than this one.

No, there was only one thing to say. Only one thing he *could* say, even though it about killed him to do it. He stood and snapped a salute.

"Sir, *yes, sir.*"

December
North Shore, Oahu
Hawaii

Lucky flipped the surfboard upright after she paddled to shore and stepped out onto the sand. It was a typically beautiful Hawaiian day—or it would have been if she hadn't just spotted the man standing cross-armed at the top of the shore break. For a second, she thought her eyes were playing tricks on her. There was no way that Kevin MacDonald was standing up there waiting for her.

But the mirage didn't fade, and her heart reacted with a crazy rhythm that made her head swim. Part of her wanted to turn around and race back out to sea. Part of her wanted to march up to him and plant a fist in his handsome face.

And part of her wanted to wrap her arms around him and hold him tight.

Lucky hardened her heart and lifted her head. She wasn't running, damn him. She thought he'd given up. The phone calls had ceased months ago, and even though it had made her ache deep down, she figured he'd finally gotten the message.

Looks like she'd been wrong.

She clutched the board tighter to her side and climbed the sharply sloping beach at Waimea Bay.

Kev stood impassive, arms crossed, chewing gum like he had no cares in the world, aviator sunglasses reflecting her wet form. Like he belonged here. Like he showed up every day and watched her paddle out to sea before turning and shooting the pipeline back to the beach.

Except he didn't look like he belonged at all. A white T-shirt stretched across his broad chest, tapering down to disappear into the waistband of a pair of faded, loose-fitting Levi's. His only real nod to beach culture was a pair of flip-flops, or *slippahs,* as the Hawaiians called them, and she knew it must have given him pause to don them. Kev was usually a cowboy- or combat-boot kind of guy.

Fresh anger flared to life inside her. But before she could speak, he said the one thing guaranteed to make her listen. Guaranteed to make her wish she were dead.

"Al Ahmad's back."

A cold finger of dread slid deep into her belly, tickled her spine, threatened to turn her knees to liquid. *Al Ahmad.*

He was supposed to be dead. She'd slept at night because he was dead. Because he could never come for her. Never force her to listen to that lovely, evil voice ever again.

6

"And what's that mean to me?" she asked. She didn't bother to ask how the bastard was still alive. If Kev was here, then he just was. It wasn't debatable.

But she wasn't about to let Kev know just how horrified that information made her or how much she wanted to sink into the ocean and never come out again.

"We need you, Lucky."

Her breath seized in her lungs. "No way in hell," she said hoarsely when she could talk again. "I'm not on active duty anymore."

As if that had anything to do with it. When she'd been active, she'd wanted to be a part of the Hostile Operations Team. She'd gotten her wish when she'd been assigned to them for interpreter duties. It wasn't the excitement of full-blown ops, but it was important.

She'd been so idealistic. Though women weren't allowed to go on missions, she'd wanted to be the first. She'd hoped she'd get the chance to train hard and save the world, but she'd learned just how unsuited she was for that task, thanks to Al Ahmad.

"We could reactivate you."

Lucky clutched the surfboard harder, the urge to gut him with it burning into her. He stood there so casually, threatening to upend her world as if it were nothing. Threatening to drag her back into that life when it had nearly destroyed her. "Mendez wouldn't dare."

"You know he would."

Lucky slicked back her wet hair with one hand, hoping it didn't shake, and bent to remove the ankle strap anchoring the surfboard to her leg. She didn't have to look at Kev to know he was following the movement of her leg as she thrust it to the side to reach the strap.

She could feel the burn of his gaze on her skin, just like she always had. And it made her sick to her stomach. Angry. How dare he make her feel *anything*.

Especially now.

She hardened her heart. She wouldn't do it. She couldn't do it. She owed them nothing. She'd done her time, and she'd gotten the hell out. She straightened and lifted her chin. "Get someone else. You've got any number of people who can interpret for you."

Those firm lips turned down in a frown. "It's more than translation. We need you on the inside."

Her heart thumped. "I'm not in that business any-more."

As if she ever had been. Her *stay* with Al Ahmad had not been planned. His people had grabbed her at a market in North Africa when she should have been out of their reach. They'd proven she wasn't. That none of them were.

Day after day, she'd thought her life was over. Day after day, he'd toyed with her. Poisoned her mind.

Broke her.

She faced Kev head-on, a current of defiance growing inside her with every second. No way in hell was she let-ting them shatter her carefully reconstructed life. It didn't matter that Al Ahmad had resurfaced, that she damn well wanted to nail the bastard to the wall with a rusty railroad spike.

If she were a different person, a braver person, she would take this chance. She'd get close enough to kill him herself. And then maybe she could forget how weak she was. How needy. How malleable she'd been in his hands. She'd fought him, but not hard enough.

Kev pulled the sunglasses from his face and tapped

them against a muscled forearm wrapped in ink. "This is too important. It's you we need. No one else."

Lucky had to remind herself to breathe when faced with the full effect of blue eyes and silky, dark hair that was much longer than Army regs allowed. But Kev was a Spec Ops soldier, and that made the rules different for him.

Women, as she knew from firsthand observation, couldn't help but fling themselves in the path of Kevin MacDonald. Which was precisely why she'd been determined not to do so when they'd first met a couple of years ago. There'd been something between them, some spark, but she'd never found out what it was. Because as quickly as it ignited, it was gone.

It still hurt, remembering the way he'd held her so close when he'd gotten her out of Al Ahmad's compound, the way he'd seemed so intent upon her. He'd kissed her. The one and only time he'd ever done so.

Even now, her lips tingled with the memory. Her body ached with heat.

But it had been nothing more than a beautiful lie. When she'd looked for him afterward, when she'd expected him to come to the hospital to see her, it had been Marco who came instead.

And now Marco was dead, and she had no right to feel anything but grief. Yet that didn't stop her belly from churning at the sight of Kevin MacDonald.

He watched her with an intensity that both unnerved and angered her. How dare he walk back into her life looking like something straight from a Hollywood movie set and calmly inform her that her world was about to be turned topsy-turvy?

Again.

She picked up the surfboard and started up the beach. "Go tell Mendez to reactivate me," she called over her shoulder. If they wanted her back, they'd have to force her. "If he could do it, he'd have done it already."

"Aw, sweetheart, don't be like that," Kev said in that Alabama drawl of his, and she stopped short, swung around as fury lashed into her.

"Don't you *dare* call me that!"

He held up both hands, backed away a step. "It's all right, I can take a hint. No sweet nothings." He dropped his hands to his sides, but not before sliding the sunglasses back into place over those beautiful eyes. "But you and I both know Mendez could reactivate you with a phone call. Don't make it happen, Lucky. Help us out, you're done. Get recalled to duty, and God knows what comes next when this is over."

Hell, yes, Mendez could do it. She knew that. But it would take slightly longer than one phone call.

"Tell him I'll think about it," she said, but she wouldn't do anything of the sort. Yes, she'd love to get Al Ahmad. But she'd like to live even more.

"He's dangerous. You know that better than most." He seemed to hesitate for a second. "Marco would want you to help us get him."

Lucky whipped the surfboard in an arc and let it go. Kev leaped backward as it crashed to the ground. He stumbled and fell against a coconut palm, the fronds shaking with the impact.

"Jesus Christ," he yelled. "What's the matter with you?"

She was shaking. "Don't you *ever* tell me what Marco

would want. Invoking his name won't get you anywhere with me."

Kev looked solemn. For the first time since he'd started talking, she felt like she was seeing the real him. The man who'd called her almost nightly for months, trying to make sure she was all right. That Marco's death hadn't killed her too.

"We all lost him, Lucky. We all miss him."

Tears boiled near the surface. Fury ate at her like battery acid. He had no idea. *No idea.*

Of course she missed Marco. And yet she'd been so wrong for him. She'd tried hard to love him the way she should, but loving anyone after what she'd been through with Al Ahmad hadn't been easy.

The guilt of her failures ate at her. She'd been doing a good job of forgetting out here in the sun and surf, of moving on and accepting her life, and Kev was wrecking it all.

"You let him die out there."

It wasn't what she'd meant to say, but she couldn't call the words back now that she'd released them. Kev looked as if she'd slapped him. She knew Marco's death wasn't his fault, but that hadn't stopped her from blaming him—blaming all of Marco's team—for what had happened.

She should apologize, but her throat seized up.

Kev's jaw tightened. "That's not fair, and you know it. Marco died doing the job. It's a risk we all take."

Yes, she knew it. And it was the thing that kept her awake at night sometimes, thinking about Marco, about Kev, wondering if he was still alive or if he'd met his end in some dank, lonely, war-torn country the way Marco had.

11

But she couldn't say any of that. They stood there staring at each other until Kev took something from his pocket. He held out a card.

"I'm at the Hale Koa. Call me when you've thought about this."

She still couldn't speak. How could she say all the things she needed to say? The things she'd bottled up for so long? How could she ever explain where it had all gone wrong?

He didn't put the card away. She wanted to leave him standing there, but her feet seemed stuck in the sand.

"Take it, Lucky."

She snatched the card from his grasp with a growl. Then she picked up the surfboard and trod up the beach, feeling his eyes on her back the whole way.

TWO

"SHE'S GONNA RUN," KEV SAID into his government-issued cell phone. He was sitting at a shrimp truck parked beside Kamehameha Highway, finishing off a plate of shrimp, macaroni salad, and white rice. He'd chosen this location because it was across the street from the road leading out of Lucky's neighborhood.

She lived in a small beach community on the North Shore. Her house was a tiny rental that sat upon tall blocks and had jalousie windows that opened to let the sea breeze in, and her car sat under the house, a beat-up blue Jeep with the top down. He'd been sitting here for the past hour, watching for that Jeep. It had not yet made an appearance.

But he knew it would. He knew it like he knew his own name.

"I won't argue with you," Matt said. "Besides Marco, you knew her better than anyone."

"Yeah," Kev replied, ignoring the sting of those words in his gut. He'd let her go, dammit. Let Marco have her. And now she hated him.

Of course she did.

"Just keep an eye out. Do what it takes to bring her in."

"Copy that."

They hung up again and Kev pushed the plate aside, his gaze focused on the street. He was still trying to process everything he felt at seeing Lucky again. He hadn't seen her in months now, not since he'd gone to her and Marco's house for a barbecue late one afternoon shortly before they'd deployed to the desert and the ill-fated mission to get ibn-Rashad. Kev had made it a point not to refuse invitations from Marco, though he'd wanted to refuse every one.

That last time, he hadn't gone alone. He'd taken some chick that he'd picked up in a bar earlier. She'd been half-drunk, half-dressed, and completely horny for him.

He'd paraded her in front of everyone like she'd been someone important in his life even though it made him vaguely disgusted with himself to do so.

But Lucky had seen through the act. She'd glared daggers at him half the night. Which, perversely, he'd found gratifying. As if she cared about him. As if she weren't married to Marco but was instead still just one of the gang, frowning at him and giving him a hard time over his choice of female companionship.

Which, God knows, he didn't have a great track record with. The trashier the female, the more flagrantly he flaunted her in front of his friends. Give him a gal with a serious penchant for short skirts and too much makeup, and he was all up in that business.

Even though it turned him off on some level. *Blood will tell,* his mama had always said. And he figured since he had the wrong kind of blood, he might as well embrace his heritage.

Except, God, he remembered holding Lucky close after he'd broken into Al Ahmad's compound. Remembered the sweetness of her lips, the beauty of her face—swollen with tears—and the hard surge of tenderness in his gut. He'd wanted her then. Wanted her more than he'd ever wanted anything in his life.

A frightening prospect for someone who knew what it was like to have everything ripped away in a moment. His life had changed irrevocably when he'd been sixteen, and he'd vowed not to need anyone ever again.

He'd done a good job of that until he'd met Lucky. She'd gotten under his skin somehow, and he hadn't liked the way it made him feel. So he'd walked away before he could fuck it up.

Kev sat up a little straighter as a blue Jeep pulled up to the main road. His heart thumped as he got a look at the woman in the driver's seat. Oh yeah, she was running all right. He could see the suitcases piled in the back seat. The trouble with an open-top vehicle was that it revealed all your secrets. Lucky wasn't making a grocery run.

Kev trotted over to his rental and unlocked it. A second later, he was behind the wheel and pulling into traffic. Surprising how much traffic there was on the North Shore. It wasn't as bad as Waikiki, but it was still damn congested. The sun shone down, and the ocean sparkled off to his right. Hawaii was frigging beautiful. He wanted to spend more time in the sun, but it looked like his stay was going to be of relatively short duration.

Traffic crawled toward Haleiwa, the town where he'd take the turn that led through the center of the island past the Dole Plantation and back over to the H2. Then it was down to Honolulu.

He couldn't see Lucky's Jeep, but he wasn't particularly worried about losing her. There was only one way off the island—one quick way—and he had no doubt she was headed for the airport. Sure, she could pay someone in a fishing boat to take her to a different island, but even then she'd have to fly back through Honolulu on her way out.

No, she was headed to the airport. She knew she needed to act quickly, and she probably hoped to catch him off guard. Probably figured he'd gone back to his hotel to await her call.

Traffic thinned out in Haleiwa as people went to other beaches or headed into the funky shops and restaurants in the beach community where more than one television show had been filmed.

Kev started up the long incline between pineapple fields that led to the center of the island. Three cars in front of him, Lucky's Jeep moved steadily along. When they reached the fork that went toward the H2 or down into another community, Lucky headed toward the H2. Soon they were rolling down the highway and heading east.

Kev stayed as close as he could manage without alerting her. When they reached the airport, she stopped in long-term parking and unloaded all her bags. Too many bags to mean she was coming back.

Kev parked the rental nearby and rubbed his fingers along the bridge of his nose. Goddamn, he hated this. Hated everything about it. But he had a job to do, and Lucky already despised him enough that one more thing shouldn't matter.

Lucky disliked abandoning her Jeep. She took another fond look at the beat-up vehicle and then pocketed the keys with a sigh. She'd find a cop inside and give the keys away, saying she'd found them. It was all she could think to do in the time she had.

Kev wouldn't wait long at the Hale Koa before he began to get suspicious, and she intended to be off the island by then. She turned away and started to arrange her luggage so she could at least get it as far as a trolley.

"Hey, great. You're all packed."

Her head snapped up to find Kev sauntering toward her as if this was the most normal circumstance in the world. Her stomach fell into her toes and blood pounded in her temples. Had she really thought she could lose him? Really?

"What the hell are you doing here?"

As if she didn't already know.

He thumbed the loops in his jeans, oh so casually, but his stare didn't waver in intensity. "I'm here to catch a flight, same as you."

"Great," she said, tossing her hair over her shoulder. "You can give me a hand with this luggage. Then we can say a tearful good-bye at the gate."

One corner of that delectable mouth turned up in a grin. "'Fraid not." He jerked a thumb in the direction he'd just come from. "Got a rental over there with my stuff. Also got two plane tickets to DC. First class."

Her belly did a swan dive into a pool of acid. "DC? Why?"

He came closer, and her heart kicked up a notch. Why did this man look so damn good in a white T-shirt and faded jeans? And why did she have to notice?

"We're based there now. HOT's moved up in the world. No more Army bullshit to deal with. Just missions now. And freedom."

"Freedom? How can you call what you do freedom? You're tied to the Army whether you think so or not."

His eyes sparkled in the light shafting down between the gaps in the structure. "We've gone deep black. We've got money, equipment—Jesus, things you can't imagine. It's different now."

She felt light-headed—and not all of it was from how close he stood. "It's not different. You still risk your life. You could still die out there, same as Marco."

The glitter in his eyes dialed down a notch, and fresh guilt assailed her.

"Yeah, I know. But we've still got it pretty damn good. And we do important work. You know we do."

The lump in her throat was elephantine. She closed her eyes, saw her husband's face—and then she didn't. All she could see was Kev. *Damn it.*

"I don't want to be a part of this," she said, forcing the words past the tightness. "I don't want to go back to that life."

He reached out as if to touch her, but his hands fell to his sides, and she knew he'd thought better of it. "I know. But we need you. Al Ahmad—" He broke off, looked over the top of her head as if he were staring at something only he could see. Then he made eye contact again, and her blood roared in her ears. "He's dangerous. You know that. And he has to be stopped. You're the only one who can positively ID him."

Her head swam. "He could have changed his face. He's vain, but not so vain he wouldn't make that sacrifice if it was needed."

Kev nodded. "He could have. But he can't change his voice."

She drew in a deep breath. That insidious voice still played in her ears sometimes late at night.

"I know this is a lot to ask of you. I know you hate us—hate me—but we need you. It's important."

She wanted to hang her head. And she wanted to step into his embrace and slide her arms around his waist the way she once had. That single, too-brief time when he'd held her after getting her out of Al Ahmad's compound. It had been everything she'd wanted—and everything she'd feared.

And it hadn't lasted nearly long enough. She'd thought he would be the one to come to the hospital when they put her in for observation. But he hadn't. Marco had.

"I don't hate you."

His eyes glittered. "That's good," he said after a long moment.

The note of caring in his voice was her undoing. "Why didn't you come to see me?"

She wanted to recall the words the instant she said them. It was weak, and she hadn't meant to show him any weakness.

He didn't ask what she meant, and she realized that he didn't have to. That he knew. His gaze dropped to her arm and her heart fell. He knew what was there beneath the long-sleeved cotton shirt she wore, the crisscross of Xs that rode up the inside of her arm to her elbow. They'd faded to silvery-pink lines now, but they would never go away.

"I couldn't bear to see what he did to you."

She hugged herself instinctively. The other arm looked exactly the same. And then there were the scars on her abdomen and back. She still felt such a mix of emotions over what Al Ahmad had done to her. Rage. Shame. Guilt.

"It's just skin," she said. "It heals."

But she felt ugly, damaged. And his rejection had only made those feelings worse.

"I know."

Anger surged inside her. She glared at him. "How can you ask me to go back, knowing what he did to me? How can you think I would want to?"

His handsome face creased. "I think you want him dead. I think you'd do anything to make it happen."

It was a direct hit and utterly true. Since earlier on the beach when she'd reacted from her gut, she'd been thinking about this mission. About Al Ahmad. About how much she wanted him dead and how, if she didn't help HOT get him, she'd have to live in fear of him coming after her.

Because he would, sooner or later.

"You're right," she said softly as the wave of her anger broke against the shore and receded.

"Then come to DC. Help us nail him."

Her heart thumped. Adrenaline surged through her veins, left her trembling and cold in spite of the bright, hot day. She wanted to rewind the clock, wanted to go back to that fateful day when she'd first been assigned to HOT and ask for another tour of duty instead. Anything to stop the boulder that tumbled down the hill toward her.

Except there was no way to avoid the boulder. Nothing to do but trust that HOT could get the job done this time. Because if they didn't, she didn't know what her life would become.

Lucky sagged beneath the weight of her decision. She had no choice. It was this, or run away and live in fear every day of her life. She'd taken Marco's name when they'd married, but that would not protect her forever. Al Ahmad would find her.

But she had other reasons to worry too. There was her mother, her stepfather and half sisters. What if Al Ahmad figured out who they were? He would kill them too, simply because she cared about them.

She couldn't let that happen.

Lucky swallowed the lump in her throat. "All right. I'll come."

THREE

A SENSE OF UNREALITY FILLED Lucky as she stepped off the plane at Baltimore-Washington International Airport in the early morning hours. DC was not where she'd expected to be when she'd headed down to the beach with her surfboard yesterday morning, but here she was, walking off a plane and feeling a bit shell-shocked. For one thing it was nearly Christmas, and it would definitely feel like winter outside, unlike in Hawaii.

There, in spite of the Christmas lights and trees and decorations, it was easy to ignore the approaching holiday because it was always hot and sunny. Here, not so much. The lights and trees on the concourse seemed to jump out at her and hammer her over the head with the idea it was almost Christmas. In just a couple of weeks, she was supposed to head to Montana to be with family. She'd tried to get out of it, but she feared if she didn't go, her mother would drag her stepfather and the triplets to Hawaii.

Which was something Lucky did not need. Dealing with the cheerfulness—and downright alien-ness—of those five was not something she wanted to do on her own

22

turf. In Montana, she could suffer a few days and then be on her way home again.

They passed down the escalator and into the baggage claim area. Kev grabbed a cart and they stood to wait for her luggage. Not his, of course. He'd traveled with carry-on only, which told her a few things. First, this trip had been last minute. Second, he hadn't been expected to stay for long. Third, Mendez knew she would come.

Of course he did. The bastard. John Mendez was one of the toughest career soldiers she'd ever run across. She had a lot of respect for him. And a lot of fury too. Especially now. He would use whatever tool for the job it took, and to hell with the consequences.

She was a tool. She knew it, and she'd come willingly. *No backing out now, chickie.* No, whatever the consequences, she was here.

Kev stood with his arms folded and stared at the baggage carousel as if he could will it to start moving. He was so quiet, so enigmatic. Always had been. All he'd ever done had confused her. Once, she'd thought he was interested in her, when she'd first arrived at HOT. He'd smiled and flirted, and she'd flirted right back.

But then came North Africa and Al Ahmad, and everything had changed. Lucky bit the inside of her lip. She'd been so uncertain of herself after that. She'd married Marco when what she should have done was run far and fast in the other direction until she could get herself together again.

It hadn't been fair to Marco. Or to her.

Dammit. Lucky pulled in a deep breath and swore she wouldn't cry. Not now.

She looked up at Kev and realized he was frowning.

23

"You okay?"

"Hell, no," she bit out. "I was minding my own business, surfing and having a good life, and then you showed up and ruined it all."

A good life. That was a lie.

"I'm sorry."

"You aren't. You're following orders and there's nothing else you would prefer. If Mendez told you to leap from the top of the Capitol, you'd ask him how soon he wanted it done."

Cool blue eyes stared at her. "I am following orders. You know that I have to. You'd do the same thing if you were still in. There's no choice. But I do care."

He took a step toward her, loomed over her while her heart kicked up a beat. Something flashed in his eyes then, and she realized there was a whole lot more emotion burning deep inside Kev's soul than she'd given him credit for.

"I'm pissed as hell that Mendez is bringing you back in. I want nothing more than for you to be back in Hawaii, doing whatever you want, far away from HOT and everything we stand for."

Lucky swallowed. She could smell the anger rolling from him, could feel the heat of his body so near hers. He smelled good, like sunshine and water, and she wanted to close her eyes and drink him in.

His anger shocked her. And touched her.

"I'm sorry for what I said about Marco. About his death." Her voice was soft, strained. She should have said this before now, but she hadn't been able to bring it up again. "I know you loved him too."

Now he was the one who seemed stunned. His jaw flexed. "Yeah, I did. If I could have taken his place out

24

there, I would have."

Her heart thumped hard. She touched him, nearly withdrew when the sensation of skin against skin was almost too much. She didn't like touching people when she could avoid it. In the months after she'd returned from North Africa, it had been everything she could do to work up to touching—and being touched—by Marco.

She swallowed. She'd gotten much better about touching, but it wasn't something she went out of her way to do. This touch was almost sensory overload. Her nerve endings leapt to attention, her skin blazing hot. It was everything she could do not to jerk away and tuck her hand beneath her armpit.

"Don't say that, Kev. He wouldn't have wanted that at all."

"No, but I do. If I could have given him back to you—"

His voice choked off as the buzzer rang for the baggage carousel. It lurched to a start, and Kev moved away from her, going to stand near the mouth of the carousel as the first bags began to disgorge. Lucky stared at his broad back, pulled in one deep breath after another.

The thought of Kev dying out there the way Marco had… She shuddered. It wasn't right, not for any of them, and yet it was what these men risked every time. They put their lives on the line to protect this country, and most people would never know it. Marco should have had a hero's welcome, but he'd come back in a lonely casket met at Dover by an honor guard. And then he'd been buried quietly at a ceremony featuring as much of HOT as could come to the funeral, and her.

No, it wasn't right, but it was what they'd signed up

for.

Lucky wrapped her arms around herself. Marco had deserved so much better than that. Than her.

She sniffed and waited for the jumpy sensation beneath her skin to ebb. Finally, Kev hefted her bags from the carousel.

When he came over to her, he was frowning again. "You got a coat in here? That sweatshirt won't do you much good outside."

She ran her hands over the soft material and frowned. "I have a jacket. Nothing thick though."

He led them off to the side, away from the crowd. "Which suitcase?"

"It'll be fine. We're going to get into a car, right? The heater will warm me up."

"It's just as easy to get the jacket now."

She sighed. "Fine. I think it's in the red one."

Kev set the suitcase on the floor, and Lucky bent to unzip it. After rummaging around for a few moments, she came up with a wrinkled jacket that said U.S. Army on it. She didn't know why she'd kept the damn thing, but she stood and put it on before zipping the suitcase closed again. Then they were rolling out of the airport and into the parking deck.

The air was a shock to her system after the months in Hawaii. Her breath frosted and her fingers grew stiff in the chill air. Kev led them to a white pickup where he slung her bags in the back and then started the engine. It took a while for the heater to finally feel warm instead of frigid, but by then she didn't think she would ever get warm again.

Soon they were on the road, and Lucky turned her

head to look at the endless buildings and land. That was one thing about living on an island—you got used to seeing ocean just about everywhere you looked. To see land—endless land—was strange after the last few months.

"Where are you taking me?" she asked after they'd passed several miles in silence.

"My orders are to bring you to HOT HQ. After that, I don't know."

"And where is HQ?"

"Not far."

She hugged herself and sniffed. "HOT has come up in the world."

He shrugged. "You know that Mendez has been trying for years. He finally got someone to say yes."

Lucky scrubbed a hand through her hair and yawned. She never slept well on a plane, and last night had been no exception. "I don't think anyone could say no to that man for long."

Even her, apparently. It hadn't escaped her attention that she'd pretty much caved in to precisely what Mendez wanted within hours of being told.

"Don't beat yourself up," Kev said quietly. "He was bringing you back one way or another. This way, you have more control."

She snorted softly. "Some control. Yesterday I was surfing and contemplating my day, and now I'm here. The power of Mendez."

Kev's fingers tightened on the wheel. "We're gonna get Al Ahmad. This time, we're getting him."

"I sure hope so. Because I won't come back again."

Kev glanced over at her, his expression fierce. "You

won't have to. Believe me. If it's the last thing I do, I'll make sure that bastard is good and dead this time."

Her heart skipped a beat. And then a current of anger whipped through her. "Don't you do anything stupid, Kevin MacDonald. I buried one of you already. I won't do it again."

His eyes flashed with some emotion she couldn't read, and then he was staring straight ahead again, his knuckles white on the wheel. Lucky closed her eyes and leaned her head back. She didn't know why she'd said that, but Marco and Kev had been inseparable when she'd first met them. They were like brothers instead of best friends, their pasts so similar it was spooky. They both had deadbeat dads, both had drunk mothers. Neither of them was in contact with their family.

She'd thought they would always be tight, but then she'd entered the picture and everything changed. Marco tried to pretend it hadn't, but he'd known it too. Kev pulled away from them both after they married, though he still accepted invitations and then showed up with wildly inappropriate women. He never stayed long, always slipping his arm around whatever trashy babe he was with and saying something about how he had to get her home. Lucky had hated thinking of him taking those women home and undressing them, caressing them in ways that made her throat dry. It hadn't been any of her business, and yet it had bothered her anyway.

"I'm not going to do anything stupid." His voice broke into her thoughts and she opened her eyes. His profile always caused that little hitch in her heart. Strong lines, handsome lines. She wanted to press her mouth to his jaw and work her way around to his lips.

It was a disconcerting thought to have, and she shifted in her seat, uncomfortable.

"I'm glad to hear it."

"What happened out there with Marco… He didn't do anything stupid. He was just the one who got picked. None of us knew what would happen to him and Jim."

Her throat ached. She'd spent so much time blaming herself. What if she'd caused Marco to screw up? What if he'd been preoccupied with her and the things that had being going on between them?

Matt Girard had told her everything that happened, but she'd still vacillated between helpless fury and self-blame.

She cleared her throat. "I talked to Karen Matuzaki a few times after… She moved back to California, you know. She and the kids moved in with her parents so she could go back to school and finish her degree."

Karen had gotten Jim's Servicemen's Group Life Insurance, same as she'd gotten Marco's. It was a substantial amount of money, but not enough to live on for the rest of your life. She'd talked to Karen a few times, and then over the last couple of months they'd only e-mailed once in a while. She'd taken it as a sign that Karen was moving on and coping with her new reality.

"I'm glad to hear she's all right."

"As all right as anyone can be after losing her husband and the father of her children."

Kev sighed. "Yeah," he said softly.

They lapsed into silence. Lucky closed her eyes. She was so tired. She hadn't slept on the plane, and her gut was churning with stress. She had no idea what Mendez expected from her, and while the prospect of getting anywhere near Al Ahmad was ulcer inducing, she was determined to do the job and get out quickly. Yeah, she'd wanted to run at first—but all night long all she'd thought about was that evil, slimy bastard and the things he'd done to her. The way he'd affected every day of her life since.

He had to die. And she would do whatever it took to make that happen.

FOUR

"LUCKY? LUCKY?"

Her eyes snapped open, and she looked up to find Kev gently shaking her. Her first instinct was to recoil; her second was to burrow her head into his chest and sob.

She sat up, rubbing her eyes, and Kev straightened. "Sorry," she said.

"No problem. It's been a long night for you."

She glanced at her phone to check the time. "It's six hours earlier in Hawaii. I'd be in bed right now."

"Yeah, that time-zone shift is always a bitch."

She blinked at their surroundings. The truck was parked in a lot near a compound that would have looked nondescript were it not for the razor wire, antennas, and satellite dishes.

"Whoa, are these the new digs?"

Kev slid his hands over the top of the steering wheel. "This is it. The Church of Mendez."

She laughed in spite of herself. "You guys don't call it that to his face do you?"

Kev grinned. "No. But we do call it the playground.

He seems to like that."

He reached behind her seat and dug into the backpack he'd set there. Then he came out with a manila envelope and handed it to her.

"What's this?"

"Your credentials."

She turned the envelope in her hands before ripping it open. A HOT restricted-access badge fell out, along with an ID and some other papers.

"Just when I'm sure nothing can surprise me." She turned the badge over. "You knew I'd come."

He shrugged. "Mendez was getting you back one way or the other. And you'll need these to get inside."

"I'm not active anymore."

"Doesn't matter. We operate our own access now. We're deep black."

"HOT was always deep black."

He shook his head. "Not like this." He popped open his door. "Come on. Mendez is waiting."

"Wow, I don't even get a shower first, huh?" She knew better, but it was still irritating to be called onto the carpet and expected to obey when she'd left that kind of life behind. No one ordered her to do anything these days, and she liked it that way.

But it seemed HOT could always drag you back in.

"He wants to see you. After that, I have no idea. But I'll do what he tells me."

"Apparently, we all will," she said bitterly. And then she opened the door, looped the badge around her neck, and started for the gate. They passed through several layers of security and into the bowels of the building.

"It still smells new," she grumbled as they passed

through yet another door controlled by a cipher.

"We're working on it."

This building was prime, nothing like the facility at Fort Bragg. If she didn't know better, she'd think she'd just stepped into the NSA. There were lasers, huge monitors, infrared cameras, ciphers, eye and fingerprint scanners, and a computer that spoke to them as they walked through the mantrap.

The doors were thick steel that thudded shut as they went deeper into the facility. Finally, they came to a room with two guards stationed on either side.

Kev took her badge and handed it to the closest guy. "We're here to see the colonel. This is Lucky San Ramos. She's HOT cleared, level three."

The guard turned and picked up a phone. A few moments later, he dropped it and entered a code into the door. It swung open and Kev led her through. Lucky ground to a halt. Around her, giant screens ringed the room. Computer banks sat in the center of the room, men and women busy at each as colored dots moved on the screen.

HOT squads out in the field. The dots lit up across several continents, and Lucky swallowed. It was surreal to be back on the inside after so long away.

And after the way she'd lost Marco. *Poor Marco.*

"You all right?"

She glanced up at Kev. He was watching her closely, and she told herself not to read too much into it. "It's a little intense, but I'm okay. It's been a while."

He smiled as if to reassure her. "I know. But it'll be fine."

"So where's the old man?" Because she wanted to get this over with now that she was here.

"The old man isn't that damn old," a voice boomed behind her. Lucky spun to find Colonel Mendez, looking intense as always as he sized her up. He wasn't a bad-looking man, though she had no intention of ever telling him that. He was tough, tall and wiry, and had that same high-and-tight, salt-and-pepper hair he'd always had.

While the other guys grew their hair out of regs for missions, Mendez never did.

"Hello, sir," she said, her old training snapping to the fore of her brain. No, she wasn't in anymore, and she could probably get away with leaving the sir off. But why antagonize the guy?

"So you gonna help us out, huh? Damn patriotic of you, Lucky."

Anger cracked through the veneer of her calm. "It has nothing to do with patriotism, I assure you."

His eyes raked her face. "No, I guess not." He held out his arm suddenly, as if he were a courtier at a ball. "Why don't we go to the ready room and discuss everything?"

After a moment's hesitation, she slipped her arm in his. No one here was going to hurt her. She'd worked hard to get over her phobias, and she was going to have to work even harder now. Besides, if he wanted to play it that way, she could go along. For now.

"Let's get it over with."

"Sergeant," Mendez said, jerking his head at Kev. Kev preceded them through the operations center and into another room. Lucky blinked at the sight of Marco's old teammates sitting at a table. They stood almost as one, a rippling wave of muscle and danger.

"Hey there, Lucky," Matt Girard said, looking as

handsome as ever. "Good to see you, *chère*."

"I'd say the same, but, well, I think you guys probably know I'd prefer to be anywhere but here."

His gray eyes were somber. "I don't doubt it."

She let her gaze wander around the table, said hello to everyone in turn. There was Billy "The Kid" Blake, the computer whiz; Jack "Hawk" Hunter, the sniper; Nick "Brandy" Brandon, the spotter; Chase "Fidler" Daniels and Ryan "Flash" Gordon, the intel guys—and two guys she didn't know at all. It hit her with a sickening thump that they were Jim and Marco's replacements.

She glanced over at Kev, found him watching her, his gaze sharp. The other guys introduced themselves, and then they all sat down at a table.

Mendez wasted no time. "Al Ahmad's been to France and Switzerland according to our sources." He pushed a dossier toward her and called up a slide show on the screen at one end of the room.

Lucky scanned the documents. It was nothing much, but Al Ahmad's name had shown up in some intercepted cables. That wouldn't have meant much, except that it was ibn-Rashad who seemed to be breaking the silence.

A power struggle in the Freedom Force? Anything was possible. With friends like ibn-Rashad, who needed enemies?

"Someone is accessing Al Ahmad's accounts here in Zurich," Mendez said, his cursor hovering over the name of a bank on a map.

"Weren't those accounts closed when he died?"

"They were. But the NSA followed the money through various pipelines until it showed up again. New accounts, same bank. Al Ahmad is a bit superstitious, it seems."

Yes, he was certainly that. As well as a psycho.

"So where does HOT come in?"

Mendez fixed his fierce gaze on her. "You're the only one who has ever seen him. The only one on our side, that is. We need you to ID him in real time so we can grab him."

Her heart thumped hard. Sweat pooled between her breasts, though she'd been cold since she'd stepped off the plane into the middle of winter. "I don't know that I can. I only saw his face once. He always wore a keffiyeh and tucked part of it around the lower half of his face. But it fell away one day…"

She tried not to let her fear show. She could feel Kev's eyes on her, feel him trying to imbue her with strength. Well, dammit, she didn't need his strength. Didn't need anyone's. She had her own. She'd worked long and hard on finding it.

She sucked in a breath and gritted her teeth. "It's possible, but I can't guarantee it."

Mendez looked grave. "You know what he sounds like, and that's the key. He never gives the orders himself, always sends them through his lieutenants. We've never captured his voice… but you would know it if you heard it."

"Maybe." She shoved a hand through her hair. "I don't know, but maybe. But how do you propose I do that? He's smart and he's not going to start making calls—or none that you can connect to him."

"No, that's true." His gaze slid over the team. "We could wait, try to capture his voice. We talked of getting recordings, transmitting them here for you to listen to. But he's too careful. We need boots on the ground, Lucky. We need the assets in place to take him once the ID is made. We want you to go in with Alpha squad."

She blinked at him, the chill in her bones creeping outward until she was certain she would freeze where she sat. It was everything she could do not to let her teeth chatter. They wanted to capture Al Ahmad, not kill him. And they wanted her to go with them.

Had Kev known this from the start? She didn't look at him as she fixed her gaze on Mendez.

"I'm not an operator."

"No. But you can be a teacher."

"I'm not following you."

Mendez tapped on the keyboard, and a new slide popped up. "He's in Qu'rim."

Her heart skipped. "Qu'rim is on the verge of civil war."

The capital city of Baq was still untouched by the violence—but it was moving closer every day. There was rebellion out in the desert, pockets of unrest near the city. She might be out of the military now, but she could watch CNN International and Al Jazeera like anyone.

Mendez looked grave. "Yes. But Baq is still safe at the moment. The airport is held by troops loyal to the king, and the king is secretly working with the U.S. on security. We've been sending arms for months now."

Lucky clenched her hands into fists in her lap. "This is beginning to sound completely insane."

"I'll grant you that. But Qu'rim is important. More important than many people realize."

He brought up another screen, and her heart nearly stopped. "Uranium," she breathed. "They have uranium."

Around the table, the guys looked grim. "Yeah," Mendez said. "They have a mine. And it's in our best interests to protect that. Should the rebels succeed—well, the balance of power could shift in the region. And that would not be a good thing for us."

She felt numb. "I thought this conflict was about fair treatment. The poor taking from the rich and all that."

"That's what they want you to think. But it's far more than that. The Qu'rimis have an enrichment program. So far, they claim it's for peaceful means, but in the wrong hands…" He shrugged.

"You think Al Ahmad has something to do with this."

His eyes flashed with approval. "Yes. The rebellion started a little over a year ago, and things have steadily gotten worse. He's there. And he knows that if the balance shifts, he'll be in a prime position. Qu'rim has chemical weapons. Al Ahmad wants them."

"Holy shit."

"Precisely."

She drew in a deep breath. If Al Ahmad had anything to do with this, if he got his hands on chemical weapons, if he got control of the uranium… it was a terrifying scenario with disastrous consequences.

"What do you need from me?"

Mendez leaned forward, his eyes sparking with intensity. "We need to know who Al Ahmad is, and we need to get him so we can put an end to the Freedom Force. For that, we need you. If it could be done any other way—" He slapped a hand on the table and she jumped. "But it can't. We need boots on the ground, ready to take him. We need you."

He turned back to the screen and pulled up another

slide before she could say anything. "This is the scenario. Baq is still doing business as usual, and there's a demand for English teachers. You speak several dialects of Arabic, and you would be able to fit in as an instructor. Naturally, you will be accompanied by your new husband."

She started, but she didn't think Mendez noticed. If any of the guys were uncomfortable, they didn't show it. Except Kev. He seemed… stiff, angry.

And then Billy shot Kev a look, and Lucky revised her estimate. That was at least *two* guys uncomfortable with the idea. Three if you counted her.

"The rest of the team will be there in various capacities. You won't be alone. And Sergeant MacDonald will be with you twenty-four seven, no matter what."

Her heart squeezed tight. Kev didn't say a word, but she sensed this was news to him the way his shoulders drew back even tighter than before. If she did this, she was going into Baq with Kev as her husband. *Kev.*

My God.

Lucky concentrated on what Mendez was saying. "And how am I supposed to find Al Ahmad in the midst of all this chaos? Baq is huge, and if he's busy fomenting rebellion in some of the more remote quarters of Qu'rim…"

"He has a daughter. She goes to school in Baq."

Lucky's heart nearly stopped. That monster had a child? Oh dear God. A chill washed over her from the top of her head to the soles of her feet. "If you know all this, how can you not know who he is?"

Irritation flashed across his features then, but she knew instinctively that it wasn't directed at her. Mendez was very proud of his brainchild and very protective of their accomplishments. The fact HOT couldn't find the most dangerous terrorist in the world and neutralize him did not sit well with the colonel.

"I wish I could tell you that. But he's careful. Paranoid. He does everything through intermediaries. We don't know who his daughter is, but we know she is in a very exclusive school for girls. The students are daughters of the wealthiest, the most privileged of Qu'rimi society."

"I'm not a teacher."

"You speak the dialect. And you speak English. It's all that's required. Many of the people who sign on to teach English in Qu'rim are nothing more than native speakers. You at least have more than that going for you."

"And won't they be suspicious when I show up speaking the language?"

He shook his head. "We're working with the king and certain high-placed people in his command. There will be no questions."

Lucky closed her eyes and tilted her head back. This was not what she'd expected—and yet there was no way she could refuse. Everyone at this table was counting on her. And more than that, her nation was counting on her. If Al Ahmad and the Freedom Force gained control of the uranium mine—or Qu'rim's chemical stockpile—the consequences would be catastrophic.

"All right," she said softly. "Tell me what I have to do."

FIVE

ABDUL HALIM BIN KHALID AL-FAIZAN sipped his tea and read the papers that his wife had brought to him. There was much unrest in the desert these days. Much unrest.

As it should be, praise be to Allah. Abdul Halim's lips curled in a small smile as he thought of all that would come to pass when opposition forces broke through the king's defenses and conquered the city. It was almost time, but not quite.

There was still the matter of the uranium to be settled first. And it would be quite soon, he was certain.

But he was a patient man these days. He could wait.

He knew the Americans would be looking for him now that his code name had resurfaced. It was regrettable that his second-in-command had allowed news of his existence to escape. That would not happen again. He'd made an example of Jassar ibn-Rashad. No one would cross Al Ahmad now, not if they wished to avoid the fate he'd meted out to his former lieutenant.

Fortunately, few people knew that Abdul Halim and

Al Ahmad were the same person. Jassar ibn-Rashad had not known. Abdul Halim made it a point never to let his lieutenants know his true identity. Those who knew were related to him by blood or marriage, and they would not tell. As his fate went, so went the fate of the family.

Abdul Halim lifted his head as his wife came into the room. Fatima was a pretty creature but empty-headed for the most part. But Lana loved her. It didn't hurt that Fatima was quite enthusiastic in bed, which was never an unwelcome thing. In fact, looking at her now, at her trim figure beneath the silk dress she wore, his body began to stir.

And then Lana ran into the room. "Daddy!"

She ran into his arms and hugged him tight, her dark curls tickling his nose as he held her. He patted her head and set her away from him. She was a precocious child, much like he had been at her age. She amused him. He would even go so far as to say he felt an emotional attachment to her.

But he did not wallow in sentimentality. If he had to one day slice himself away from her, then he would do so. He would do whatever it took to achieve his goals.

"What is it, my pet?"

"I want a puppy." She stuck her little lip out in a pout. Perhaps he should be angry with the blatant attempt at manipulation, but she was too much like him. At the age of six, Lana had a very high opinion of herself. He admired that greatly.

"Lana, did I not tell you not to ask your father for a puppy?" Fatima was standing with hands on slim hips, looking furious.

Abdul Halim ruffled his daughter's hair. "I will think about it, *habibti.* Now get ready for school."

Lana stomped her foot and ran from the room. Fatima sighed. "I'm sorry. I told her not to bother you about a puppy."

He shrugged. "She is a child. She does not understand delaying gratification." He set the papers aside and picked up his phone when he heard the telltale buzz. There was a message from one of his lieutenants. It would be in code, of course. He opened it and began to read. Fatima knew better than to disturb him at such a time. She left the room in a cloud of silk and sweet perfume.

Abdul Halim finished reading the message and picked up the paper again. Nothing much happening other than more foreign arrivals in the city today. The world media was coming more steadily now because of the unrest in the desert.

Just wait until riots broke out in the city. They would be positively gleeful, the ghouls. Abdul Halim smiled to himself.

The doorbell rang and Fatima went to answer it. He heard the rustle of silk as she came back to the sitting room. His brother was behind her.

"Greetings, brother," he said as Farouk came into the room and took a seat. Fatima left them and closed the door behind her.

Farouk accepted a cigarette. "What do you need me to do?"

"I need you to find the woman. She is dangerous to us now."

Farouk blew out a column of smoke. His eyes flashed. He knew who Abdul Halim meant. The only person to ever escape once the Freedom Force had taken her hostage.

"We should have gone after her sooner."

"We did not have the resources," Abdul Halim snapped. "Once we were attacked, we had to scatter. It was impossible."

Farouk had been there in North Africa, and he knew what had happened. The Americans had rescued her. And they'd shot Abdul Halim and left him for dead.

Now that his secret was exposed, Lucinda Reid was dangerous. He remembered that she'd insisted she was called Lucky. He'd laughed at that, but little did he realize at the time just how lucky she was. She was not only lucky, she was also spirited.

And she'd been defiant. So defiant. He did not like defiance, especially from a woman, and yet it had fascinated him too. His people had taken her from the street because he'd wanted to kill an American. He'd wanted to watch their government panic and posture, and he'd wanted to sow the seeds of fear in their tourists and in the local government. When Americans were scared, they reacted out of proportion to the threat. He liked how easily manipulated they were, and he'd thought to use it in his aims against the state.

He should have killed her immediately, but she'd fascinated him. He hadn't known she was military until they'd gone through her purse and found her identification. She'd been doing work for her government, interpreting for the military commanders that were propping up the state on orders from the American government. He'd taken her capture as a sign, and he'd been determined to break her utterly before he killed her.

At first, he'd tormented her with words. And then he'd used his knife to mark her body. He had been so close to breaking her. To taking her for his own. He did not often mix sex and punishment, but there were times when it was necessary.

It had been necessary with her. She was disobedient and she'd inflamed him with the desire to punish. He'd wanted to prove to her that she was nothing, that her military couldn't save her. He'd been looking forward to it so much.

But the Americans had busted in and taken her from him, and then he'd spent the last two years reestablishing his network. Abdul Halim viciously stubbed out his own cigarette. He'd wanted to deal with her sooner, but he was methodical and logical—and she'd presented no threat when he was thought to be dead.

But everything had changed with ibn-Rashad's betrayal. Lucky Reid was now a loose end, and though it galled him to let her off so easily when she really needed to pay for her sins, it was his only choice.

"Find her, Farouk. Find her and kill her."

Kev didn't like the way Lucky sat there so quiet and still and chewed on her lip. He wanted to tell Mendez to leave her the hell alone, tell them all that there was no way in fucking hell she was going to Qu'rim and facing the prospect of Al Ahmad.

And, Jesus Christ on a cracker, how in the hell was he supposed to play her fucking husband? Lucky wanted him anywhere but where she was. She said she didn't hate him, but he knew she despised him—despised all of them. He understood why.

If somebody had to pretend to be her husband, let one of the other guys do it.

Any of them would be better at it. Chase or Ryan—or maybe Sam, though he was pretty hot and heavy with that English professor they'd bailed out of trouble a couple months ago and might find it difficult to pretend.

Yet the thought of them—any of them—pretending to be Lucky's husband made him want to growl. Mendez had chosen him for a reason—probably because the colonel knew that Lucky had been tight with him and Marco back in the day—and he would see it through. Even if it killed him.

Because being near her twenty-four seven was certain to kill him. He'd spent years thinking about her, months calling her, and hours fantasizing about kissing her again. He still didn't know why he'd kissed her, except that he'd been so damn relieved she was alive. He'd been the one to find her, and in those few moments before the other guys arrived, she'd clung to him. It had killed him to see her so vulnerable. So he'd just lowered his head and kissed her. Maybe to impart strength, maybe because he just had to.

Whatever it was, it had rocked him to his core. Shaken his foundations. And now he wanted to do it again.

Jesus, he was one sick bastard. She'd lost her husband—a man he'd called his best friend—and she didn't need his fantasies intruding on her life.

She glanced over at him. He didn't give away, by word or deed, what he was thinking. Her gaze darted back to Mendez and what he was saying. Kev heard it all, but his eyes remained on Lucky.

There would be some hard training first, so they didn't just haul her back into the danger zone and expect she could handle it. She'd been out of the Army for over a year, and she needed to be recertified in weapons. Then she needed to get her combat skills up to snuff. She went a little pale at that, but Kev was the only one who seemed to notice. He knew that Lucky didn't like to be touched. He remembered Marco telling him once, a sad note in his voice, how Lucky flinched whenever he reached for her.

Marco wouldn't tell him details—nor would Kev have wanted to hear them—but he could imagine. Kev had gone home that night and punched the shit out of the bag he'd kept in his apartment when what he'd really wanted was to bury a knife in Al Ahmad's throat.

"Big Mac."

Kev's head snapped up. "Yes, sir?"

Mendez was looking at him with narrowed eyes. "You're with Lucky twenty-four seven starting now. We're training hard for the next few weeks and then we're going in. You'll start practicing your cover story right now."

"I'd rather not." Lucky's voice was hard as she looked at Mendez. "All I need is a hotel and a rental, and I'll be here every day as required. I don't need a babysitter."

"Not negotiable," Mendez snapped back. "This mission is too damn critical, and I need to know if you two can work together or if one of the other boys needs to play the part."

Her chin lifted. "I've agreed to help. But I'm not active and I don't take orders."

"Yes, ma'am, you do." Mendez's voice had that edge to it that all the guys knew meant serious business. "You're active, soldier. We don't send civilians into combat."

Lucky's jaw worked. "You said if I came willingly —"

Mendez's chair scraped as he stood. Everyone else in the room snapped to attention. Except Lucky. Kev watched her sitting there, that militant look on her face, and prayed Mendez was amused rather than irritated.

"This is war, Sergeant San Ramos. You know it as well as the rest of us. Just because you leave active duty doesn't mean you can't be called back, which you also know since you had to sign papers to that effect. You can consider yourself recalled to duty."

Lucky scraped to her feet and stood rigidly. Kev wouldn't have quite called it attention, but it was close enough. "Sir, *yes, sir!*"

Mendez nodded in satisfaction. "It's one operation, Sergeant. One and done." His eyes drifted across the rest of them. "You're dismissed. Get to work."

"That rotten old sonofabitch!" Lucky took a swig of the beer the waitress had set in front of her and shivered inside her sweatshirt. She still wasn't used to this damn cold weather, but she was going to have to get used to it in a hurry.

She'd spent the morning going over some paperwork with the guys, but when it came time for training, Matt told Kev to take her home and come back tomorrow. Apparently, her jet lag was showing.

But instead of taking her wherever he was supposed to take her, Kev had asked if she was hungry. She'd been surprised to realize she was. Now they were here, in a bar, drinking beer and waiting on cheeseburgers and fries to arrive.

"He knew he was activating me. He knew it all along, but he just had to sweet-talk me first."

Kev sat at a right angle to her, nursing his own beer and looking distinctly unhappy. No doubt because he'd been tasked with babysitting her for the foreseeable future.

His gaze strayed to the blond waitress with the big breasts and fake nails as she walked by their table again. Lucky didn't miss the way the girl looked at him or the tip of his chin he gave her in return.

Irritation flared inside her. "Would you like me to wait in the car?"

His gaze slid over to her. "What? Why?"

Lucky couldn't help the little hitch in her chest every time he looked directly at her. Why did Kevin MacDonald have to be so damn gorgeous? And so, well, dark and dangerous and unfathomable? Marco had always been an open book, but Kev... Kev was like a locked vault in Fort Knox. On the outside, he was amiable good-old-boy friendliness. But on the inside... Well, she wasn't sure anyone knew what was on the inside. Kev didn't share—not even with Marco.

"I asked if you'd like me to wait in the car. After you pick the waitress up, that is. You can take her home and

49

fuck her brains out and I'll wait in the car until you're done."

Kev's face was granite. "I'm not taking the waitress home."

"But you want to."

He took a drink of his beer. "Maybe. So what? It's not against the law."

Lucky ran her finger up and down the side of the cold mug, playing with the condensation. It wasn't any of her concern, and yet she was irritated. What did that say about her?

"I'm sorry if I'm cramping your style. I didn't know Mendez would put us together. And I don't think you did either."

Kev leaned forward, both elbows on the table, and gave her a hard look. "I didn't know he was going to activate you. All I was tasked with was bringing you back. I didn't know the plan, and I didn't know he'd want you to go with us."

She bit the inside of her lip. And then she sighed. "I believe you. It's not Mendez's style to share his plans before he needs to. He sent you because of Marco." Her throat hurt to say the name aloud to Kev, but she was getting better at it. She dragged in another breath. "He knew I'd listen to you."

One of his dark eyebrows arched. "Seriously? I called you for months and you blew me off." He leaned back and took another long drink of beer, trying to look casual when she could feel the tension rolling from him. "Hell, *I* didn't think you'd listen to me. I also didn't think you'd try to brain me with a surfboard."

Lucky closed her eyes and tried to shrug some heat

into her shoulders. "I was pissed. And I didn't brain you."

"No, you didn't. But you did ignore my calls."

She darted her tongue over suddenly dry lips. How could she explain without revealing things about her life with Marco that he wouldn't understand?

"I didn't want to talk to you. Any of you. Ever."

"Yeah, I get that. And I understand."

She forced a smile. "Well, looks like I didn't get that wish after all, so what now?"

He shrugged. "We finish these beers, eat the burgers we ordered, and go home. Tomorrow's an early day."

"Home." The word sat in her gut like a stone. She didn't have a home, not anymore. Unless you counted a zillion acres in Montana where she'd never felt like she belonged. Her mother had begged her to come home after Marco, but she just couldn't face all that wheat-blond perfection. Her mother, her stepfather, and her half sisters were all cut from the same golden cloth while she'd been the odd one. Her hair was more brown than gold, her skin olive whereas theirs was milky pale. It had been difficult enough to deal with as a teenager. Now? No way.

"Don't worry. I've got two bedrooms, and the place is clean."

"You'd think with a new facility like that one Mendez would turn loose of a little cash to let me stay in a hotel. Or at least in billeting."

Except she wouldn't be quite so easy to control that way. Mendez knew all about breaking a soldier down in order to build them into what he wanted them to be. Taking her independence out from under her was the first step.

"Well, he didn't, so we gotta live with it." Kev sipped his beer. "Not only that, but he's right that we have to spend time together before heading to Qu'rim. Our cover has to be seamless, and for that we have to be comfortable together."

As if she could ever be comfortable with him.

"I'm supposed to go to Montana for Christmas. Wonder if Mendez will call my mother for me?"

She wasn't serious, but Kev shrugged. "You'll think of something."

She sipped her beer. Yeah, she'd think of something. *Mom, I've been recalled to active duty. The world needs me to stop a terrorist.*

The waitress showed up with their burgers then and flashed Kev a smile. He smiled right back, and Lucky could hear the woman's breath catch.

"Anything else I can get you, sugar? Anything at all?"

"Not just yet, darlin'," he said in that Alabama drawl he liked to exaggerate for effect.

Lucky rolled her eyes as the woman flounced away. "Same old Kev," she said as she shook salt on her fries. "Dazzling the ladies with Southern charm."

"Not my fault if they're dazzled."

"No, of course not." She dredged a fry in ketchup and put it in her mouth. She didn't usually eat like this, but then she didn't usually get dragged halfway around the world and recalled to active duty either.

She looked up and found Kev watching her, his eyes unreadable. The air between them seemed to grow thicker. Her skin prickled with heat and an awareness that shocked her after so long of feeling nothing. Before she could figure out how to deal with it, how to push it away again, Kev spoke quietly.

"You were never dazzled."

SIX

"I WAS PLENTY DAZZLED," SHE said before looking down at her plate and carefully selecting a french fry. "But then I learned you can turn that drawl up or down for effect. It kind of killed the magic. Besides, you had enough women hanging on you. You didn't need another one."

Kev didn't know why he'd said that. Except they were sitting here in this restaurant, the waitress was flirting with him, and he was wondering why just about every woman he'd ever met flirted with him when Lucky never had. He remembered her walking into HOT HQ at Fort Bragg that first day. She'd just been assigned interpreting duties with them, and she'd shown up in her cammies and boots, her hair twisted upon her head, and a take-no-prisoners look on her face.

He'd been cleaning his weapon and he'd looked up as someone—he couldn't remember who now—brought her in and introduced her. He'd reached out to shake her hand, turned on the charm, and watched her brown eyes go soft. And he'd thought, *Yeah, man, I am so in.*

He'd thought about asking her to join him for a beer

later, but things came up and it was another week before he'd seen her again. By then, her eyes were no longer soft when she looked at him. They were... unimpressed. That had knocked him for a loop. And yet there'd still been a current of heat between them that only grew stronger the more they worked together.

He'd wondered if it was just him most of the time, but then sometimes he'd catch her looking at him in a way that said it wasn't. And then there was Marco. She'd seemed a lot freer with Marco than she had with him. He'd taken that as a sign, especially when Marco indicated he wanted her.

Kev drained his beer while his heart throbbed with old memories. The waitress was back before he set the glass down.

"Another?" she asked, lowering her lashes and gazing at him sideways from beneath them.

"No thanks. Just water now, Lisa." He winked. "Gotta drive tonight. The missus will have another though."

Lisa's expression registered confusion as she glanced at Lucky. Kev felt a like an asshole because, yeah, he had been flirting with her. It was second nature to him, but he shouldn't have done it tonight.

Lucky calmly ate another fry as Lisa walked away. "You just crushed all her hopes."

The knife twisted a little deeper in his gut. "I'm a married man now, darlin'. No time for one-night stands with cute waitresses."

Not that he felt like taking Lisa home, but hell, it would probably be better for him. It would take Lucky off his mind for a little while at least. Jesus, he still couldn't believe he had to play her husband. That he had to spend every waking minute with her for the foreseeable future. And every sleeping minute too, because she would just be in the next room.

Goddamn.

Billy had come up to him earlier and asked how he was feeling about it. He'd lied and said he was fine. But he wasn't fine, and Billy knew it. They'd worked a lot of hours together in the aftermath of Marco's death, and Billy knew how frustrated he'd been when Lucky wouldn't answer his calls. How worried he'd been for her.

"I argued against it," Billy had said. "But the others think it's a good idea for you to be the one who goes in with her."

"It's fine," he'd replied. "Marco wanted me to take care of her. So I will."

Billy had looked at him with that grave look he had. And then he clapped Kev on the shoulder and left him standing there alone.

Lucky sighed and Kev glanced at her. "I hope this isn't a bar you frequent. Otherwise, she'll know it's a lie."

"Unless I ran off to Vegas recently."

She snorted. "Right. Can't imagine the woman who could get you to do that."

Annoyance pricked him. "Nope, me neither."

He ate a couple of fries, and they lapsed into silence. The sooner they got out of here, the better. He'd get her home, show her to her room, and then he'd go for a run. A long, ball-busting run that drained him of any energy and made him so exhausted he'd fall into bed and sleep for six hours straight.

"So how did we meet then?" She broke off an edge of bun and popped it in her mouth.

"That will depend on our story. You're a teacher, but we don't know what I am yet."

HOT was still working on the details of the plan before they went into Qu'rim, so it was no surprise they didn't have that piece of information. It would come soon.

"Doesn't mean we can't come up with a plausible explanation of how we met. If it doesn't fit the official story, we'll change it."

"Why don't we just wait until Mendez gives us the rest of the story?" Because he didn't feel like sitting here and hashing over the details of some imagined story they shared. A fucking love story, for God's sake.

Her gaze fixed on him. "Humor me, Kev. I need something to think about other than what this job means I have to do. I don't relish the idea of being in the same time zone with…" She swallowed. "With him again."

Jesus. It was an indication of how twisted up she had him that he'd managed not to think about what this mission meant for her. About how she had to be feeling at the idea of facing Al Ahmad again. He knew what was on her skin, what that bastard had done to her. He'd spent a lot of time wondering in the aftermath if it had broken her. It hadn't, but she had definitely changed.

"Yeah, all right." Because how could he say no?

Lisa returned with Lucky's beer and plopped it down in front of her. Kev smiled and winked out of habit and the waitress's expression softened. "Anything else I can get you two?"

"Naw. Thanks again, Lisa."

"Sure thing, hon," she said, her voice low and smooth once more.

Lucky blinked as the waitress walked away. "She

tried to pick you up again. Right in front of me. *After* you said I was the missus. Unbelievable."

"Curse of the MacDonalds," he said, shrugging.

She rolled her eyes. "Yeah, some curse." She went back to her hamburger and took a bite. He'd noticed that she was picking at her food, but at least she was eating it.

"We met at a picnic," Kev said, and her head snapped up.

"A picnic?"

"Yep. A fundraiser for the local school in our beloved hometown."

Lucky laughed. "You're so clearly from down South. I'm not."

"Do you honestly think anyone in Baq will know what the hell that means? Besides, no one says we grew up together. Just that we met in the same town and started dating. It's plausible."

"All right. So we met at a picnic. How long did we date before marrying?"

"Not long. Three months. And yeah, we went to Vegas."

"It sounds a bit far-fetched."

She'd wanted to talk about this, and now she was criticizing him? Unbelievable. "You got a better idea?"

She looked thoughtful for a moment. "We met in Hawaii. You went there on vacation, we had a whirlwind romance, and then we kept in touch on the Internet. But it wasn't enough, so we planned to get married. I made all the arrangements, and then you came to Hawaii and we got married. But since your job is here, I came back with you."

He couldn't help but imagine it. He pictured her naked and lying on a bed, waiting for him. His cock began to throb to attention. *Fuck.* He shifted in his seat and forced his mind elsewhere. *Way to fucking go, asshole.*

When Marco had asked him to take care of Lucky, Kev was pretty sure he hadn't meant *imagine how it feels to bury yourself inside her.*

"If it fits what Mendez comes up with for me, it will work."

She sighed and dropped her gaze, her long lashes sweeping down over her brown eyes. "Marco always said the best lies were the ones that were closest to the truth."

Kev closed his eyes and then shifted his gaze to the football game playing on the television over the bar. He gritted his teeth so hard his jaw hurt. God, he missed Marco. And he had no right to sit here and think about his friend's widow in any capacity other than as a teammate and fellow soldier.

He heard her chair scrape back, and he whipped his gaze back to her. She stood there looking pale and upset. "I have to pee," she blurted. "Too much beer."

He watched her hurry toward the restrooms. He sank his head into his hands and sat there with his elbows on the table, breathing hard and staring at the plate below him. He had no idea what had happened just now. Part of him wanted to get up, follow her into the bathroom, and make her tell him what was wrong. The rest of him wanted to sit right here and pretend this wasn't happening.

He argued with himself for five minutes, and then he started to stand and go after her. But she emerged from the rear of the restaurant, and he sat down again.

"Everything okay?" he asked as she stopped beside the table.

"Of course. Why wouldn't it be?"

"You seemed a little upset."

She pushed a hand through her hair. "I'm tired. And yes, I'm upset too. I thought this part of my life was over, and now here I am, back with HOT and trying not to sink before I can learn to swim."

Kev stood and tossed some bills on the table. "Let's get out of here. You'll feel better after some sleep."

They went outside and he opened his truck door for her, frowning when she shivered noticeably. She wasn't used to this weather after so long in Hawaii.

"We need to get you some warmer clothes."

She looked up at him, her eyes shining in the lights from the parking lot. "Agreed. But no stops at the mall tonight, okay?"

"Fine."

They drove the few miles to his townhouse. He parked and went around to open the door for her, but she was standing on the pavement when he got there. Hugging herself.

"Come on," he said when she went to reach for a suitcase. "I'll get the bags after you're inside."

"Don't be silly. I can carry at least two."

"You're cold." His breath frosted in the air and she shivered.

"Yeah, but lugging suitcases will take care of that."

"Not arguing with you, Lucky. Get inside, and I'll get everything." He handed her a key and pointed at his door. He thought she might argue, but she clamped her mouth shut and went toward the house.

When he got everything inside, she was standing in his living room. "I see you've hired the same decorator as always," she said.

Kev's gaze flickered around the room. There was a couch and chair, a giant-ass television, and a weight bench and punching bag in what was supposed to be the dining room area. Naturally, the walls were bare. And Lucky was looking at him with one eyebrow arched. It made him snort.

"Cute." He picked up her luggage. "Come on, I'll show you to your room."

Lucky grabbed her carry-on and followed him up the narrow stairs. The house wasn't big, but at least it had two bedrooms. He led her to the guest room, which he did have set up with a bed, considering that one or another of the guys sometimes crashed here after a night spent watching movies and drinking beer.

There was a table with a lamp beside the narrow bed. No pictures in here either, but he hoped she wouldn't care. She stood against the wall while he set her things down. He straightened and met her gaze.

"Thanks," she said softly.

"No problem." He wanted to pull her into his arms and hold her close, tell her it would all be okay. But he didn't know that. And he didn't have the right. He went to the door, then stopped and turned back to her. "For what it's worth, I'm sorry about this. If I'd known what Mendez's plan was, I wouldn't have agreed to it."

He felt like it was important to say. She looked at him sadly. "I know you think so, but the truth is you do what you're told. It's the way you're wired. Every last one of you."

He felt her words like a blow. It wasn't a bad thing in his line of work to obey orders. It's what made the team work so well. They trusted each other—and they trusted

Mendez. Yet he was pissed, just a little bit, about the way this had all gone down.

"Maybe so, but I didn't know he intended to stick us together on this mission. I'd have fought against it if I had."

She waved a hand. "Just go, Kev. It's fine."

He wrapped a hand around the edge of the door, trying to think of something to say. In the end, he said nothing.

SEVEN

LUCKY WOKE AT FOUR IN the morning, groggy and disoriented. It took her a few minutes to remember where she was and why. As soon as it dawned on her that she was in Kev's house and that he was in the next room, her heart flipped. How was she going to do this? How was she going to spend every waking moment with Kevin Mac-Donald and not go mad?

God, last night in the restaurant when she'd mentioned Marco, the look on Kev's face had gutted her. She hadn't meant to do it, but then his name popped out, and she'd found herself wondering how she could be so stupid.

She sat up and shoved a shaking hand through her hair. What would Kev think of her if he knew the truth?

She shouldn't have married Marco. She shouldn't have married anyone after her ordeal. But he'd been so gentle and kind, and she'd fallen for him. Eventually, she'd realized there'd been more friendship between them than raw passion. And they'd both realized it wasn't ever going to change.

They'd been two damaged people trying to forge a

life together, and it hadn't been working out. They'd been heading for divorce for months. She hadn't been surprised when Marco had said he wanted one.

She'd been relieved. And that bothered her to this day because he'd deserved better than that. He'd deserved better than her.

She heard Kev's door open and shut, and she pulled her knees up to her chest. He didn't want her here. Why would he? He'd called her for months, but she'd never answered. Surely he'd gotten pissed off enough to stop caring how she was doing.

He'd even told her last night that he would have fought against them being paired up for this mission if he'd known ahead of time it was going to happen. She believed he would have, too. Hell, he still might. And maybe it would be best—except she couldn't imagine going after Al Ahmad with anyone but Kev at her side.

Lucky got up and dressed in a pair of jeans and one of the few sweatshirts she had. She went into the bathroom and brushed her long hair before pulling it back in a ponytail. Lucky frowned at her reflection. She'd gotten pretty tanned in Hawaii, and she'd stopped wearing makeup because it always ran in the heat anyway, but she'd kill for some mascara, concealer, and a little bit of lip gloss right now. It would help hide the dark circles and make her look more alive.

Since she needed to shop for winter clothes, she'd add in a trip to the drugstore and pick up some cheap beauty supplies. Her frown deepened. She didn't have a car or any way to get around other than to rely on Kev. She knew he'd take her wherever she needed to go, but dammit, she'd rather be on her own for the training part of this mission.

Mendez wasn't going to allow it though. Maybe he thought she'd run, or maybe he just wanted her within reach at all times. Whatever the case, he'd made sure she had little choice but to do as he asked.

Lucky finished up and went downstairs around a quarter to five. Kev was in the kitchen, fixing coffee and microwaving something out of a box. She took a deep breath and went in to join him.

"Aloha," she said, and he turned toward her, an eyebrow ticked up.

"Morning. Coffee?"

"Sure." She took a step into the kitchen and stood there with her arms folded over her chest. She wasn't cold—Kev had made sure the heat was turned up—but she was self-conscious. It was strange to be standing here with him when there was so much going on beneath the surface.

Kev poured coffee in a cup and slid it toward her on the counter. "Cream's in the fridge. Sugar's there if you need it," he added, pointing to a jar.

"Thanks, but I drink it black." She picked up the cup and blew on the steam.

"Didn't think you'd be up so early. It's still, what, midnight or something in Hawaii?"

"Or something." She didn't want to do the calculations because it would just make her tired all over again.

"I've got toaster waffles or frozen breakfast trays. Help yourself."

Lucky wrinkled her nose. Such a bachelor. "Any bread?"

"Yeah." He took a loaf from a breadbox and slid it toward her.

Lucky took out two slices, looked carefully for green spots, and pulled the toaster closer before popping the slices in and pressing the lever. She thought back with longing to the ripe pineapple she'd left on the counter in her rental. In Hawaii, she'd often fix toast and fresh fruit—pineapple, papaya, mango, whatever was available that day—and head out onto the lanai with her coffee. She could see the ocean through the trees and hear the power of it as it pounded the shore. She'd gotten used to that and damn if she didn't miss it. One day gone and she was already homesick for the beach.

Not to mention it was fricking freezing here.

The microwave dinged, and Kev took out a tray that looked like it contained scrambled eggs, pancakes, and sausage. "What?" he said, and she knew she'd made a face.

"Nothing."

"Of course it's something. You disapprove of microwave convenience, apparently."

"Not at all. I just think fresh tastes better."

Kev shrugged as he stabbed a fork in the tray and speared some eggs. "Maybe, but who's got time for all that?"

Lucky found some butter in the nearly empty fridge—no surprise it was bare—and buttered her toast when it was finished. "It doesn't take much time to scramble an egg and cook a few sausage links."

Kev snorted. "Since that stuff will kill you anyway, what's it matter if I get it frozen or fresh?"

He had a point. Lucky bit into the toast and waved it at him. "Probably doesn't. But like I said, fresh tastes better."

Kev made a noncommittal noise.

"Maybe we could stop at a grocery store today," she said. "Pick up something for this cold empty box you have here."

He shook his head slowly. "Wow, just moved in and already taking over. I think I want to go back to Vegas and have a do-over."

Lucky laughed. "Sorry. By the power vested in Mendez, we're hitched until this operation do us part."

Something crossed his features then, some expression she couldn't quite read, and she wished she'd kept her mouth shut. But then he was looking at her again with an easy smile on his face. "Guess we gotta make the best of it then."

"That's what I was thinking."

She chewed her toast in silence, leaning against the counter and trying very hard not to look at him. He finished up the microwave meal and tossed the tray in the trash. Then he stretched, and her mouth went dry at the bulge and pop of muscle rippling across his chest and arms.

"It'll probably be a long day today, but I'll see if I can't talk Mendez into giving you a car at least. I know you'd like to come and go on your own."

Lucky swallowed. "I would."

"I could try to talk him into giving you a room on post. I don't think he'll go for it though."

Her stomach clenched. She knew Kev didn't want her here. It was uncomfortable for them both. "I don't think he will either, but it's worth another try. And I'm sorry he dumped me on you like this. But I can handle it. I was startled when you found me on the beach. I won't fly off the handle like that again, I swear."

His eyes were unreadable. "What did you say that I didn't deserve? You didn't expect me to show up like that. Or tell you we needed you to come back."

"But what I said about Marco… it was wrong. The job killed him, not any of you."

His jaw tightened. "I hate that it happened. You have no idea how often I've thought of it, how many times I've gone over it all in my head and wondered what we could have done differently. We were betrayed by our source, and we paid a high price. It's the job, but fuck yeah, I still wonder if it could have been avoided. We all do."

Lucky put down the remains of her toast. She couldn't swallow now if she had to. "I asked him to leave HOT."

Somehow, she got the words out past the tightness in her throat and then immediately wished she could call them back. Why had she told him that? It was private, and yet there was a part of her that felt a sense of relief that she had shared it with someone.

She'd never been certain if Marco had told Kev about their problems or not, but she could see by the look in his eyes that he was surprised.

"He didn't tell me." Kev straightened and pulled in a deep breath. She thought he looked troubled for a second, but then he looked the same as always. Stoic and closed in. But he was probably pissed at her all over again. Pissed that she'd fucked with Marco's head like that, that she'd tried to take away the job he loved.

"But if he had told me," he continued, "I'd have told him to go. It's no life for a married man."

Lucky blinked. That certainly hadn't been what she'd

expected him to say. And somehow it released the knot of tension in her stomach just a little bit.

"It can be. A lot of the guys and their families handle it just fine. Anyone who marries a soldier knows what they signed on for. And I knew it better than most, since I was also a soldier."

He was studying her, his blue eyes giving nothing away. "After what you went through, I think it was a normal reaction to ask him to leave HOT."

She picked up the toast again and took a bite. It was cold now, but she needed something to do. She chewed slowly, though it tasted like ashes in her mouth now. She didn't talk about what she'd been through with anyone. It was too ugly, too shameful, and it made her feel less than human.

She hated those feelings.

"So what's on the agenda today?" she asked brightly, once she choked down the toast.

His brows drew down but he didn't question her. "We head over to HQ and start your training."

She kept the bright smile on her face though her insides churned at the thought of all she would face in the coming weeks. "Sounds great." She threw the remnants of the toast in the trash and turned to face him. "Ready when you are."

He picked up his keys from the counter. "Let's go then."

They were putting on their coats when she stopped and looked up at him. "Do you really think this is going to work?"

"It has to. We can't let the Freedom Force get that uranium."

She nodded. But she didn't tell him she wasn't sure she'd ever be able to pick out Al Ahmad in real time without giving away the game.

It turned out that training for a HOT mission was not like going to the gym and taking a spin class. Nor was it like surfing. Thank God for the surfing, however, because without the level of endurance required for the sport, Lucky would be in a whole lot worse shape than she currently was.

She stood bent in half after their current training session, panting, sweat rolling down her face as Kev sauntered toward her. He didn't even look winded after the latest circuit of the obstacle course. But he was sweaty. Damn. *Hot and sweaty.* His T-shirt clung to hard muscles and his brow glistened. His dark hair stuck to his head and his eyes gleamed hot as lasers.

"You okay?"

She straightened, putting a hand in the small of her back and huffing in a breath. "Yeah, fine."

He frowned. "Sorry to push you so hard, but it's gonna be rough in Qu'rim. You have to be ready."

"I realize that." She shivered. They might have been working up a sweat, but as soon as she stopped moving, the cold air got to her. It wasn't too bad, in the low fifties today, but it might as well have been a hundred below to her.

"You need to go inside for a while?"

She firmed her jaw. "No."

"It's okay if you do. You can't do everything in one day."

"I want this over with. I want to go into Qu'rim, get Al Ahmad, and go back to my life. If I have to run this course ten times a day to make that happen, I will."

"I know you will." He shook his head. "Come on, let's go in. We'll do some target shooting next."

"You don't have to pull punches for me."

He lifted one eyebrow. "It's the first day, Lucky. I think switching it up is acceptable. By the time we go on the mission, you'll be ready."

She wasn't so sure about that, but what choice did she have? He started toward the compound, and she fell in beside him. Other guys were on the course, going through their paces in full gear. She'd gone through with nothing but the clothes on her back this time. Kev was also wearing only his workout clothes, and she knew it was so she wouldn't feel self-conscious about her lack of conditioning compared to the rest of them.

They passed into the building, and Lucky wrapped her arms around herself. She was never getting warm again, apparently.

"Go take a shower," Kev said when they reached the women's locker room. "Then meet me at the indoor range."

She didn't argue. The shower felt damn good on her sore muscles, and she spent more time than she probably should have under the spray. But then she got out, dried her hair just enough so it wouldn't frizz once she pulled it back in a ponytail, and dressed in a fresh sweatshirt and yoga pants before going to join Kev at the shooting range.

It was strange to walk around HOT HQ after so long away. But this building wasn't the same building she'd been used to at Fort Bragg. And she wasn't the same person. She passed people in the hallways who nodded at her. No one thought she didn't belong, though women weren't numerous in this outfit. But things were changing at the highest levels of the military, and women could go into combat now. It was only a matter of time before they were actually on the teams.

Lucky found the range and stepped inside. Kev was talking to Jack Hunter, and she stopped to watch them. Kev was dark and intense while Jack was golden and equally intense. Jack was one of the best snipers in the world. She'd heard the stories about Jack's kills back when she was a part of the organization.

But not all of them were official, so he didn't hold the record for confirmed kills that he should have.

And that was the thing about these men in HOT. They weren't in it for the glory. Kev's head lifted as if he sensed her presence, and then his eyes met hers across the distance. Jack turned and nodded. He wasn't much of a smiler, that man. Then again, doing what he did, she figured he had to be partly inhuman anyway.

Maybe they all were. She walked toward the two men, relieved in a way that she didn't have to smile and pretend she was happy. A row of handguns lay on the table in front of them, magazines ready to go.

"How long's it been since you qualified?" Kev asked her.

"Two and a half years. And I haven't shot a weapon since I left the Army."

Kev picked up a pair of goggles and earplugs and passed them to her. She put them on while he put his on. Jack picked up his own gear and went over to a different station.

Lucky stepped into the lane and picked up the MK 23. It was smooth and cool in her hands, and she adjusted her position. The target was suspended from the ceiling downrange, and Lucky took her time lining up the shot. Then she squeezed off a round. The sound was deafening indoors, even with earplugs. The gun kicked a bit, but she wasn't unprepared for it. Still, the shot went a little wild, missing the target completely.

Frustrated, she aimed and squeezed again. And again the shot missed the outline of the body, though it did hit the paper this time.

Lucky growled in frustration. She didn't have time to be so bad. She had to get this right because her life depended on it.

She lifted the gun again, determined to hit the mother-fucking outline this time.

And then she felt a warm body behind her and she went utterly still.

EIGHT

"HERE," KEV SAID, PUTTING HIS arms around her, gripping her wrists gently and guiding the gun into place. But Lucky couldn't concentrate on what he was doing because her entire body had just gone on red alert.

She could feel his warmth right behind her, his hard, taut body pressing into her, and though she should want to run, she wanted to turn in his arms instead. Perversely, she wanted to slip her arms around his waist and put her cheek against his chest. And then she just wanted to breathe him in.

No one had held her in so long. She and Marco had ceased being intimate in the last few months of their marriage. She'd understood why and she'd thought it was for the best.

But it was a shock to realize now that she wanted to be held. But not by just anyone. By this man. She shivered. If Kev noticed, he didn't say anything.

Instead, he bent until his cheek was next to hers, the profile of his handsome face right there in her peripheral vision. If he turned just a little bit, she could press her mouth to his. She could feel, once more, that firm, gorgeous mouth claiming her own.

Did she want to do that? She did, and it was overwhelming as hell.

The heat rolling off him distracted her, shook her to her core. She hadn't felt anyone's heat like that in a very long time. She'd vaguely thought she was fine with that, but now she realized she wasn't. She *wanted* comfort and connection.

Lucky blinked as she tried to process the tsunami of feelings roiling inside her.

"You're trying too hard," Kev told her, his arms around her, his cheek so, so close.

Her heart was about to pound right out of her chest. She gripped the gun in clammy fingers as her pulse rocketed into the danger zone. He was touching her and… she didn't want to shrink from it.

"You gotta concentrate on the weapon, on the way it feels in your hand. You have to let it be a part of you. Imagine you're pointing at someone and the gun is an extension of your finger." His hand caressed hers like a lover. "Don't think so hard. Just point… and then squeeze as you let your breath out. Don't hold it."

She pointed, because she had to do something, but she didn't squeeze. She couldn't think with him so near. Or, rather, all she could think about was being a part of him. Not a part of this damn gun, but of *him*.

God, she was so pathetic. After so long shutting herself away from the world, her senses came roaring back to life with the wrong man. A man who'd already shown her once before that he didn't want her.

"Stop touching me," she choked out. Because she had

to get away from him before she did something stupid. Before she leaned into his heat and melted against him.

Kev's arms dropped as if he'd touched a hot stove. He took a step back.

"I'm sorry," he said softly. "I forgot."

Her stomach clenched. He knew about her difficulty with being touched. She shouldn't be surprised, because Marco and Kev had been best friends and would have talked, but it made her feel like a freak. What else had Marco told him?

She gritted her teeth and sighted down the gun. Marco had sworn he'd told no one that he'd asked her for a divorce. He'd wanted her to be able to say she'd broken it off. He'd wanted to leave her with a shred of pride. She closed her eyes as tears welled in her throat. Marco would have kept that promise. He wouldn't have told a soul.

But he had told Kev she didn't like to be touched. That much was clear.

And she couldn't tell him that what she'd really wanted was for him to hold her. He'd think she was crazy. Or pitiful. She couldn't explain a damn thing.

Lucky lined up the shot and fired, determined to get on with this. To move past the awkwardness and just be normal for a few minutes. But of course she missed. She put the gun on the table and shoved the goggles off. It was no good. She sucked, and she was going to put them all in danger in Qu'rim.

Kev's arm shot up, trapping her in place when she would have stalked out of the lane. Once more he was close, and she could feel the heat rippling off him. The anger.

"You aren't walking away from this."

She pressed her back against the lane divider and stared up at him. It was dim in the range, almost intimate if not for the gunpowder and the methodical sound of Jack firing rapidly and no doubt accurately. She couldn't see Jack, but she could hear him.

Kev loomed over her, his brows drawn low, a question in his eyes as he searched her face.

Emotion welled inside her, but she swallowed it down and glared hard because she didn't want him to see the boiling feelings below the mask. Her voice was laced with sarcasm because she needed to lash out. "You never walk away, do you, Kev?"

His jaw flexed, his eyes glowing bright. His mouth was a flat, hard line. And she knew that he understood exactly what she meant. Embarrassment threatened to turn her beet red. Why had she gone there again? Why had she brought up the hospital and his failure to show up when nothing was ever going to change it?

"I walk away when it's the right thing to do."

"And how do you know when it is?"

He looked wild for a minute. And then he looked determined. "I couldn't be what you needed. I wasn't going to give you false hope."

Her stomach clenched into a knot. She should know better than to tangle with this man. He might be big and tough and cocky, but he was intense and intuitive. And he damn sure wasn't stupid.

"I'm mystified that you could have possibly known what I needed when I didn't know myself."

She turned and picked up the goggles. Then she grabbed the gun. She wasn't giving up, damn him. She wasn't walking away.

Lucky braced her feet apart in the lane and sighted the target. She breathed in and out, in and out, channeling her anger and frustration into her determination. And then, finally, when she let her breath out one more time, she squeezed the trigger.

And the shot connected with the silhouette. It wasn't perfect—a shoulder shot—but it was progress.

"That's how it's done," Kev said from behind her, as if they hadn't just been on the brink of an argument. "Do it again."

They spent another hour target practicing. She knew it was nothing like what Kev usually did, but then she was getting an abbreviated session today anyway. HOT operators fired for hours at a time, until they could do it blind. She wouldn't ever be able to shoot blind, but she could practice until her accuracy improved.

Which it started to do after an hour. She fired the last of her bullets and Kev appeared in her periphery.

"That's enough for today."

The range smelled like spent ammo, all flinty and smoky, when they finished packing up the gear and walked out into the staging area again. Lucky felt oddly calm after obliterating pretend bad guys for the past couple of hours.

Perhaps she'd be even calmer if she could forget what it felt like standing there with Kev's arms around her, his breath in her ear, his lips a whisper away. He'd rattled her with that move, but not for the reasons he thought.

"You did good in there," Kev said. "You still need practice, but not as much as I worried you might."

"Thanks." The silence between them was starting to grow awkward when they reached the locker rooms again.

Kev's expression was grave as he faced her. "You're doing well, but you know we have to do the hand-to-hand stuff soon, right?"

She swallowed. "Yes."

"I can't go easy on you, Lucky. Because the other guys certainly won't. I hope you know that."

She lifted her chin. "I do. And I'll be fine."

And then, on impulse—just to prove she could—she reached out and touched his arm. It jolted her down to her core, but she didn't jerk away. "I know what has to be done. I'll handle whatever you throw at me. Because there's no other choice."

His gaze dropped to where her hand rested on his arm. Then he looked at her again with a heat that almost took her breath away. But he hid it so fast that she found herself wondering if she'd imagined it.

His expression was placid now. Bland. As if nothing bothered him. "We'll start early tomorrow. For now, there's more paperwork to do. And Mendez has some briefs about the Freedom Force he wants you to catch up on."

She pulled her hand away and tucked it under her arm. "Then I'd better get going," she said. "Any progress on a car for me?"

He shook his head. "Not yet. Maybe in a few days."

She tried not to frown too hard. Damn Mendez anyway. "So I'll meet you somewhere when it's time to go?"

His voice was soft and deep. "I'll find you."

He turned and walked away, and she found herself rooted to the spot, staring at his broad back, his words echoing in her head. *I'll find you.*

They were simple words, but they got under her skin,

made her think of other times, other places. North Africa. Hawaii. He'd found her in those places too, just when she thought she never would or never could be found.

Kev always found her. But then he left her alone.

"You doing okay, Big Mac?"

Kev looked up from his desk to find Matt standing over him. He hadn't even heard his team CO come in. He tossed his pen down and leaned back in his chair. Was he doing okay? Hell no.

He was fighting so many confusing feelings that his head was spinning.

What had he been thinking to wrap himself around Lucky like that? To have her in his arms but not for the reason he wanted her there? She'd stiffened immediately, but still he hadn't let her go. He'd stood behind her, his hands on her wrists, the flowery scent of her hair in his nostrils, and his body had hardened. It took everything he had not to pull her back against him and let her feel what she did to him.

But then she'd told him to stop touching her, and he'd realized what he was doing. And that she didn't like it. How could he have forgotten it for even a second?

What a fucking mess. He was holed up in a house with her, thinking about her sleeping in the bed next door to his room and wondering how in the hell he was going to survive the next few weeks.

"Sure," he lied. "Why do you ask?"

Matt sank down in the chair beside Kev's desk, leaned back, and folded his hands over his abdomen. His eyes were sympathetic and Kev's gut clenched.

"I know it's got to be hard on you, being responsible for Lucky."

An understatement. Marco had asked him to look out for her, but fantasizing about her naked probably wasn't what he'd meant. Worse, it wasn't what she wanted, regardless of her questions about why he'd walked away after she'd been rescued.

She was still hurting over losing Marco. That much was obvious. And he was a bastard for wanting to take advantage of that.

"She's been through enough thanks to us, don't you think?"

Kev refused to take the bait and talk about the way Lucky's presence made him feel. Enough of that and he'd be spilling his guts like a little girl. Worse, he'd probably be off the mission and sent to the shrink to discuss his inappropriate thoughts about his friend's widow.

"Yeah, I do." Matt frowned. "But we need her. You know how crucial this is."

Kev gritted his teeth. "Yes."

Matt leaned forward then, elbows on knees. "She needs to be ready. And I need to know you can keep your emotions out of this."

Kev wanted to deny there were any emotions involved. But what was the point? They both knew otherwise. Except Matt thought the emotions were because Lucky was Marco's widow. And Kev wasn't about to let him think otherwise.

"We watched our brothers die out there," Kev said, his throat tight. "If I didn't fall apart then, what makes you think I will this time?"

Matt's gaze searched his for a long moment. And then he straightened. "All right. That's exactly what I wanted to know." He got to his feet, but he didn't walk away. "If this changes for any reason, I need to know. If you prefer one of the other guys to take on the role of her husband in Qu'rim, you have to let me know soon. Once we go in, there's no changing places."

Kev didn't even blink. Let one of the other guys be responsible for Lucky's safety? No way in hell. "Copy that."

In another hour, Kev logged off his computer and went to find Lucky. She was in a briefing room, film of the Freedom Force running on screen, her eyes shining suspiciously as she turned to see who'd interrupted her.

She hit the pause button and turned away, and he knew she was working to regain her composure. There was no film of Al Ahmad, of course, but they had ibn-Rashad and many of the others. Not to mention shots of the terror they wrought—suicide bombings, massacres, beheadings. It wasn't light viewing, and it wasn't for the weak of heart either.

"We have to stop them, Kev."

He came inside and pulled out one of the chairs around the conference table. "Yeah, we do."

She drummed her fingers on the tabletop. "I guess I thought I could make it all go away by running as far as possible and trying to be someone different. But the reality is that it didn't go away. Guys like you are still fighting these bastards while people like me pretend they don't know what's going on." She looked up at him, her eyes still shiny. "How do you stand it?"

He sighed. "I don't think you do. You just get numb deep down. And you keep on fighting because you know it's the right thing to do. People like that can't be allowed to win. Whatever the cost."

She leaned her head back on the chair. "I know. Poor Marco."

A tear leaked out of the corner of one eye and slid down her cheek. His heart twisted. He wanted to drag her into his arms and hold her close, tell her it would all be okay someday, but how could he do that? He had no right.

"I'm not going to tell you that he died doing what was right and therefore that makes it okay. It's not okay. But he made a difference, Lucky. What he did made a difference."

She sucked in a deep breath. "He deserved better."

"He did, and we're going to get those assholes and make them pay."

She didn't say anything. Her chin trembled, and he felt like an asshole himself. He wanted to give her the comfort she needed, but he didn't know how to do it. She was vulnerable in this moment, and he knew he couldn't take advantage of her emotional state. It wasn't right.

Instead, he cleared his throat, hands on his knees, gripping them tight to keep him from reaching for her and saying to hell with it.

"Hey, you ready for some shopping? Let's blow this joint and get you some warmer clothes."

She swiped beneath her eyes almost angrily and then she gave him a watery smile that wasn't quite genuine. "Now you're speaking my language. What woman can resist an offer like that?"

He shot her a smile. "None that I know."

She snorted softly. "That's a lot of women, I bet."

His grin widened, though he ached deep down. He didn't want to play the part of the womanizer right now. He wanted to show her there was more to him than that.

But he couldn't.

"Sure is."

She rolled her eyes and he knew that teasing her was working. He wanted to tell her that he had feelings, but he kept them locked away for a reason. He'd seen the dark side of emotions. Seen the destruction they could cause.

In Kev's world, sex with a variety of women was easy. It was love that was impossible.

NINE

LUCKY SAT IN KEV'S TRUCK and stared out the window at the darkening sky. They hadn't said much of anything since getting into the truck back at HOT HQ. She closed her eyes and tried to catch a little sleep since her schedule was still so off, but all she saw in her head was the footage of the Freedom Force wreaking terror on innocent people. They had no scruples, no morals, no conscience. They blew up babies and old women just as easily as they did those whom they considered enemy combatants.

Lucky shivered.

Evil people. Al Ahmad was the worst of all. He wasn't a zealot like some of his followers. He didn't fight for a cause because he believed in it so much as he wanted to dominate weaker souls. And he wanted power. He was addicted to it. She knew it quite well, since he'd held the power of life and death over her for many days. Days she'd tried to forget but which still sometimes made her wake up in a cold sweat, a silent scream on her lips.

She gave her head a little shake and tried to push the

images away. She wouldn't descend into fear. She couldn't. She had a job to do, and she was going to do it. With the help of this man at her side, and the other men on the team. She would find Al Ahmad in Qu'rim—before he found her. She had to, or more innocent people would die. He couldn't be allowed to get chemical weapons. The things he would do with them would make all those videos look so simple in comparison.

Kev was looking at her with brows drawn low when he pulled into a parking slot at the mall. "You want to do this now or do you need to go home instead?"

Home. The word slid into her brain and wound itself around and around. What was home? Where was home? It was a strange word to her. Always had been in so many ways. Because she didn't feel like she belonged anywhere.

Not in Montana, not in the Army, not with Marco.

She'd called her mother earlier when she'd had a break. She could hear the triplets in the background, giggling and screaming as they watched some television show. They sounded so happy and carefree. Had she ever been that way? If so, she didn't remember it.

"They have a horse show coming up," her mother had said.

Lucky had made the appropriate response. Everyone in her family rode horses. She was terrified of them. Yet another thing that made her feel out of place.

She'd managed to explain she wasn't coming for Christmas, that she'd been recalled to duty with the Army. Her mother had been upset at first, but Lucky explained how important it was. There were things happening in the Middle East, blah, blah, blah, and her language skills were important.

Her mother accepted it, but Lucky could tell she was disappointed. She'd hung up feeling like she'd said the wrong things, but not knowing what the right things were.

"Lucky?" Kev said, and she shook herself.

"No," she said, remembering that he'd asked if she wanted to leave. "We're here and I need warm clothes."

They went inside the mall. Lucky thought Kev would leave her to do her shopping in peace, but he took Mendez literally and stuck to her side like glue the entire time.

She hadn't been shopping for more than shorts, flip-flops, and T-shirts in months, but now she had to buy jeans and sweaters and boots. It took longer than she thought it would, but she finally had enough warm clothing—and in-between clothing—to get her through the days in DC before they went to Qu'rim.

In Qu'rim, her wardrobe would change again. Cool cotton clothing beneath a long abaya and a hijab. In truth, she looked forward to the Arab clothing so she could hide inside it. It wouldn't protect her from Al Ahmad, but it would make it harder for him to recognize her.

"You hungry?" Kev asked when she finished paying for the last of her purchases.

Her stomach rumbled then as if to prevent her from saying anything but yes. "I could eat something."

"Come on then. I know a place not too far from here."

They piled into his truck with all her bags, and then he drove to a little restaurant sitting beside one of the many waterways that fed into the Chesapeake. It wasn't Hawaii—too brown and cold for that—but the restaurant by the water was familiar in a way that nothing had been yet. She could almost relax—except that relaxing didn't come easily to her since finding out Al Ahmad was still alive. The film today hadn't helped.

"You okay?" Kev asked after they'd ordered.

She dragged her gaze from the leaden sky and fixed it on him. "Sure, why wouldn't I be?"

He shrugged. "It wasn't a great day for you. It's a lot to get hit with at once."

"I feel like the lives of so many innocent people depend on me. Yeah, it's a lot to get hit with at once." She took a sip of the soda the waitress put in front of her. "What if I can't find him? What then?"

His eyes were hard. Determined. "You'll find him. But even if you don't, HOT will. We won't let him get those weapons. We won't let the region fall."

She sighed. "We've been propping up the people we want to be in charge for decades in that part of the world, and it doesn't always work out. You know that."

"I do know it. But we've learned from those mistakes. Al Ahmad won't win."

"I wish I was as confident as you are."

"Just do the work and stop worrying. That's the part you have to learn. All you can control is the work, so be as strong and relentless as you can be when it comes to training. The rest will fall in place. We have good intel, we have the assets, and we're going to get that bastard."

He was so fierce and certain, and her heart swelled with emotion. But she wouldn't tell him she didn't find it as easy as he did to put the worry aside.

As if he knew what she was thinking, he reached out and took her hand. Once more, electricity pulsed through her veins at the touch of skin on skin. Kev's skin. Her skin. Oh, it was almost more than she could bear.

"I won't let him take you again. I swear it, Lucky. I'll

die before I let it happen."

She squeezed his hand suddenly. "If you don't promise me not to die, I'll ask Mendez for another bodyguard. I won't have you on my conscience."

He smiled that soft smile of his. "Ah, babe, what you don't understand is that all of us will behave precisely the same way. It doesn't matter if it's me or Matt or any of the others—we'll die before we let Al Ahmad take you again."

Lucky swallowed the lump in her throat. She knew that what he said was utterly true. HOT would, to a man, die to prevent her from being taken hostage by that madman. They all knew what she'd been through the last time, and they wouldn't let it happen again.

It got to her in a way nothing else could. Her heart swelled with hot emotion. It was a combination of joy, anger, frustration—and something very like belonging.

"Don't die, Kev. Swear you won't."

He reached up and ghosted a finger along her cheek, and she realized a tear had slid down it when her skin felt cool.

"I swear it. For you, I'd swear just about anything."

Lucky blinked at him, her entire body hot and achy. Had he really just said…?

He looked down at their hands, and she thought he might pull away. But he didn't. She found herself leaning toward him, so slowly, as if she were being pulled by a string. But he was the only thing she could see as her heart pounded and the blood throbbed in her ears. The restaurant fell away, the clink of silverware and porcelain and glass faded, the soft chatter of voices ceased. There was nothing but her and him and the silent pull of attraction that had them moving closer together.

Kev's eyes dropped to her mouth then, his gaze focusing there while her skin sizzled beneath that hot look.

Her lashes dropped down as her eyes landed on his mouth. That hard, sensual mouth. She wanted to feel it against hers. She wanted it so badly. Maybe, if he kissed her, she'd feel alive again.

"Here you go, hon." A plate plopped down on the table with a clang, and Lucky straightened with a jolt. After the waitress set their plates down and asked if they needed anything else, she walked away and Lucky finally managed to look at Kev.

His jaw was hard, his eyes completely cool now. He looked farther away from her than ever, and she wanted to scream in frustration.

"I'm sorry about that," he said, his voice tight. "It won't happen again."

She didn't know if he was talking about the almost-kiss or touching her cheek or what he'd said about dying. She wanted desperately to ask, but how did you ask something like that? Lucky dug her fork into her crab cake and shrugged as if it were no big deal.

But what would have happened if the waitress hadn't interrupted?

Kev punched his pillow and flipped onto his back. He'd almost kissed Lucky. Right in the middle of a damn restaurant. For a few short moments, he'd forgotten why he wasn't supposed to do so. Jesus.

If not for the waitress arriving when she had, Kev would have pressed his mouth to Lucky's and taken everything he could get away with. He was such a bastard. He had to remember that she was vulnerable. Frightened. She was being forced to go after a terrorist who'd tortured her, an organization that had killed her husband, and she was no doubt feeling a whole range of emotions that made her especially vulnerable right now.

And he'd been ready to take shameless advantage of it. Because he was a dawg.

Take care of Lucky for me.

"Yeah, I know that's not what you meant," Kev said into the darkness. "I'm trying, Marco, but it's not easy."

It wasn't just because Lucky was beautiful. She was, of course, but he'd never had a problem controlling himself with a beautiful woman before. It wasn't even that he'd been attracted to her before Marco had expressed interest in her.

It was something behind those eyes. Something deep and wounded and hidden. Lucky needed protecting more than any woman he'd ever known, but she was also the least likely person to accept it. She hid her vulnerabilities from the world, but she couldn't hide them from him. He'd always seen them, even before the Freedom Force had snatched her from a market in broad daylight. There'd always been something inside Lucky that drew him.

Something he wanted to explore. He wanted, quite simply, to drown in her. To take her in his arms and hold her close, to make her feel safe and sheltered. And then he wanted to peel her clothing off her body and explore every curve and line.

He was growing hard thinking about it. Kev threw the covers back and sat up with a curse. He'd go downstairs and work out for an hour or two, exhaust himself, and hope he could get to sleep without thoughts of Lucky rolling around in his head.

He stood in the dark and pulled on a pair of shorts and a T-shirt he'd thrown on a chair near the bed. Then he grabbed his shoes and started for the door.

A noise stopped him. He stood in the dark and listened hard, his ears straining for the sound. He didn't expect anyone was trying to break in, not really, but it didn't stop him from reacting like he'd been trained to react. He took everything as a threat until he determined otherwise. It was safer that way.

This time when the noise came, his heart fell into his toes. *Lucky*.

Kev grabbed his weapon, then tore out of his room and down the short hall to the room next door. He thought about knocking, but dismissed it as an option that would take too much time—not to mention alert a potential intruder—and simply shoved the door open and burst into her room.

It was dark, except for a small night light that he knew he didn't own, and undisturbed. Except for the woman in the bed. She'd thrown the covers off and lay there in nothing but a T-shirt that had twisted up to reveal the smoothness of her belly and the tiny panties she wore.

Kev swallowed as he lowered the gun. She was asleep, but whimpering. And then she said a word. *No*.

It tore his heart in two and halted any idea he'd had about backing out of the room and leaving her to dream. He set the gun on a small table by the door before he went over to the bed and perched on the edge.

Then he reached out and smoothed the tangle of taw-ny-gold hair from her face. "Lucky? Wake up. You're dreaming, sweetheart."

She pulled in her breath on a sob—and then her eyes snapped open. They fixed on his face, their chocolate depths wide with terror and sorrow. She blinked once. And then she sobbed again, turning away from him and pulling the pillow to her face to muffle the sound.

Kev's heart was a mangled organ right now. It squeezed hard. "It was a dream, Lucky. A dream. I'm here. I won't let anyone hurt you."

Her crying slowly subsided as he rubbed her back. Finally, she turned her head and looked up at him, her eyes glistening with moisture. "I'm sorry."

"For what? For having a bad dream? For crying?" He shrugged. "I'd be lying if I said I'd never done any of those things."

That day so long ago when he'd walked into his boy-hood home after storming out earlier that morning had been a good day to cry. He hadn't, but he'd certainly had bad dreams. For years. If he hadn't left that day, would he be dead too? Or could he have prevented his father from killing everyone and then turning the gun on himself?

It was a question he'd never ceased asking—and a question that would never have an answer.

Lucky pulled in a shaky breath. "Why are you so good to me?"

Kev blinked away the bad memories and focused on the woman before him. *What?* "Why wouldn't I be?"

She looked away and swallowed, as if she couldn't quite voice why she thought he shouldn't be nice to her. In spite of himself, his gaze traveled down her back to the exposed curve of her hip. She had tan lines, and he found it erotic as hell. Her panties were white, flimsy, and lacy. He wanted to put a finger beneath the elastic and slide the silk down.

Kev pulled in a breath and tried to calm his raging testosterone. His cock was so hard it hurt. He closed his eyes and told himself not to look at Lucky's skin. Not to think about the silkiness of all that smooth flesh beneath his palms. He wanted to drop his head and bury his nose in the wavy cloud of her hair. And then he wanted to kiss every inch of her while she writhed beneath him.

But he could do none of those things. He forced himself to stand. Then he squeezed his hands into fists at his side so he wouldn't be tempted to use them.

Lucky sat up, her expression swinging toward confusion as she lifted her knees and wrapped her arms around them. And then her gaze fell down his body, and he knew what she was seeing. He didn't try to hide it. What was the point?

Their eyes met again, and they stared at each other in silence for a long moment.

Busted.

"I'm not being good to you because I want to fuck you, if that's what you're thinking," he finally said. And then he decided to be brutally honest with her. "But yeah, I want that too. I've always wanted it. But that's not enough for a woman like you. And it's definitely not cool now, given the circumstances."

She tilted her head to the side like a puppy trying to understand something curious. "What do you mean it's not enough for a woman like me?"

Of all the things he'd expected her to say.

"Jesus, Lucky." He raked a hand through his hair and then rubbed his palm over his face. "I mean you deserve better than a random fuck from a guy like me. You always have."

Her brows arrowed down. "Don't you think that should be up to me? What gives you the right to decide what I deserve?"

He blinked. He was at a total loss. It was clear he would never understand women. He'd just told her she was nothing to him but a body, and she wanted to know why that was a bad thing.

So he'd try to explain as best he could. Maybe he should be subtle. Maybe he should walk away and keep his mouth shut.

But he wasn't capable of subtle right now. He wanted her to know the truth—and then he want her to tell him to fuck off, like he deserved.

"Marco wanted to marry you and put you on a pedestal. I never wanted that. I wanted you naked and beneath me, hot and sweaty and incoherent with pleasure. I wanted it pretty damn badly, but I also know myself. Once I'd had that from you, I'd have moved on to the next woman. I didn't want to hurt you."

She stared at him for a long moment. Then her expression clouded.

"Fuck you, Kevin MacDonald," she said, her voice tight and angry. She got onto her knees on the bed, her finger jabbing at him. "Fuck you for thinking you're so damned amazing that I'd have been ruined forever just because you took me to your bed. Did you ever stop to think that maybe all I wanted was sex too? That I was no more interested in happy ever after with you than you were with me? Fuck you, you arrogant prick."

There was the fuck you, but not the way he'd expected. It was shocking to hear her say such a thing—and hell if it wasn't arousing too. As if he needed more arousing.

His gaze dropped from her fiery eyes to her nipples, beaded tight and pressing against her T-shirt. He wanted to lick them and his cock jumped in response.

Goddammit.

There was a reason he couldn't do this. "It doesn't matter what either of us wants anymore. You're Marco's widow," he said, his voice suddenly raw. "And as much as I want you now, that's a line I can't cross."

Her breath hitched. And then she glared at him. "There you go again, assuming things about me. I didn't say I wanted you now, did I? That ship sailed a long time ago."

He swallowed. It's what he deserved to hear... and he almost believed her. But her eyes gleamed feverishly as her gaze raked over him. She couldn't help but let her gaze linger on his cock, and a surge of something very like triumph shot through him. Her nipples were erect against her thin shirt and her pulse thrummed in her throat. She was lying, and that knowledge both pleased and angered him.

He wasn't letting her get away with it, though he should. He should walk away and let sleeping dogs lie. But he just wasn't capable of it. His emotions were too raw, too close to the surface.

"You didn't have to say it. It's obvious."

Her eyes flashed, but instead of hiding from him, she knelt there proudly, hands on hips, breasts jutting forward, their curves so round and tempting. "Nipples? That's your proof? I haven't been warm since I landed in this icebox and you think my nipples are hard for any other reason?"

Stop now, dude. Just stop. "Yeah, I do."

She snorted. "We all want you, don't we, Southern boy? You turn up the drawl and we fling our panties at you." She flicked her fingers at him. "Take your drawl down to the bar and get laid so your brain will be clear again. I'm going back to sleep."

He should do exactly as she told him. He should walk out of this house, go down to the nearest bar, and pick up a woman. Or he should scroll through the contacts on his phone and call one of his last hookups.

But he couldn't leave her here alone. And he damn sure couldn't bring another woman back to his own house and fuck her next door while Lucky lay here in her little T-shirt and flimsy panties.

No, she was the one he wanted. And he was going to go fucking crazy living with her for the next few weeks and not being able to touch her.

"You know what I think?" he said, his voice like a whip in the semidarkness of the room. She made him crazy, and he'd be damned if he was going crazy alone. "I think you're every bit as horny as I am. I think you want me."

What the fuck was he saying? Why was he pushing her? This was not what he'd promised Marco.

He could hear her breathing sharply, see her chest rising and falling in the soft glow of the night light, and he knew he'd hit a nerve. *Tell me to fuck off, Lucky. Tell me I'm wrong.*

"Maybe I am horny," she said hoarsely, and he took

an involuntary step toward her. "But if you touch me now, if you dare to touch me, I'll go to Mendez and tell him I can't work with you."

He stalked toward her. "Maybe I want you to do just that. Did you ever think of that? Maybe being near you without being able to touch you is driving me crazy, and maybe I'll have some peace if you get me kicked off this op."

He stopped beside the bed. She was still kneeling there, her head tilted back to gaze up at him, her eyes searching his face. Her lips were so pink and moist, so lush. He wanted to taste them one more time. Needed to taste them. If he did that, maybe he could shake this inconvenient attraction to his friend's widow. Maybe kissing Lucky was nothing like he remembered. There would be no spark, no need rushing through him, no desire to ravage and claim.

There would be nothing but emptiness, and he could go back to life the way he understood it. He could stop thinking about this damn woman and what might have been if he'd not walked away and given her to Marco.

She didn't shrink away from him. Her gaze sank to his cock again and need speared into him. Kev reached for her, cupped his hands on either side of her head, and thrust his fingers into her gleaming hair. She didn't try to pull away and a surge of possessiveness rode hard through him.

He lowered his head toward hers.

"Kev…," she whispered.

He stopped for only a second, his pulse pounding a beat in his temples, his cock. "I'm going to kiss you. And then you can complain to Mendez all you damn well like."

TEN

LUCKY'S HEART WAS ABOUT TO beat right out of her chest. She knew she should object. Strenuously. She should put her hands on his chest and shove. She should tell him to get the hell out of her room and leave her alone.

She'd told him she didn't want him. She'd said he didn't make her horny, and she'd said she would tell Mendez if he touched her.

God help her, she'd lied.

Her hands didn't go to his chest. They went to his arms, gripped his heavy biceps, and held on for dear life. Her pulse hammered hard, and her nipples strained against the cotton of her shirt. No, she wasn't cold, damn him. She was excited. Nervous. Scared.

She hadn't been touched by a man in so long, and even then, even when Marco had been gentle and sweet, she'd been edgy. She was edgy now for a different reason.

Adrenaline pumped through her veins as his head descended. He dragged her closer until her body was plastered to his, his mouth a whisper away from hers. She wanted it more than she wanted her next breath.

He hesitated. "Tell me to stop, Lucky."

She licked her lips, her eyes wide on his. "I... I can't."

He stared at her for a long moment. And then he swore before his mouth claimed hers.

A lightning storm of sensation exploded in her belly, her limbs. Her sex. Liquid heat flooded her as her skin sizzled and burned. She ached in ways she'd forgotten were possible. She hadn't been with a man since Marco. He'd been thoughtful and tender, but he hadn't made her burn. It had probably been her fears getting in the way—and yet she burned now.

God how she burned.

Kev tilted her head back and thrust his tongue between her lips. Lucky moaned softly as she clung to him. He tasted like toothpaste and man and she wanted more of him, so much more. Her hands slid up his biceps, and then she looped her arms around his neck. He groaned and pulled her tighter against him until her breasts were flattened against the hard planes of his chest.

His hands drifted down to cup her ass as his tongue demanded more from her. Lucky met him stroke for stroke. The kiss they'd shared so long ago had been sweet compared to this one, tender. This kiss was hot. Sensual. Sexy.

It was the kind of kiss that two people shared when they were desperate for each other.

Kev's hands drifted back up, shaped her waist, her ribs, before cupping her breasts. He could have gone beneath her T-shirt, but he stayed on top of it. That little bit of consideration made her heart pinch.

His mouth left hers, slid hotly down the column of

her throat, and then fastened over one tight nipple. Lucky gasped at the heat and sensual shock. Her fingers curled into his shoulders as she arched her back, thrusting her breasts toward his mouth. She wished she could feel his tongue on her naked flesh instead of through the cotton.

But oh, it was wicked good to feel his mouth at all.

He nipped and sucked, softly, and Lucky realized she was making little panting noises. He stopped and lifted his head, his blue eyes lasering into hers.

"I thought you didn't want me."

She gripped his shoulders harder. "I don't."

It wasn't true and he knew it. He laughed softly. "No, you definitely don't. If I slid my hand into your panties, what would I find?"

She lifted her chin. "I imagine you know very well what you'd find."

He kissed her again until she was soft and pliant and clinging to him. She felt the change come over him, felt him fighting with himself. "We can't do this," he said against her ear. "It's wrong."

She wanted to howl. She knew why Kev thought it was wrong, and she knew she should think so too. But she didn't. Not anymore. "It's not."

Kev took a step back until they were no longer touching and stood there with his brows drawn low and his chest rising and falling as if he'd just run a marathon.

"Marco was my best friend." He shoved a hand through his hair, his eyes growing wild. "I can't want his wife. I can't want to do the things to you that he should be doing."

Her heart hurt. How could she tell him that Marco hadn't wanted to do those things to her anymore? That it had been over? To admit that would be admitting there was something wrong with her.

And she just couldn't do it. Not now.

She crossed her arms and hugged herself, sinking down on the bed as she did so. "He's not here anymore, Kev. He won't ever be here ever again." She swallowed. *Tell him.* "And even if he was, you have no idea what our life together was like or what path we were going down. Don't make assumptions."

He looked angry. "What the fuck is that supposed to mean?"

She ought to be offended, but in truth she was just tired. So tired. She'd spent months running away from herself, from her feelings, from the crumbling foundations of a marriage that had been going wrong long before her husband went on a mission that cost him his life.

"It means there are things about my life—and Marco's—th...that you don't have a right to know."

She couldn't say it. She couldn't tell Kev that Marco had wanted free of her. She didn't blame him because she'd wanted free too. But what did it say about her that the man who'd married her and wanted to take care of her—put her on a pedestal, as Kev thought—had changed his mind?

Kev looked confused. And then he grew angry again. He was so beautiful it hurt to look at him. His eyes were clear and hot, his shoulders were broad, and a wave of inked muscles flexed in his arms as he curled his fingers into fists. "It's clear we can't work together anymore. If you don't ask Mendez for another bodyguard for this assignment, I will."

Her stomach twisted. She knew he was right, that she

should ask for one of the other guys—but she wouldn't. She couldn't. "If that's what you want, go ahead. But you're the only one I trust."

It was the truth.

He swore softly. "That's not fair."

"Life isn't fair. If it was, Marco would be alive and Al Ahmad would be dead—and all those innocent people he killed would still be alive too." She closed her eyes and shook her head. How had she let this degenerate into such a mess? "I'll go after him no matter who Mendez assigns to guard me, because he has to be stopped. But I want it to be you. You're the one I know best, the one I'm not afraid of being alone with."

And that was the truth. He'd touched her tonight in ways that would make her come out of her skin if anyone else had done it. She was still reeling from the realization she'd really wanted more. Not just in her head, but her body had wanted it too.

His jaw tightened. "You *should* be afraid. We both should."

He turned and walked out the door, shutting it firmly behind him.

Lucky stepped into the darkened room at the HOT training facility and gazed at the obstacles in her path. She knew Kev would attack her at some point, and she had to be ready. Her ears strained to hear movement in the darkness and her heartbeat slowed as she regulated her breathing.

Christmas was coming in just three days, but that didn't mean that training for a mission eased. In fact, Lucky's training had shifted into overdrive. Every day for the last two weeks, she'd hit the obstacle course, the pistol range, the outdoor range, and the gym.

It was necessary on two accounts. First, she had to be ready or the mission could fail. And second, it kept her busy and exhausted enough that she didn't keep dwelling on what might have happened if Kev hadn't backed away from her after that kiss.

He was still her bodyguard, her trainer, her constant companion—but they didn't talk much anymore. She asked again for her own car and a room, thinking she needed some time to herself before they went to Qu'rim and she and Kev were forced to play husband and wife. Mendez did not approve the request. Not that she'd expected he would.

Though it was awkward as hell, she'd awakened early every day, showered, put on her jeans and a sweatshirt, grabbed breakfast and coffee, and piled into Kev's truck to ride the few miles to the military base that housed HOT's facility.

And then she spent the days honing her skills with the men who would be staking their lives on her ability to find the evil needle in the sand dune. It wasn't the same intensity of training they'd gone through to become HOT operators in the first place, but it wasn't easy either. She worked hard, and every night she went home exhausted and fell into bed before eight o'clock. She didn't dream because she was too tired to dream.

Lucky forced herself to focus on the terrain. She crept from one point to the next, ever aware of what was happening around her. There were noises—loud bangs, animals, people moving—and then there was silence. She moved forward slowly, trying to be aware of what was happening around her.

And then someone grabbed her from behind and shoved a gun beneath her jaw. Lucky forced down the panic that was her constant companion during the hand-to-hand stuff and let her instincts take over. She just did what she'd been taught, grabbing the wrist holding the gun and twisting from beneath her assailant's grip. Another flip and twist followed by a sharp blow to the elbow and she had control of the gun.

Kev grinned at her as he shook his arm out. "Great work."

She dragged in a breath and willed her heart to slow. She knew that if he'd reacted as *he'd* been taught, she wouldn't be standing here with the empty weapon. But he'd been acting as an assailant without Special Ops training, and therefore he hadn't prevented her from taking the gun. She knew he could have done so with terrifying speed, and she shivered beneath her sweatshirt.

"Thanks." She flipped the gun and handed it back to him grip first. The hand-to-hand combat had been her biggest worry, but she'd made it through. Because of Kev. He'd been the one to initiate her, and he'd been the one to direct her training. He'd told her he couldn't go easy on her, but he'd in fact been harder on her than anyone else. When she'd faced the others, they'd been tough—but not as tough as Kev.

He'd forced her to work hard and to concentrate on

her actions rather than on what he did to her. And that had been the key to making it work. Once she let go of her fear and reacted on instinct, she succeeded.

"Hey, Big Mac," a dark voice cut in. Lucky spun toward the entrance, her heart kicking up. Her adrenaline was already pumping hard, but the interruption only served to ratchet it up because she was already in fight mode.

Jack Hunter stood silhouetted against the door, as quiet, deadly, and coolly handsome as always. Man, he gave her the shivers. "Mendez wants to see us in the ready room."

"Give us a minute." Kev's voice came from behind her, equally calm and cool.

"Sure."

Jack disappeared and she turned back to Kev. His gaze pierced her. "It's not too late to ask for another partner on this mission."

Lucky's belly flipped. "I told you I didn't want anyone else."

He stared at her for a long moment. And then he shrugged. "Just thought you should know that I understand if you've changed your mind."

"I haven't." But she knew he wished she had. After that hot kiss they'd shared, after the way he'd had his mouth and hands on her starved flesh, his indifference hurt more than it should.

He turned away from her while her heart throbbed with hurt. Lucky sucked it down and followed him. He put the weapon and their gear away, and then they walked through the corridors to the ready room. Mendez sat at one end of the conference table while the rest of the guys ranged around it in positions of utter relaxation or knife-edged readiness.

Lucky took a seat and concentrated on the colonel. He looked grim—but when didn't he?

As soon as they were all there, he launched into it.

"We've had information. The king's forces are strained at the seams, and there's been some dissension in the ranks. We think someone on the inside is communicating with the Freedom Force, but we can't be sure. And the king is unwilling to believe anyone in his inner circle would betray him."

"The mine?" It was Matt who'd spoken.

"Still in the government's hands, but we're no longer certain that matters as much as we thought it did. If someone is conspiring with Al Ahmad, the government could collapse much sooner than we expected. The balance of power could shift at any moment. I don't have to tell you that we can't let that happen."

The men murmured agreement. Lucky's heart pounded as she thought of the film and what Al Ahmad would do if he had that mine. What if he changed his mind about the chemical weapons and someone gave him nuclear technology instead?

The looks on the male faces around the conference table told her they'd all thought the same thing.

"We're inserting before New Year's," Mendez said, and Lucky's stomach dropped. She'd always known they were going to Qu'rim, always known she would be that much closer to Al Ahmad—but having a definite date rattled her in a way that all the training and planning hadn't yet managed.

She glanced over at Kev, found his eyes on her, and jerked her head back to the front of the room as Mendez punched a button, and a PowerPoint presentation flared on the screen in front of them.

"Here's the plan..."

ELEVEN

KEV READ OVER HIS BRIEF again and glanced at Lucky, who was still reading hers. He was a photographer covering the unrest in Qu'rim, and she was a teacher. They were newlyweds, which kicked him deep in the gut and made him want to howl in frustration. How was he supposed to play the newlywed with this woman? He had the part down about being unable to keep his hands off her— but he wasn't going to let that happen.

He couldn't. What would it say about him if he did? About his respect and love for Marco?

It was bad enough he'd kissed her. That he'd done more than that and had his mouth on her breast, even if there'd been a T-shirt between him and her flesh. He'd been wrong to push her and helpless when she'd admitted that she wanted him too.

He should have walked away before things got out of hand. But he hadn't.

And now he'd spent the last two weeks thinking about the way she'd looked, kneeling on her bed, her head thrown back and her breasts thrust toward him. He'd been thinking about the way she tasted, about how he wanted to taste her again. Worse, he'd gone to bed hard and aching every night, knowing she was there, knowing she'd been ready to melt beneath his touch.

He had to get his head around the fact she was going to Qu'rim with the team. This was the first time they'd gone on a mission with a woman as part of the operations team, and if anyone had told him he'd be the one pretending to be her husband, he'd have laughed his ass off and told them it was too far-fetched for belief.

But HOT was evolving, and so too were their missions. He was a Special Operations soldier, but it seemed he was also an actor these days as well. Whatever it took to get the mission done.

They'd been planning the mission for a while when Mendez scraped back from his chair and stood. Everyone snapped to attention—including Lucky.

"As you were," Mendez said. "It's been a long day, so why don't you all get some rest? Back here tomorrow at oh seven hundred."

Everyone looked at each other as Mendez walked out. "You heard the man," Matt said. "Go home for a few hours. Come back in the morning ready to work. And oh," he said, turning back to them when he reached the door. "Evie's cooking Christmas dinner. Since nobody's going home for the holidays, we're happy to have you celebrate with us."

The guys all said their thanks and Matt left with a nod.

"Who's Evie?" Lucky asked, leaning in close so no one else could hear.

"His fiancée. Our Richie Rich went home for his sister's wedding this summer and came back with a woman."

Lucky's mouth formed a soft O. He found himself wanting to press his lips over hers and experience the fire and sweetness of that kiss again. He clamped down on the desire and forced himself to think of something else. Cleaning the toilet. Washing dishes. Anything to get his mind off her mouth.

"That's awesome. I guess she's not military, hmm?"

"Nope. They were childhood friends." Kev huffed a laugh as he thought back to the drama of the summer. It hadn't been fun at the time, not when he and the guys had used HOT assets to help Matt—against orders not to get involved—but everything had turned out all right in the end. They'd busted an organized crime ring and dismantled a huge illegal operation. That kind of thing was always satisfying. It was the reason he did this job—to make a difference and stop the bad guys. He hadn't been able to stop his father, but he damn sure could try to stop as many men like Dan MacDonald as possible.

Soulless, conscienceless bastard.

The guys filed toward the door. Billy called out, "We're going over to Buddy's for a few beers. You two want to come?"

Kev opened his mouth to say no, but Lucky turned with a smile on her face—she didn't smile like that at him, dammit—and said, "Thanks, that would be great."

He waited until everyone else was gone before he spoke. "You need to rest, Lucky. Once we go in, it'll be nonstop."

Her pretty eyes were solemn. "I know that. But I think we deserve a night out for once, don't you? Maybe we can forget, for a little while, what's about to happen."

He knew from experience that wasn't possible but he nodded anyway. "All right, if that's what you want."

They drove to Buddy's in silence. When they arrived, Billy waved them over to a round table tucked into one corner of the bar. It was a dive in some ways, but Buddy always welcomed the guys warmly and the food was good. Around the table, the guys laughed and joked as if there wasn't a critical mission coming up. Lucky sat down next to Ryan Gordon, who turned his killer smile—part of the reason his team name was Flash rather than just the obvious Flash Gordon reference—on her while Kev tugged out the only remaining chair across the table and tried not to scowl as Flash leaned in and said something that made Lucky tilt her head back and laugh.

Billy shoved a beer at Kev and gave him a sympathetic look that made Kev frown all the harder. He didn't like that knowing look at all.

Garrett Spencer got up and ambled over to the jukebox while a waitress hustled over with more beers and some extra menus. Kev studied his menu intently, which was ridiculous considering he knew everything Buddy's had, and tried not to lift his gaze over the top of it to look at Lucky sitting there with Flash, laughing at every third thing he said and tossing her mane of hair playfully over her shoulder.

"Maybe Flash should play her husband," Billy said *sotto voce*, and Kev stiffened. "They look a lot more natural together than you two."

Kev turned a page in the menu. He didn't see what was written on it anymore. "Fine by me."

Billy snorted. "No, it's not."

"Mind your own business, Kid."

Billy lifted a bottle of Sam Adams to his lips. "I am minding my business. I know what Marco meant to you, and I know you care about Lucky too. And if you can't do this job without emotional attachment, you put us all at risk. Let someone else play the part, dude."

Kev resisted the urge to punch something. "I already tried. She trusts me—and I'm sticking with her because I promised Marco."

Billy let out a breath. "Copy that. Just be careful, okay?"

Kev nodded as Billy took another pull from the beer. He knew his teammate cared, but there was no easy way through this job when Lucky twisted him up on the inside the way she did.

Iceman must have made a selection because the juke-box rattled to life and the strains of a dance tune filled the air. It wasn't too fast, but it wasn't slow either.

Flash stood up then, and Lucky stood with him. Kev started to stand too, but Billy gave him a look that made him sink back down as the pair of them walked over to the area that had been cleared off to make a dance floor. Kev sat stiffly, waiting for Flash to take her into his arms and praying he wouldn't—because Kev would probably bolt off this chair and rip her out of them.

But nothing of the sort happened as Flash and Lucky lined up and began moving in sync. Kev realized then that it was a stupid line dance and he let out a long breath. Iceman joined them while Knight Rider stood and went over to the door as his professor fiancée walked inside and launched herself into his arms.

Sam wrapped his arms beneath her ass and lifted her up while she put her legs around him and kissed him like no one else was in the room.

"Damn, those two could ignite a rocket," Billy said softly.

No kidding there. Sam set Dr. Georgeanne Hayes down and they walked over to the table, wedged tightly together as if they couldn't bear to be parted. He pulled a chair over for her, but she plopped down on his lap instead and wrapped one arm around his neck. He certainly didn't seem to mind.

"How are y'all doing today?" she said in her Texas drawl, plucking Sam's beer off the table and taking a drink.

"Great, ma'am," Billy said. "How about you?"

Georgie laughed. "Fabulous now that I'm here with my man."

The waitress came back to the table, and Kev ordered a burger. The other guys had already ordered and the waitress said she'd come back for Lucky's order when she was done on the floor. Kev took a long draught of the beer she'd set in front of him and tried not to scowl as Lucky laughed and kicked up her heels with abandon.

He hadn't seen her that relaxed in... well, he couldn't remember.

It wouldn't last, though. Tonight, they could all pretend nothing was wrong, that life was normal, but tomorrow they'd be back to work, worrying about the mission and how they were going to find—and extract—Al Ahmad. Kev wished like hell they were killing the bastard, but the order from the top was to capture.

It wasn't going to be easy, nor was it going to be like other missions since they were taking Lucky along for the ride.

The song finished and Lucky came back to the table with Flash behind her. He pushed her seat in for her and then looked up at Kev. Whatever he saw on Kev's face wiped the smile from his own, and he sat down and grabbed his beer. He made sure not to sit too close to Lucky after that, and Kev felt like an asshole.

He wasn't supposed to be possessive of her. He was just supposed to protect her. And it was in her best interests to be at ease with the guys. If she could manage it, he had no right to interfere in any way. If Flash flirted, it was her call if she let him. Not Kev's.

Jesus.

Billy slapped him on the shoulder in sympathy. If it was obvious to Billy how much he was struggling watching Lucky with another man, was it obvious to the others? And what did they think about him, knowing that she'd been Marco's wife?

But no one said anything or shot him any looks, and they subsided into conversation and laughter for the next couple of hours. They scarfed burgers, wings, and assorted fried junk, and knocked back a few beers. The talk around the table covered many topics, though not the one foremost on anyone's mind: Qu'rim. Instead, they steered clear of that subject until finally Georgie Hayes—who'd ended up in a corner with Lucky, talking about whatever women talked about—caught Sam's eye and the two of them rose as one and said their good-byes.

After that, the gathering grew subdued as everyone eyed cell phones and watches. One by one, they started to sort out their bills and head for the door. Kev opened the truck door for Lucky, and she climbed inside and put on her seatbelt while he went around and got in the other side.

The air was colder than it had been as a front came in from the west and sent temperatures spiraling downward. There was even talk of a white Christmas for a change.

"That was fun," Lucky said as they pulled out of the parking lot. "Thanks for taking me."

"I didn't think I had a choice."

She sighed. "Well, thanks anyway." She paused for a moment. "I like Georgie and Sam. They're so perfect together. It was strange at first, seeing him and knowing he was Marco's replacement. But now I just think of him as one of the guys."

"It was for me, too. But that's the way the military works. I told myself for a long time that it was the same as if Marco had taken another assignment and moved away."

Her voice grew subdued. "I thought I saw him in Hawaii sometimes. There are so many military guys there, and I'd be somewhere, and there'd be a guy in ACUs who looked so familiar. But he'd turn and I'd realize it wasn't Marco at all."

Kev swallowed the lump in his throat. "Yeah, I get that. I'm sorry it happened though. I can only imagine how hard that was for you."

He glanced over at her. Her head was bowed, and she was fiddling with her cell phone. Then she pocketed it and sighed.

"I miss him, but my life isn't over."

He didn't know what to say to that. "No, I know."

"Do you?" She tapped her fingers on the armrest and stared straight ahead. "The closer we get to going on this mission, the more I worry about the things I never did. What if I never get to do them at all?"

A chill slipped down his spine. "That's the beer talking."

She shook her head. "I don't think it is. I think it's a real concern. These next few days could be all I have left."

Kev gripped the wheel tight. *Dammit.* "I told you I won't let him get you. You're coming back. We're all coming back."

"You can't guarantee that."

Kev whipped the truck into a fast-food parking lot and shoved the gearshift into park before turning to look at her, fury rolling through him. He didn't want to hear her talk that way. He didn't want to hear the fatalistic tone in her voice. It wasn't right.

He'd lost Marco out there. He wasn't about to lose Lucky, and he wouldn't have her talking as if fate had already decided it for her. Her eyes were wide as she stared at him.

"Attitude is everything out there," he grated. "You can't go in with the idea this is the end. You have to be comfortable with yourself, sure, but it doesn't do any good to think this is where you will die. If you think like that, you put us all in danger."

"All right." Her voice was soft. Her eyes slipped over his face, and her throat worked. He had a sudden urge to haul her into his arms. He resisted, but barely.

"Just stop thinking it's over, okay?"

She nodded. "But there are still things I never did. Things I wanted to do. It's not fatalistic to wish I'd had the courage to do them."

He shoved a hand through his hair and growled. "What is it you want to do so bad? You have a few days yet if it's important to you."

The air in the truck grew thick with silence. And then

she reached out with trembling fingers and touched his mouth. Her fingers were light, soft, ghosting over his lips so carefully. His blood beat hard in his veins, and his chest grew tight. She was going to drive him insane before this was over.

"I want to be with you."

TWELVE

KEV'S EYES GREW WILD, HUNTED, and Lucky's heart hammered. She was feeling braver than she'd thought possible. Was it the beer talking? Maybe it was, though she'd only had two and she didn't feel tipsy.

Or maybe it wasn't the beer at all, but the gravity of this mission. She'd watched Georgie Hayes with Sam, and she'd envied them. They were so clearly in love, so clearly hot for each other. She didn't know what that felt like, not really, but she wanted it.

She'd told Kev she wanted him, and saying the words was a relief. She hadn't been brave enough to tell him before—before Al Ahmad, before her capture and rescue, before that first kiss. Before she'd married Marco.

If she had, what would have happened? Maybe they'd have had sex, and maybe she'd have still married Marco. Or maybe she wouldn't because she would have known she was the wrong woman for him. Maybe Marco would have figured it out sooner if she'd been honest with herself about her feelings for Kev.

No matter what Kev said, she had to be honest with

herself now. This mission might go sour. She might not return. It was reality, nothing more.

And reality demanded she not deny her feelings right now. For the first time in forever, she wanted a man. She wasn't afraid of Kev touching her. She knew instinctively that he was the only one who could.

"Lucky... Jesus."

"No one has to know."

"I'll know." He put his head on the steering wheel. She could hear him breathing. And then he sat up and shoved the truck into gear. She turned and laid her forehead against the cool window, embarrassment and fury twining together in her belly as he drove in silence toward home. Why had she said anything? Why had she put herself out there like that?

They reached his townhouse and walked toward the door. She stood behind him while he shoved the key in the lock and twisted. And then they were inside the hall, and she shut the door behind her, feeling awkward and embarrassed and wondering what to say before she excused herself and went to her lonely bed.

But Kev turned to her in the dimly lit hallway, his eyes ablaze with anger.

"Why me? Why not Flash or Iceman—or, hell, anyone else?"

Lucky's heart twisted. "I don't know. I just know you're the only one who can touch me. The only one who won't make me shudder in horror or feel sick."

His throat moved. "Marco never said... he said you had difficulties with intimacy."

She'd already figured out that Marco had told Kev about her issues with being touched. Yet it was still embarrassing. And maybe it was a relief too, because what if he'd taken her up on her offer and then she freaked out?

"It was too soon after…" She dropped her gaze from his. "He tried. I tried. It worked, but not the way it should have."

There'd been no fire between them, but she'd felt safe enough with Marco.

"And you think it'll be different with me." He wasn't asking a question.

"Maybe it won't," she said, her head bowed. "But I want to find out. I need to find out—" She swallowed hard. "I want to know if I'll ever be normal again. If I can be with a man without fear, or if I'm doomed to always fear the power he has over me."

"You said Al Ahmad didn't…" His eyes were wide.

"He didn't. But he used his power. He took mine away, and he used his to hurt me."

After a long moment, Kev reached out and started to unbutton her coat. He slipped it from her shoulders and hung it on the coat rack behind him. Then he unbuttoned his own and did the same. He was so big and powerful standing there, broad-shouldered with lean, hard muscles and piercing blue eyes. But she wasn't afraid of him, and she didn't think she could be. But she really didn't know what would happen.

"Marco asked me to take care of you. I don't think this is what he had in mind."

She tilted her head back to look up at him. "This isn't Marco's call. It's mine. And yours. He's gone, Kev. We can't bring him back, and we can't hurt him."

He closed his eyes for a long moment. "I feel like I'm betraying him."

"How?" Her voice grew thick with emotion. "He's gone and we're alive. We didn't die with him. And I don't think he'd want us to act like we did."

She took a step closer to him, lifted a hand, and palmed his cheek. Electricity flooded her system. And his, if the way his head jerked up was any indication. He put his hand over hers, held it against his cheek as warmth spread through her belly.

And then he spoke. "You'll tell me if you want to stop. You won't endure something just because you think you should. Those are the rules, Lucky."

She was beginning to tremble deep inside. "I understand."

He took her hand and led her up the stairs to his room. He switched on the lamp on the bedside table and then turned to look at her. They stood a foot apart and just stared. Her breathing grew shallower, her belly tightening—

Then he tugged her into his arms and kissed her. His tongue slipped into her mouth, tangled with her own, gently at first and then a bit wilder, and she clung to him as her body melted, dissolving into a million little sparks of flame. This was Kevin MacDonald she was kissing, the man she'd once wanted so desperately, the man she still wanted even when she shouldn't.

She knew why this was illicit, forbidden. They would be judged on more than one level if anyone knew. First, there was Marco. And then there was the idea they were on the same team and sex clouded thinking.

But, dammit, Mendez had ordered them to stay together. To pretend to be newlyweds. What did he expect would happen?

Lucky slid her palms over his chest, down the soft cotton of his T-shirt and the hard, corrugated abs beneath until she reached the swelling of his cock. She rubbed it beneath his jeans and he made a noise of approval in his throat.

Then he reached for the hem of her shirt and tugged it up and over her head. The room wasn't cold exactly, but it was cooler than she'd been in her warm sweatshirt. Her nipples beaded beneath the silk of her bra, though it wasn't all due to the cold. She pressed her chest against Kev's— and then she yanked his shirt from his jeans and pushed it up so she could feel her skin against his.

Things began to happen fast after that. Kev unsnapped her bra and tore it off her shoulders, dropping it on the growing pile of clothing. Then he dropped to his knees and took one of her taut nipples in his mouth while she clutched his shoulders and let her head fall back as tears gathered in the corners of her eyes.

It felt good. So good. And she wasn't afraid, though her heart raced and adrenaline tripped through her veins. Kev sucked her nipple hard and soft, then licked around the areola before doing it again. Every tug of his mouth on her breast created an answering spike of slick pleasure in her pussy.

As if he knew what she was feeling, he unbuttoned her jeans and slid them down her hips along with her lacy panties until she stood before him in nothing, her body bared to his eyes. For the first time, a tendril of unease uncoiled in her belly and knocked around. Not because she was afraid of him, but because she was afraid of his reaction to what he would see.

Her belly was crisscrossed with fine silvery-pink

scars, like her arms and her back, and Kev sat back for a moment, just staring at her. She crossed her arms self-consciously, her brain beating with the refrain that she'd been stupid, so stupid, that he wouldn't want her, that he would find her horribly ugly now.

He took her arms and pulled them apart. And then he pressed his mouth to her belly and her eyes flooded with tears. He licked his way over her scars, his hands on her ass as he pulled her in closer. What he did next nearly undid her.

He turned his head and pressed his cheek between her breasts and just held her close.

Lucky put her hands in his hair and clutched him to her with trembling fingers. She wanted to sob. Her entire body shook from head to toe, but not out of fear.

"You're perfect, Lucky. Perfect."

"You don't have to say that." Her voice sounded choked, and she was beginning to think she'd made a mistake, that this would be far too emotional and she wasn't prepared for it after all.

She'd thought she could divorce herself from the process in such a way that it was only about the physical, but she should have known better. When had it ever been just about the physical with this man?

"Why wouldn't I? It's the truth."

Kev got to his feet then and swept her up like she weighed nothing. Then he carried her the few steps to his bed and laid her down on the cool sheets.

"You still want to do this?" he asked. His voice was tender, sweet, and she knew if she said no, he'd understand.

Her pussy chose that moment to throb, as if to remind

her that her body was still very much in this game.

Lucky nodded at the man standing over her.

He gave her a grin as he unzipped his jeans and shoved them down his hips. Her mouth went utterly dry as all that skin and muscle was revealed. She thought she should do something—kiss his ridged abdomen, lick his cock—but all she could do was watch.

"You're the perfect one," she said hoarsely. And he was. Like something carved out of marble and made flesh. Even with the ink that scrolled across his chest and arms punctuated by battle scars, he was perfect.

He came down over the top of her, his body not quite touching hers though she could feel the heat of him above her. "Not me," he told her, his lips gliding over her collarbone. "I'm far from perfect. I'm greedy, Lucky. I want everything you have. I want to taste you and tease you and pleasure you until you can't walk. I want to touch every curve, explore every hollow, and taste every inch of you. If you can't handle that, you need to tell me now."

She lifted a finger to his mouth, traced the hard sensual lines of his lips. Her tummy felt tight, and her pussy was achy. She didn't want to think about what her heart was doing.

"You're ruthless, aren't you?"

He let his gaze slide lazily down over her body before he met her eyes again. "Just thought you should know what you're asking for. I've wanted you for a long time. And that kind of want takes a lot of time to satisfy."

His body hurt with the need spiraling through him, and yet he didn't want to let it loose the way it demanded. If this were any other woman, he'd take this faster. He'd make her come first, and then he'd plunge into her body and thrust hard and deep.

But this was Lucky, and she'd been tortured. The fine scars on her belly had nearly undone him. Between that and Marco, he was a mess of emotion right now. He wasn't used to his emotions being so close to the surface. He'd spent years shoving them deep, burying them under work and numbing them with sex.

He had a feeling that sex with Lucky wasn't going to numb a damn thing though. It was supposed to feel wrong, being with her this way, but it didn't. He hoped Marco would forgive him as he lowered himself and took Lucky's mouth tenderly, thoroughly.

She'd asked for this, he told himself. She'd asked and he couldn't deny her. He should have been able to do so, but the truth was that he was worried about what could happen on this mission too. And he didn't want to go out there without tasting Lucky at least once.

Oh, it was wrong on so many levels. Wrong because of Marco. Wrong because of perspective. How could he make love to her and then maintain the distance he needed in Qu'rim to protect her and get the job done?

He didn't know at the moment, but he would figure it out. Because nothing short of a bomb blast in his living room was going to stop this train from leaving the station.

Lucky's arms went around him as she arched her body toward his, and all thoughts of taking this slowly flew out of his head. He deepened the kiss, shaped her body with his hands as he rolled to the side and took her with him. She threw a leg over his hip and arched her pelvis toward him.

Kev groped for his nightstand, jerked open the drawer, and yanked out a strip of condoms.

Lucky tore her mouth from his and worked her way over his neck, his chest. His breath was coming faster now, his cock straining and aching as he put the strip in his mouth and tore one free.

Lucky looked up, her dark eyes slumberous and sensual, her hair wild. Then she laughed softly.

"I know I should be all prissy about the fact we're doing this in a bed that's no doubt seen tons of action—as your condom supply proves—but the truth is I don't care."

He wanted to deny it, but how could he? He'd had sex with other women in this bed, but not as many as she supposed. It was easier—and less of a hassle, usually, to take them back to their own place instead of bringing them to his.

"That's not what matters right now," he said.

She laughed as she shoved him over the rest of the way and straddled him. Then she took the condom wrapper from his hand and opened it.

"No, it's not."

Kev swallowed as his fingers glided into the softness between her thighs. She was wet and hot, and she shuddered as he found her clit and flicked it back and forth.

"Oh," she said, stilling. Her eyes closed and her head

tilted back, and he knew then that he had to taste her first.

Kev gripped her hips and pulled her toward him. Her eyes sparked, but then she came to him on her knees until he could lift his head and lick her right where he wanted. Her soft cry was ample reward for the effort.

"Put your knees on either side of my head."

She did as he told her and then she gripped the headboard for support as he thrust his tongue into her softness. She tasted sweet and hot, like warm honey, and he parted her with his fingers so he could gain better access to all of her.

"Kevin. My God," she gasped, her body jerking as he licked and sucked her clit again and again. He was mad with the desire to make her come, to make her feel so good she had to scream his name or burst holding it in.

It didn't take long. He felt her stiffen, felt her entire body vibrating—and then the tension burst as he tugged on her clit harder than before.

"Kevin!"

He loved that she said his name like that, in a way no one else did. He'd been Kev since he'd been a kid—Kevvie to his mother and sister—but no one ever called him Kevin, besides the military and his father.

But the way Lucky said it. God. It sounded sweet, not filled with hate or anger or pain or command. Sweet and beautiful, and he wanted to hear it again.

When she stopped trembling, he looked up at her, at the way she looked shell-shocked and satisfied all at once. A prickle of unease filled him then. What if she regretted it now? What if the lustful haze was gone, and she was horrified by what they'd done?

She blushed and turned her head away, and he felt

that same kick in the gut he'd felt the first instant he'd seen her again on the beach in Hawaii.

"Do you want to stop this and go back to your room?"

She didn't look at him, but she shook her head.

"Lucky. What's wrong?"

She eased away from him, until she was straddling his chest rather than his head, and then she lifted her gaze to his and he saw the tears there. His gut clenched hard.

"I haven't felt like that in a long time," she whispered. "A long damn time."

He sat up and hugged her to him. He didn't want to think about when she'd last felt that way, or about the man who'd done these things to her before tonight. If he let his mind go there, the emotion would break through the thin membrane holding it beneath the surface.

He didn't want to think about what would happen if it did.

Her legs were around his waist and her ass was between his legs. She put her head on his shoulder and clung to him. He could feel her heart hammering in her chest, and he pushed her back until he could see her eyes. They were shiny and liquid and she bit her lip as if that could keep the tears from escaping.

Kev pushed her hair out of her face. She'd been through so much. Too much. He wanted to make it all go away, but he knew he couldn't. All he could do was give her this night, if she still wanted it. This experience.

"The night's not over yet."

Her smile almost broke his heart. "I'm glad. Because I need more, Kev. More of you."

THIRTEEN

SHE WAS SCARED IN A way, and yet she felt brave too. Because Kev was holding her close, his naked body solid and warm, his hands rubbing a sizzling trail up and down her spine. She hadn't known what to expect or how she would react, but she didn't want this to stop. For the first time in forever, she felt almost normal.

Kev's eyes were serious as he gazed at her. "Are you ready?"

She almost could have laughed, but she knew he was being careful because of her. Because of what he knew about her.

She realized she was still clutching the condom in her hand, and she tore it open and slid it down his hard length. He didn't utter a sound as she did so, but she knew by the jerk of his body that her touch affected him.

He shifted her closer, lifting her up and entering her body as they sat facing each other. Lucky's breath caught at the intensity of his invasion. His cock stretched her open, but it wasn't unpleasant. It was… intimate. Arousing.

The closeness, the rawness, made her heart thrum. She forced her mind from going to the most obvious place, to the last man she'd made love with. No way could she go there. Not right now.

"You're so wet," he growled. "So perfect."

Lucky breathed him in, his slightly spicy, earthy scent, and shuddered with the feelings he called up inside her.

They sat face to face, his body deep inside hers, until she began to squirm with the need to have him move, to have something happen so her brain would stop trying to go where she didn't want it to go.

"Kevin. Please… oh, please."

He captured one of her nipples in his mouth and began that sensual tug-of-war he'd done to her earlier. Her fingers curled into his hard shoulders as she arched her back and tried to catch the edge of pleasure that lay just out of reach. It was so close, so close…

When she could wait no more, she lifted her hips and sank down on him. He made a noise deep in his throat that thrilled her, so she did it again. And again.

She understood then that he was letting her take control, letting her set the pace, and her heart pinched.

She pushed him back until he lay on the bed and she was straddling him once more. Then she kissed him so she didn't have to look into his eyes, so she didn't have to wonder if he was trying not to think about Marco too.

Kev gripped her hips in tight fingers and helped her move, thrusting up inside her with every downstroke of hers.

It had been so long since she'd had sex that it felt as if he would split her in two, and yet it felt wonderful at the same time. Because she was so wet. Because he moved hotly, slickly, perfectly.

She gasped and groaned and kissed him harder until he tore his mouth from hers.

"I need to take control. Can you handle that?"

She looked down at his beautiful, taut face, saw the restraint there. For her sake. He was being careful for her. It melted something inside her, some last little barrier that she hadn't known was there.

"I trust you."

He pulled her down with a groan and rolled until she was beneath him. Vaguely, she thought that she should feel a moment of panic at being under such a big, powerful man. At being within his control, his power.

He dwarfed her, but it didn't waken the terror within her. Lucky closed her eyes and gave herself up to the chaotic feelings rolling through her. She was with Kev for the first time ever—and maybe the last time too—and she wasn't going to allow anything to ruin the experience.

Not yet.

He put a hand under her ass and lifted her to him— and then he thrust hard and deep, making her cry out at the sensation this new angle created.

"More," she moaned when he would have stopped. "More."

She could feel his heart beating hard in his chest as she ran her hands over his skin, and it made her breath catch. He took her deeper into the abyss of pleasure with every hard thrust, every perfect roll of his hips. She wrapped her legs around him and let him take her wherever he wanted her to go.

He went slow at first, sliding hard into her, and then

faster, his body relentless as it pushed hers toward the edge. And then she caught fire, her body tightening, straining toward release, aching for that perfect moment when her orgasm would hit her.

It happened suddenly, hitting her with a sharpness that made her gasp his name again and again as her body shattered and dissolved beneath his expert ministrations.

Vaguely, she was aware of his release, a hard, thumping orgasm that jerked through him and left him groaning brokenly in her ear.

His hand slid down her side, over the slickness of her skin—and then he lifted himself off her and left the bed. Lucky prayed the awkwardness of sex with a man she wasn't supposed to want wouldn't appear yet, but of course it did.

She could hear him in the bathroom, disposing of the condom and maybe hoping she would get up and go before he returned. She sat there a heartbeat too long, debating with herself over whether or not it was cowardly to slink away, when he came out of the bathroom and their gazes clashed.

He looked… troubled. It was the only word for it, and her heart fell. She'd asked him to do something that caused him pain. She slid from the bed and started groping for her clothes where they were strewn across the floor. Her vision was blurry, and she rubbed her arm over her eyes as she kept feeling for which garments were hers.

"Lucky."

She straightened, a pile of clothing in her arms, and clutched the garments to her. She couldn't face him. "It's okay. I'm going."

His hands settled on her shoulders. And then he

pulled her back against his naked body, and she shuddered with renewed heat.

"Do you want to go?" he asked, his voice a soft rumble as he bent his head and whispered in her ear.

She should. She should go and curl into her own bed and try to forget everything that had just happened between them.

But she knew she wouldn't. She couldn't. She shook her head, and Kev reached around and gently took the clothing from her arms and dropped it on the floor. She shuddered again as he led her to the bed and flipped the covers back for her. She climbed in, her heart pounding anew as she lifted her gaze and let it glide over his muscled form. He was half-hard already and an answering ache set up a drumbeat in her core.

She wanted him again with a need that surprised her. He sank down beside her and then rolled her under him again. He dwarfed her with his size, but she wasn't afraid. Not of Kev.

His lips found hers again, and her hands glided over smooth, hard muscle. She was lost, lost...

His phone rang and he swore softly before reaching for it. This close to a mission, she knew he couldn't ignore it. He answered with a clipped "MacDonald."

And then he rolled away and sat up, scrubbing a hand through his hair. "No, I'm not busy. Be right down."

Kev yanked on his clothes and pounded down the stairs. He wanted nothing more than to ignore his visitor, but if he didn't go down and answer the door, Billy would know all his protestations about everything being fine were a lie.

When Kev opened the door, Billy stood with his hands shoved in his pockets, looking serious. One eyebrow rose as he took in Kev's hair—sticking up where Lucky had run her fingers through it, no doubt—and the rumpled state of his clothing.

"You look as if you just got out of bed."

"I did." The best lie was the closest to the truth, after all. "We've had early mornings and late nights these days. And no end in sight, right?"

"Yeah." Billy looked down at his feet. "Look, I'll just go. You should have told me you were sleeping."

A pang of guilt lanced into him. "Come in, man. It's cold out there."

Billy came in and took his jacket off and hung it on the rack. Then he went into the kitchen and grabbed a beer from the fridge, just like always. The guys often showed up unannounced at each other's places. It was just part of the brotherhood. They were close, and when they were about to go on an op, there were all kinds of thoughts ramming around in their heads.

"Want one?" Billy asked, as if it were his house instead of Kev's. Also normal.

"Sure."

Billy took out another one and twisted off the top before handing it to him. Kev took a long drink—he'd worked up a helluva thirst, after all—and looked at Billy evenly.

"Everything okay?"

Billy leaned against the counter and shoved a hand through his hair. "I didn't go home after we left the bar. Been driving around and thinking."

"About?"

"The mission. This one, the one where we lost Marco and Jim." He shrugged. "A lot of things."

Kev took another drink. He didn't want to think about that mission right now, but God knows he had been. It was never far from his mind.

Billy's eyes looked heavenward. Or, in this case, to the second floor. "Must be hard, having her here. Being responsible for her."

Kev's heart thumped painfully. "It's not easy, but it's the job."

Billy sighed and rolled his neck to pop out the kinks. "I know how much Marco meant to you. And I really want to know your head's in the right place for this. Because it's your ass—all our asses—on the line out there. It's risky taking a noncom like Lucky into battle, and yet we have no choice. Every fucking thing about this mission makes me uneasy."

Kev felt the guilt flare in his belly. His teammate was worried about him, about the mission. "My head's in the right place."

Billy frowned. "I know what it was like for you after we came back with the caskets. You forget I was there when you called her and she never answered. And I've seen the way you look at her now, man. Like you'd eat her up if she'd let you."

"Jesus." Kev slammed the beer down on the counter, though he knew he should maintain his cool. Blowing his stack only made it worse, and yet it was personal. Between him and Lucky.

"Have you seen her? She's hotter than fuck. Of course I'd like to nail her—*if* she wasn't Marco's widow. But she is and I can't."

Liar. He'd just been buried balls-deep inside her and not thinking about anything but how good it felt. He'd wanted his name on her lips as she came. It was fucking addicting to hear her cry out like that.

Guilt flashed through him as Billy held up a hand. "All right, dude. I crossed a line there." He set the beer down, twirled it absently on the counter. "There's something else."

"What?"

"I've been thinking about what it was like when we got her out of there the last time."

Kev's gut twisted. They'd burst into the house she'd been held in like a cyclone, and they'd systematically taken out every last tango on site. But Al Ahmad hadn't been there. The CIA had him pinned down in another part of town. They'd claimed their sniper got him, but it obviously wasn't true. Lucky had been chained to a bed in her underwear, the sheets stained with her blood. She'd been weak and scared. Kev had found her first. Billy had been his partner on that op, and he'd come into the room next.

They'd cut the chains, and Kev had scooped her against his body while Billy whipped a blanket off a chair that sat in the room. He'd covered her with it, and then they'd humped it out of there before more tangos arrived. No one else had seen her chained to that bed but the two of them.

"I don't think either of us will ever forget it."

Billy shook his head. "She went through a lot with Al Ahmad. Do you think she can handle this? Do you think she'll find him for us, or are we asking too much of her?"

This was the part Kev couldn't be certain about. Oh, he was certain she wanted to find the target. And that she would work hard to do so. But what if Al Ahmad was too smart for them? What if she'd forgotten his voice—or his face, since she'd only seen it briefly? What if he found her first?

Kev's spine was ice at the thought.

If Al Ahmad took her again, Kev would tear Qu'rim apart trying to find her. He wouldn't care about uranium or chemical weapons. He'd only care about finding Lucky. And that was what scared him shitless in the middle of the night.

"I think she'll do her best. And I think her best is pretty damn good for someone who isn't a special operator. She wants to find him as much as we do. Maybe more."

"Yeah, but what happens when she gets out there? It's going to bring up bad memories."

Kev picked up his beer again and took a long draught. He thought of Lucky's scars, of the way she'd tried to hide from him. He'd wanted to obliterate the man who'd done that to her. How had Marco lived with it?

Kev gripped the beer bottle tight. He didn't want to do this right now, but there was no graceful way out. "All we can do is make her feel safe and give her room to operate. She'll find him."

Billy's gaze flickered behind him, toward the stairs, then back again. Kev wondered if Lucky had come down, but he wouldn't turn to look. He wouldn't give himself away like that. Besides, she would have put her clothes on. There was nothing to worry about. But she didn't appear, and Billy pushed away from the counter.

"Guess I better get home. Thanks for the beer."

After Billy was gone, Kev went back upstairs, determined to hold Lucky close for the rest of the night. Right now, he didn't even care if they had sex again. He just cared about being next to her, smelling her skin, feeling her heat against his body.

But when he opened his bedroom door, Lucky wasn't in his bed. Her clothes were no longer on the floor. He sagged against the jamb and stared at the rumpled sheets while his heart squeezed and his lungs worked to pull in air against the sudden tightness in his chest.

She'd gone back to her own bed. He thought about going after her. But he'd let her call the shots tonight, and she was clearly calling another one.

Kev shut the door and peeled off his clothes. Then he got into bed—and promptly threw the pillow that smelled like her shampoo on the floor.

FOURTEEN

December 28th
Baq, Qu'rim

QU'RIM WAS LIKE AN OVEN inside a blast furnace after the frigidness of DC. Lucky walked down the gangway and onto the tarmac as a wall of heat assailed her lungs. She'd put on an abaya and a hijab before they'd left Morocco, and now she was wishing she could strip it off and bare her skin to whatever air might be moving out here.

She shaded her eyes—though she was wearing sunglasses—and gazed across the tarmac at the mobile missile launchers parked on the other side of the runway.

Kev stopped beside her, his brow glistening with sweat, his eyes hidden behind aviator sunglasses. And then he grinned at her—the first time he'd done so in days— and her heart turned over. Jeez, he was handsome. And not hers, no matter what they were pretending.

"Well, darlin'," he said, turning up the drawl, "you sure are a good little wife to want to come with me to this hot place while I take photos for the magazine."

Lucky's heart thumped. He'd been blasting her with Southern charm for hours now. It was for the mission, but it was starting to grate. "That's me, sugar dumpling. A good wife."

They'd spent the last five days preparing for this mission, with the exception of Christmas Day when they'd gone to Matt and Evie's place for dinner and conversation. These guys had even managed some excitement in those few days when Billy Blake had stumbled onto a conspiracy to sell faulty weapons to the Pentagon, and the team had gone to work to dismantle a defense contractor's falsified test results. And Billy had reunited with the woman he loved. If anyone was surprised at the speed with which he'd entered a committed relationship, they didn't say so.

Lucky remembered Olivia Reese from Fort Bragg, but she'd never known her well. Good for Olivia for getting her man finally. And poor Billy, having to leave her so soon after they'd gotten together again. Lucky knew what it was like to stay behind and worry. She only hoped this mission would be of short duration, and they'd all go back home in one piece.

Ryan Gordon came down the stairs and stopped beside Lucky and Kev. He was the reporter to Kev's photographer, which would enable the two of them to work closely together while they searched for Al Ahmad and the Freedom Force. The other guys were here in various capacities—engineers, computer gurus, geologists, relief workers—that would enable them to communicate and work together in teams of twos and threes.

The team had flown commercial air from Morocco, which was unusual, but they'd felt that a military transport would be too obvious for anyone paying close attention. A couple of the guys had come in on an earlier flight. There were five of them on this flight, plus her. The last two would come a little later. It was simply to keep from arousing suspicion, but Lucky wasn't sure guys who looked like these could manage to go unnoticed for long.

They were all tall, broad, and utterly lethal. Not that they appeared lethal right now. Kev looked casual and somewhat harmless in his khakis, flip-flops, and navy T-shirt. Flash was wearing a Hawaiian shirt and a pair of shorts. She caught sight of Jack Hunter and nearly swallowed her tongue. He was handsome, sure, but he was also the epitome of a totally rad surfer dude. He had two days' worth of stubble, a faded T-shirt, and board shorts with flip-flops. His hair gleamed golden in the bright sunlight, and when he smiled his teeth were blindingly white.

"Darlin'," Kev said, edging closer and putting his hand on her elbow. "I thought I told you I was the jealous type."

"I have eyes only for you. But that guy is hot, you have to admit."

Flash laughed. Matt Girard came down the stairs next, swaggering like he didn't have a care in the world. She wished she knew what he'd smoked to get that way. Matt didn't go on missions very often anymore, but this one was the exception. They all wanted to be involved in capturing the world's most wanted terrorist. It was personal to them.

Lucky pulled in a hot breath and threw up a quick prayer that everything worked the way it was supposed to as they started toward the shelter of the terminal.

She didn't miss the guards with machine guns or the military vehicles parked nearby, and she knew the guys didn't either. The troops wore the colors of the king's government, which was a good thing. Control of the airport was vital during the crisis, and the Qu'rimis still held it. So far, the opposition forces were confined to the desert—but if they got into Baq and took the airport, things would not be good for the king and his government.

Lucky prayed that didn't happen. And definitely not while they were here.

They went inside the coolness of the terminal and processed through immigration. Then they all ranged around the baggage carousel, waiting for their luggage. Lucky knew the guys had sophisticated equipment in some of those bags, and she hoped the Qu'rimis hadn't been too curious. Nothing looked military grade, of course, which was good.

Eventually, the carousel started to rotate and the bags spilled out in slow motion. By the time everyone had everything, a man with a sign that said Royal Baq Hotel on it had arrived and was standing near the entrance.

"That's us, darlin'," Kev said before grabbing her hand and tugging her toward the man. The others followed suit along with a few people she didn't recognize. They left the terminal and went out into the heat again, crossing the road that ringed the airport and stopping beside a rickety bus with faded paint. The windows were down, which was not a good sign so far as she was concerned.

The driver helped stow the bags—though the team held on to some of theirs—and then they filed onto the bus and sat down for the ride. Kev slid in next to her and put his arm around her.

It was strange, considering how they'd avoided each other—and any uncomfortable conversations—for the last several days, but it was totally in character. None of the guys even blinked.

Kev's head dropped until his mouth was next to her ear. "Relax. You're strung tighter than a tick on a dog. This is the easy bit, so sit back and enjoy the scenery."

In spite of the heat, his breath on her ear sent a shiver tripping down her spine. She turned her head until their mouths almost met. It looked intimate to anyone watching, but she wasn't concerned. They were here now, and this was their cover.

"How do you stand this kind of thing?"

"Usually, the objective is a little clearer. We know where we're going and what we're after. This time, we sit and wait and hope what we're after comes to us."

She laid her head against his shoulder because she could and looked out the window as the bus began to move. The traffic grew thicker toward the city itself, and there were tanks parked at crossroads and entry points into the city. The traffic slowed to a crawl as they rolled deeper into the city.

The air was stale and dusty and the heat oppressive in the metal confines of the bus. Sweat pooled between her breasts, rolled down her belly. The slower they went, the less the air moved. Lucky sat up and moved away from Kev, not because she wanted to get away, but because it was too hot to stay plastered next to him.

Outside the bus, the city was a mixture of modern and ancient. Mud-brick buildings coexisted with skyscrapers, and donkey carts moved down the streets along with SUVs. It was this mix, this blend of the haves and have-nots, that made Al Ahmad's rebellion possible. The city was prosperous, but it had pockets of poverty. The desert was a different story. Out there, people existed on the edge of ruin—and they knew it.

Years of bad policies had set Qu'rim back, though the current king was working to fix the mess he'd inherited from his father. They passed carts laden with fruit and vegetables, refrigerated trucks, and in one memorable instance, a group of nomads on camels.

Lucky turned to look at Kev. He'd leaned his head back on the seat and was looking at her from beneath his lashes. Sweat glistened on his face and ran down his neck, pooling in the notch at the base of his throat.

Sexy.

Lucky swallowed. "How much farther do you think?"

Kev rolled his head on the seat and looked out the window. "We've passed the third perimeter. The city center is up ahead. Twenty minutes at this pace."

Lucky sighed and stuck a finger under her hijab to scratch her head. Her hair was damp. "I'll need a shower the minute we get there."

Kev grinned. "Me too. We can conserve water together, darlin'."

Her heart flipped. "You're a little too into this," she hissed under her breath. Because she was already wired enough. She didn't need the added strain of dealing with Kev's enthusiasm for his role.

He shrugged and went back to studying the insides of his eyelids. Twenty minutes later, they rolled beneath the shaded overhang of the Royal Baq Hotel's circular drive. The hotel wasn't precisely a luxury hotel, in spite of the name, but it looked decent enough. They'd passed buildings that had been sprayed with bullet holes earlier, so the fact this one didn't have any was a good thing.

There were quite a few Westerners in the driveway and ranged throughout the lobby. Many of them had cameras, but they didn't move with the casualness of tourists.

"This is where the media stays," she whispered.

Kev nodded. Then he put his mouth next to her ear. "It's inconvenient in some respects, but better too. We'd stand out somewhere else. Here, we're part of the crowd. And hopefully we'll blend in as just another set of Americans who've come to report on the unrest."

"Don't you think interested parties will pay attention to this hotel in particular?" Not all the women wore abayas, but they were wearing hijabs to cover their hair. Lucky could have done the same, but she felt safer this way. She was shapeless and anonymous, and it helped her to breathe easier when she thought about Al Ahmad and the Freedom Force being out there somewhere. Watching.

"Of course they will. But they don't have the resources to background check everyone who checks in, so unless someone stands out in some way, they'll ignore us."

Lucky frowned. For some reason she'd thought they'd be a whole lot more inconspicuous than this. "I hope you're right."

They left the bus and entered the lobby to stand in line with everyone else. Kev put his hands on her shoulders and turned her toward him. His expression was dead serious. "We're on it. This is what we do. Have some faith."

She firmed her jaw as she gazed up into his eyes. This was probably the longest they'd made eye contact since the night they'd had sex, and it shook her deep in her core. A thrill of sexual awareness flared to life inside her as his hands held her in place and his eyes seemed to burrow into her soul.

She'd felt so close to him when they'd been wrapped around each other in his bed, and not just physically. She wanted that feeling again, but she knew it was all on her side. Kev didn't have that same need. He'd warned her he'd only wanted sex, and then he'd move on.

Well, she'd moved on for them both. She'd overheard him and Billy talking that night, and she knew she had to give Kev the space he needed. She'd seduced him, put him into a position where he had to lie to his teammate, and she wouldn't do it again.

Still, she'd gone back to her own room and lay there listening for him. She'd heard him go into his room. She'd half-hoped he would fling her door open and demand to know why she'd left. But he hadn't. He'd gone to bed alone. The next morning, he'd acted like nothing had happened.

Well, almost nothing. He'd asked her if she was okay. She'd said yes. And then he'd stood there for a long moment, hands in pockets, looking like he wanted to say something. The longer he hesitated, the more she knew she didn't want to hear it. So she'd given him a smile and told him thanks for the stress relief. He'd blinked. She'd poured her coffee into her go-cup and gone to put on her coat. By the time he'd joined her, he didn't look like he was having trouble figuring out what to say anymore.

Now she nodded at him. "I trust you, Kev."

His throat worked and she knew those words affected him in some way. And then he gave her that cocky grin he'd adopted since they'd started this mission. "That's why you married me, sugar."

His hands dropped, and she stood there for a moment,

uncertain what to do. Then she pulled her cell phone from her purse—a newly issued phone, of course, not her personal one—and checked for bars. There were two.

She looked up when Kev spoke again. "Why don't you have a seat with the luggage while I check us in, babe? It was a long trip, and I know you'd like to rest. In your condition and all."

Lucky's eyes widened. Flash leaned over Kev's shoulder and grinned. "Congratulations, you two."

Lucky shook her head at their antics as she plopped on a nearby bench. If Kev needed her for translation, he'd call her over. But in this hotel it was likely everyone spoke English. Kev and Flash were still grinning like crazy asses as she opened up a game on her phone and ignored them. About twenty minutes later Kev was back, an envelope in his hand.

"All set?" she asked.

"Yep."

They dragged their luggage to the elevator and stepped inside. It took its sweet time getting started, but soon they were on the fifth floor and heading down the hallway toward their room. The hotel definitely wasn't luxurious, but it had elements of faded Old World grandeur. The floors were tiled mosaic. Crystal light fixtures that had seen better days lit the hallway.

They reached a room at the end, and Kev slid the key in the card reader—at least they'd updated the locks—and threw the door open.

Lucky tried not to groan as she followed Kev inside. There was only one bed. It was not quite queen-sized, but the white linens were crisp and looked inviting. The walls were salmon colored, and the plaster was chipped away in places. But again there were hints of Old World elegance in the crystal chandelier and the antique carpets scattered over the floor.

Lucky pushed away thoughts of the bed and walked into the bathroom. It was large and had a sunken tub, a shower, and two sinks. The floor was tiled in mosaic and the wall over the sinks had a carved wooden mirror inset with mother-of-pearl around the ornate frame.

Lucky returned to the room. Kev was dragging in the last of the luggage, and she put her hands on her hips as she faced him. "What's with that business about my condition?"

He looked grim as he shook his head and she clamped her lips shut. He picked up his carry-on and unzipped it. Then he pulled out some equipment. A few moments later, he was sweeping the room with what looked like a small handheld radio. Lucky sank onto the edge of the bed and waited.

He was completely focused on his task, so she used the time to study him. His hair was damp and sweat glistened on his arms. His shirt stuck to his skin in places, delineating all that smooth, hard muscle for her gaze. Geez, he was delicious. Even sweaty.

Especially sweaty. Lucky closed her eyes and swallowed at the unwelcome wetness between her legs.

Kev finished his sweep for bugs and deployed a small item that looked like a speaker, setting it on a shelf to face the room. Then he took out his phone and dialed.

"All clear," he said when someone answered. "Yeah, copy." A few seconds later he put the phone back in his pocket and looked at her. "You can speak freely. But always be careful. If it doesn't need to be said, don't say it.

Got it?"

"I think so. What's that thing?" she asked, tipping her head toward the speaker that wasn't a speaker.

"Basically, it's a white-noise generator. But much more effective than the sort of things you can buy from your local spy shop. If anyone's trying to listen in to conversations in this room, they won't get anything but white noise."

"All right. Now care to tell me why I'm suddenly pregnant?"

He grinned. "You mean you don't know? Do I need to demonstrate for you again, sugar?"

She rolled her eyes even while a sharp pain pierced her heart. He was just playing around, but she couldn't help but think of them twined together again. "Stop it for two minutes, okay? I can't keep up. Besides, that wasn't part of the cover."

He sobered. "No, it's not, and we don't have to play it that way. I was just trying to make you laugh. I know this is all a bit intense for you."

"It is, but I'll cope." She stood and unwound the hijab from her hair. "I'll cope even better once I get out of these hot clothes and into a cool shower."

At least the room was cool, the central air rattling through the vents and circulating thanks to the ceiling fan that whirred softly overhead. She shook her head and scrubbed her fingers through her damp hair. The ride in the hot bus hadn't been much help, that was certain. Next, she lifted the abaya over her head and almost moaned as cool air wafted over the cotton shift she'd worn beneath it.

She tossed the abaya on a chair and lifted her hair off her neck. Kev sat down at the desk and opened his computer.

"So what happens now?" she asked.

"We wait for everyone to get here."

Lucky sat on the bed again, her heart kicking up a little as she contemplated all they had yet to do. It was maddening to think that all she could do was go to work teaching children to speak English and wait for Al Ahmad to show up. What did they think he was going to do? Come to a parent-teacher conference?

She'd asked Mendez that very question. He'd told her they had no idea what would happen, but they hoped that watching the class and waiting would result in something that would lead them to him.

Kev was tapping on his computer, his back to her. She glanced around the room again. When they'd told her she was going on a mission with HOT, this wasn't what she'd expected at first. She'd envisioned them rappelling down a line from a helicopter, dressed all in black, and busting into a secret hideout, even though she knew it wasn't always like that.

"I always wanted to be an operator, you know. Before, I mean…"

Kev turned toward her, one muscled arm hanging over the back of the chair. He didn't ask before what. He knew she meant before North Africa. "And now?"

She laughed softly. "It's a little maddening, to tell the truth. I think I believed there would be a lot more action. Instead, there's a lot of waiting."

"Every mission is different. Sometimes you go in and the metal of your barrel is so hot it glows. Other times, you don't fire a shot."

"I'm hoping this is one of the latter, to tell the truth."

"Yeah, me too."

She stood and stretched. His eyes dropped over her and she found herself wishing she could walk over and put her arms around him. Wishing she could press her mouth to his and just find comfort in his kiss.

But she didn't know that he would welcome it. Besides, this wasn't the place. So much remained unresolved from the last time they'd let restraint go out the window. It was always there between them, the purple elephant in the room that they'd both been pretending not to notice.

The last couple of days before they'd deployed, they'd spent their nights in the dorms at HOT HQ. There'd been no opportunity to talk alone, much less anything else.

Maybe she was the only one who felt itchy and achy, who couldn't get the images of his naked body out of her head or stop thinking about how it had felt to have him moving deep inside her.

Now she could feel her nipples beading as she thought of it, feel goose bumps forming on her flesh. She dropped her arms and wrapped them around herself, hoping to hide her reaction from him. He was watching her with an expression she couldn't quite fathom.

"I think I'd better take a shower," she said. She left him sitting there and went into the bathroom, closing the door behind her and then twisting the lock at the last second, as if he was the one who needed a barrier between them when she was the one who couldn't seem to stop thinking about the night they'd spent together.

It was only when she turned around and looked at the shower that she realized she'd forgotten toiletries and fresh clothing. Lucky sagged against the door and let out a frustrated breath.

It was going to be a long, *long* mission…

FIFTEEN

TODAY, TWENTY MEN. FOUR WOMEN. Same place.

Abdul Halim lifted his head from the message on his phone and gazed out the window of his high-rise apartment building. His contact was telling him that twenty-four Westerners had arrived today and checked into the Royal Baq Hotel, the place where the government liked to corral the media. It was ostensibly to protect them, but Abdul Halim knew that it was also to control their access. The king and his government preferred to paint a picture of complete and utter control of the situation in Qu'rim when nothing was further from the truth.

He could see the Royal Baq Hotel's domes from here. This influx of Westerners was not unexpected, but still he found it prudent to keep a watchful eye on their comings and goings through his contacts at the airport.

There were more new arrivals in the city than ever these days. Reporters come to stir up the world about the situation in Qu'rim, no doubt. Certainly some of them were CIA and MI6 operatives who were here for other reasons. And then there were the military teams like the ones that had been sent for him so many times before. He did not doubt that the Americans in particular would try again now that he'd seemingly returned to the land of the living.

But first they had to find him, and that was not going to be easy. He took a drag on his cigarette and blew out the smoke. He'd spent a lot of time building this life he had now. He was a wealthy Qu'rimi citizen. He had contacts in the government. He provided a service to both sides of the conflict, though he would prefer that part stayed private.

Yes, it made his goals a little more difficult to achieve, but it enriched his coffers so he could realize his ultimate aims in the end. He was a man with a plan, and he was on the brink of his greatest triumph. Soon the Freedom Force would be the equal of any nuclear power on the planet. They would not dismiss him so easily then.

Yet he still worried about the tiniest things. He picked up his phone again and hit redial. His brother answered.

"Any news?"

Farouk blew out a breath that no doubt contained cigarette smoke. Abdul Halim liked a cigarette now and again, but Farouk always had a lit one in his fingers. His brother knew precisely what he meant.

"Nothing. We've let too much time go by. We're still searching for her near military bases in the US. But so far there's nothing."

Abdul Halim gritted his teeth. It had been three weeks since Farouk had sent word to the network that Lucky Reid had to be found, and yet they'd had no progress.

He told himself that three weeks was nothing to worry about. He had bigger things to concentrate on here. Bigger goals. He could not spend his time worrying about the slim possibility that the United States government was somehow using Lucky Reid to find him. She'd seen his face once, briefly, and she'd been in a lot of pain when she had. Besides, he was careful not to be photographed, ever. There were no pictures of him circulating in a file, nothing anyone could set in front of her and ask her to find him.

He needed to stop obsessing over this and move on to other things. Indeed, it was time for a diversion in Baq. Something to occupy the Qu'rimi government and their supporters. The populace—and the reporters—needed something new to worry about. And he needed something to look forward to.

"Keep looking." He did not like loose ends. "And inform the faithful it is time for Baq to feel our presence."

Everyone was in country and checked in by 2100 local time. The guys ranged around the room Kev shared with Lucky, all looking relaxed but on edge in a way that only a special operations team could be.

Matt had decided after a perimeter check that this room would do for their meetings. They couldn't meet often, not the full group, but the first night was crucial as they confirmed plans and discussed findings. Several of the guys had gone out that afternoon, ostensibly to see the sights but really to check the city's defenses. Baq wasn't an especially large city, but it was packed with military equipment and personnel.

The king was scared and with good reason. The situation in Qu'rim was rapidly deteriorating—as evidenced by the bullet holes in those buildings earlier—hence the reason they'd moved up the go date on this op. Kev only hoped the situation would hold out while they searched for their needle in the haystack.

Another team had been sent to the desert to help with security at the mine. It was all very hush-hush, but surely it was a move the Freedom Force would expect. This mission, however, was something he hoped they never considered possible. Sending the only person in the world who could identify their leader into a war zone with a counter-terrorism force at her back bordered on insanity at the best of times. At the worst of times, well, he had no idea how to quantify it.

It was just fucking psychotic. And maybe that's why it would work. If Al Ahmad didn't see it coming, then maybe they had a chance.

"I've made contact with the embassy," Matt said. "Lucky and Kev will go over there tomorrow so Lucky can apply for a teaching job through the embassy. She'll be assigned to a girls' school near the palace where intel indicates that Al Ahmad's daughter goes. The school is very exclusive and small, so every student there will attend the same classes. There's already one English teacher, but she's about to be reassigned."

Kev glanced at Lucky. She was frowning, and he knew she was thinking about the teacher who would be moved simply so she could get into place. It couldn't be helped, though. They needed whatever access they could get, and this was the way it worked. The teacher would get another job—and maybe she'd get her old job back when they were gone, assuming the country hadn't disintegrated into all-out civil war by then.

"The hotel is being watched," Knight Rider said. "Not that we didn't expect that."

"Two different groups, we think," Iceman added. "Obviously, the Qu'rimi military is watching. As for the other group… could be the Freedom Force, or it could be the Opposition."

"We need to assume those are one and the same at this point," Kev added.

Matt nodded. "Agreed. We have no idea what information they're sharing, but if Al Ahmad is behind the rebellion—and all the indicators say he is—he's got his fingers in the hierarchy."

"Do we have any idea how old his daughter is yet?" Lucky asked. She'd been quiet the entire meeting so far.

Matt looked over at her. "Unfortunately, no."

"You guys aren't making this easy."

"They're still sifting the data back home, but so far we've got nothing else, *chère*."

Kev frowned at the way Matt hesitated for a moment before he went back to the briefing. It could just be that he felt badly about not being able to give Lucky more information, or it could be that he knew something he wasn't sharing.

Whatever the case, Kev's senses went on high alert. They talked for a few more minutes, everyone reporting in on his findings, and then they split into twos and threes, going back to their rooms so they could start fresh in the morning. The guys would take short shifts during the night to stay awake and monitor the channels and perimeter for any suspicious activity.

Kev, of course, didn't have to participate in that. His

sole duty was Lucky. But when he walked Matt to the door, he glanced over his shoulder at her. She was sitting on the bed, leaning back against a pillow she'd propped up, her eyes closed.

"What aren't you saying, Richie?" he asked as they stepped into the hall.

Matt looked up and down the corridor before meeting his eyes again. "It's nothing she needs to know, you understand?"

His heart thumped. "Yeah."

"Her name is on the latest intercepts." He shrugged. "He's looking for her, but he doesn't know she married Marco. They're still looking for her maiden name."

A cold chill snaked through him, turning his spine to ice. "Jesus."

"The good thing is they're looking Stateside."

That *was* a good thing, but just knowing that Al Ahmad was actively searching for her now... it lit a hot fire deep in Kev's belly that he couldn't extinguish.

Matt put a hand on his shoulder. "Go back inside and keep her safe. That's your job. We'll be with you all the way, man."

Kev went back into the room. Lucky looked up as he shut the door behind him and gave him a little smile. She looked tired. She couldn't be called pale, not after several months in the Hawaiian sun, but she seemed more sallow than he'd yet seen her. For a minute, he wondered if she'd heard them talking. But that was impossible unless she had supersonic hearing.

She pushed a lock of hair behind her ear, and he thought back to when she'd come out of the bathroom earlier, nothing but a towel wrapped around her body, her tanned legs smooth and lean beneath the white cotton. Her hair had been wet then and she'd pushed it back just like that.

His dick had gone from zero to sixty in about half a second when she'd leaned over her suitcase and the towel had ridden up her thighs. She'd dragged out some clothing before clutching it to her and retreating to the bathroom again. When she'd emerged, she'd been covered from neck to ankle in a long dress that skimmed her curves.

She was still wearing that dress, and the blue swirling pattern set off the golden undertones of her hair to perfection.

"You feeling all right?" he asked, shoving away thoughts of her in a towel before he embarrassed himself.

She wiped her hands along the tops of her thighs. "I'm fine. Just tired. And worried."

He walked back to the desk and sat down. Then he rubbed a hand through his hair and yawned. "Yeah, I understand. It's eleven at night here, and we've been awake for nearly twenty-four hours. Why don't you get ready for bed? We need to start early in the morning."

She looked around. "I haven't wanted to address this before now, but where precisely am I supposed to sleep?"

"The bed?"

She arched an eyebrow. "And where are you sleeping? They only gave us one bed."

Of course he had no intentions of sleeping with her, but to hear her state so baldly that she didn't want him in the same bed—especially after that explosive couple of hours they'd shared in his townhouse a lifetime ago—rubbed him wrong. It wasn't the first time she'd said it, considering she'd thanked him for the stress relief the morning after, but it bugged him more now than it had then.

Still, that wasn't what they were here for. This wasn't personal. It was a mission and it was critical. He tamped down on his anger and hurt—yeah, he could admit he was hurt—and gave her an even look.

"I'll sleep on the floor."

Her eyes widened. "It's made of tile."

"And I've slept on worse. Besides, I'm equipped for it."

He stood and went to his duffel. When he pulled out a sleeping bag, her jaw dropped.

"You brought a sleeping bag?"

"And a first-aid kit, ammo, MREs, and a lot of other things you wouldn't believe." He dropped the bag on the floor near the door. "This is a mission, not a spa retreat. If I don't get the soft bed or the hot-rock massage complete with New Age music and incense, I'll live."

Her expression tightened. "I'm fully aware this isn't a spa retreat."

She rubbed her hands along her arms and her eyebrows drew down as she studied a tile in the floor. Naturally, she made him feel like an asshole. Which he deserved for snapping at her.

"Poor choice of words. I just meant I'm prepared, same as always." Some of it he'd brought in and some of it the CIA had made sure the team got once they arrived.

Kev unzipped his jeans and shoved them down his hips. Lucky was looking at him again but she averted her gaze when his tightie-whities came into view.

Just as well. If she watched him undress, he'd probably get hard. And then what?

He walked over and took a pillow from the bed, and then went back and climbed into the sleeping bag. Then he put an arm behind his head and lay there staring up at the plaster ceiling and the whirring fan.

He very much feared, as she stood and began to pull the covers down on the bed, that this mission would be the death of him. And not for the usual reasons.

An explosion jolted Lucky awake and she shot upright in bed, her heart pounding hard as she tried to process what she'd heard. Her gaze slid over to the window to find Kev standing there, his face lit with an orange-and-red glow. Outside, she could hear the blare of sirens and the shouts and screams of people.

It took her another moment to process that what she'd heard had been a bomb blast. A shudder of horror rolled through her. "What happened?" she asked, though she knew.

Kev looked her way. "I'm waiting to hear from Iceman or Hawk, but it was a bomb in the city center. There's no doubt about that. But where and how and why—I'm guessing we don't know that yet."

"It's the Freedom Force."

He came over to the bed and sat down on the edge. "We don't know for certain. But yeah, this is one of their tactics, and so far the Opposition hasn't used bombings in the city. But with the pace of the unrest accelerating—it was only a matter of time." He swore softly. "I'd hoped we'd be gone by the time it started."

It wasn't the first time she'd been in a city wracked by bomb blasts—she'd been active duty, and she'd spent time in the Middle East on interpreter duties during Operation Iraqi Freedom—but it certainly didn't bring back any fond memories.

She brought her knees up and hugged them. "Do you think he knows we're here?"

Kev shook his head. "Us specifically, no. But he knows there's a price on his head. And he wants to finish this so he can bargain with the Chinese and drive the king's government out." He blew out a harsh breath. "And then there's the possibility that the Opposition has the manpower to escalate things now and it has nothing to do with Al Ahmad. For all we know, he's fled the region."

She thought of that beautiful, evil voice and his latent narcissism and knew it wasn't true. If he'd returned from the dead and sown the seeds of unrest, he'd want to stay around and see it come to fruition.

"He's here. He's too arrogant to flee when his plans are working. Besides, he escaped death once before, so he'll feel invincible. The CIA thought they had him, didn't they? Claimed their sniper put a bullet in his brain and they watched him go down? Well, they obviously didn't. And Al Ahmad is the kind of man who would stroll through the center of a battalion dressed as a poor beggar just to laugh and say he'd fooled us all." She shook her head. "He's here. And he'll stay unless he feels threatened."

Kev was looking at her with his head cocked to the side. She never found out what he might have said because there was a knock at the door. He got up. After a whispered exchange through the crack in the door, he opened it the rest of the way and Iceman walked in. Hawk was with him. They were both winded.

No one turned on a light. She thought she should find that odd, but considering this group, perhaps not.

"Bomb in a market stall about a mile away," Iceman said. "One person killed. No one has claimed responsibility yet, but it seems to have been a warning."

"The government's had a military checkpoint near that market for weeks now. We can be thankful it didn't go off tomorrow morning during rush hour," Hawk added. He tapped Iceman on the arm. "Let's roll, dude. Knight Rider needs us out there."

"Thanks for letting us know," Kev said as he let them out again.

"We'll have your back tomorrow," Hawk said, and then the door closed and they were alone.

Lucky's heart was beating hard and fast when Kev came back over to the bed. This was getting real, fast. And it was just a small bomb a mile away. What happened next? She ran her hands over her arms as dread tap-danced down her spine.

"Are you scared?"

She met Kev's gaze. "I'm not thrilled, but I'm not scared." *Yet.* She fisted her hands in the covers. "We came here to do a job. We're going to do it."

His teeth flashed in the darkness. "That's what I like to hear. Now, you want me to slide in next to you and hold you tight or can you manage to go back to sleep on your own?"

She wanted him to slide in next to her, but not to

sleep. The visceral tug in her belly—and lower—had nothing to do with sleep. Lucky bit her lip to keep any sound from escaping. He was teasing her again, trying to make her laugh, but she wished he was serious. Still, she couldn't show him how pitifully needy she was where he was concerned. She simply couldn't handle the rejection right now.

"Go away, Kev," she said tightly.

He laughed softly, like it was nothing but a joke. She heard him get into his sleeping bag, and her heart throbbed with regret and frustration. She turned on her side and punched her pillow viciously.

It would be a long time before she fell asleep.

SIXTEEN

THE CITY SEEMED SUBDUED THE next morning when Lucky finally dragged herself from bed. Her eyes felt like they had sand in them, and her reflection in the mirror made her groan. The bags under her eyes could qualify as extra luggage today.

Instead of going out early, they had to wait because of reports that traffic was still snarled at the bomb site, which was on the way to the embassy. And since the embassy was currently in lockdown, very little traffic was getting in or out. They might have a mission, and that mission might require the embassy's assistance, but no one was getting in there this morning.

Lucky had a cup of strong, sweet Arab coffee that Kev brought back to the room, and then she showered and dressed in a cotton halter dress before slipping on the abaya and fixing the hijab over her hair. When she was satisfied that only her face and hands showed, she walked out of the bathroom.

Kev gave her a once-over. He was sinfully handsome in khakis and a white button-down with loafers. She knew he was packing a weapon—possibly two or three—on that gorgeous frame of his.

"Isn't that going to be hot?" he said.

She looked down at the tan garment. "Not too bad, really. And it's a chance I'm willing to take."

"It makes you feel safer."

She lowered her gaze as her pulse thumped. He knew her better than she would like sometimes. "I think that's probably obvious."

"I understand why."

She shrugged. "It's silly in a way. I doubt he's out there on the street searching for me."

Kev seemed to stiffen for a second, but then he went over to his gear and opened a flap on the backpack where he'd stowed his camera equipment. "No, he's too busy for that."

Lucky wished she could say that Al Ahmad had probably forgotten her, but she knew that wasn't true. But he had bigger fish to fry right now, so he probably wasn't thinking about the only person to ever escape him. Much.

"Kev?"

He looked up from the camera he was fooling with. He'd had a crash course in using this particular model, a Canon EOS professional model with different lenses and tripods, monopods, and who knows what else. He looked like a very convincing photographer to her.

Except for that badass *I'd-tell-you-but-I'd-have-to-kill-you* vibe he had going.

"Yeah?"

"I have a bad feeling about this."

His brow furrowed. But he didn't scoff, and he didn't dismiss her fears as ridiculous or amateurish. "About what specifically?"

And this was the hard part. Articulating what she meant.

She'd felt uneasy since the plane landed, and she knew it was this mission and the enormity of what she had to do. But she'd felt something else, too. Some sense of unease that came from more than just the fact Al Ahmad was here and they were hunting for him.

She'd listened to the people talking in the hotel lobby, listened to the Qu'rimis and felt their fear and unease as if it were her own. They didn't openly say the government was failing, but as the military presence grew stronger, they feared it.

And now the bomb.

"Everything," she said. "The Qu'rimis look at us—and by us I mean the people in this hotel—with suspicion and distrust. The people—ordinary, everyday people—will start protesting in the streets soon. Especially if there are more bombs. The entire city could implode in a matter of days if that happens."

He closed his eyes for a second. "Yeah, I know."

"Al Ahmad knows it too. At a certain point, all the outside help in the world won't prevent a revolution. We've seen it happen in other places too often. Once it begins, our government won't step in because of the way we'll be seen on televisions around the world. We'll be perceived as an Imperialist power, a heretic power come to impose our will on the people. And you know what happens then."

"We'll be pulled out."

"And Al Ahmad will live to fight another day."

The look on his face was deadly calm. "We can't let

that happen, Lucky."

"We might not have a choice."

And that was what scared her. Because if they had to go before they got him, she had no doubt he'd do something terrible, something the likes of which had not yet been seen. Something that would leave the world a much worse place than it currently was.

Kev came over and put his hands on her shoulders. She tried not to let his touch feel so vital, but she couldn't help the shiver of longing that flooded her in response.

"The city hasn't fallen apart yet and the king is still in control. Let's get you into that school, and then let's find that bastard."

He pressed a chaste kiss to her forehead and then went back to his camera while she stood there with a knot in her throat. And not only because she feared Al Ahmad.

No, she feared Kev. The way he made her feel. Her emotions were scraped raw in this environment. There was no room for deceit or obfuscation. She feared the way the simplest touch could light her up inside and make her long for so much more. If she'd thought for one moment that a single night with him would ease this longing, she'd been very wrong.

And that scared her more than anything else could. Because it was clear he didn't feel the same way.

It was midafternoon by the time they got into the American embassy, but they made it in after undergoing a security check and filling out what seemed like a ream of paperwork.

Kev was on edge by the time they reached the person they'd been told to see. A woman with short brown hair and an easy smile greeted them and took them into an office. Then she left them alone.

The office wasn't especially large or interesting. It was lined with bookshelves and a large desk sat at one end. Mini American flags sat on the desk, crisscrossed, and a larger flag stood in one corner.

Lucky sat quietly with her hands in her lap, but she worried her lower lip incessantly. A nervous tic of hers. They hadn't spoken since sitting down, but he reached over and took her hand in his. They were supposed to be newlyweds, after all, so he indulged his desire to touch her.

Her head lifted and her brown eyes met his. He felt the jolt of that gaze all the way to his toes. He wanted to protect her. Wanted to wrap her up in his arms and not let a damn thing happen to her. It was a gut feeling that sat inside him like a ball of iron, especially after last night. Between the explosion and Matt's news that Lucky's name had been heard in intercepted chatter, Kev was sick with the thought he might not be able to protect her.

He knew what it was like to fail at protecting someone, and he simply couldn't make that mistake again. Not with Lucky.

He'd lost Marco. He'd lost his mom and sister. He wouldn't lose Lucky too.

"Thanks," she said, smiling.

He knew she was worried, but he didn't think she was petrified. Lucky was too tough to be petrified. Still, she had reason to worry. Training to get Al Ahmad was one thing. Actually being in-country and looking for the sick bastard was something else altogether. But it was more than that. It was her knowledge of the facts and how quickly the situation in Baq could change. They were racing against time and they all knew it.

"Hey, what's a husband for, right?"

She laughed softly. "A few things, I think. Dishes, yard work, fixing the car…"

He arched an eyebrow. "And hopefully a few other, more pleasant things."

She dropped her gaze for a second but he didn't miss the wash of color that highlighted her cheekbones. Why had he said that? Why had he reminded them both about that night?

Hell, as if he'd forgotten it for a moment. Yeah, it was best they didn't go there again, but damn, he'd felt things with her that shocked him.

As if he'd expected anything less. He'd been fascinated with this woman from the first moment he'd met her. And he'd walked away from her when he'd never walked away from any woman in his life.

If it had been just about sex, he'd have hit it and quit it, same as he always did. Instead, he'd shoved her toward Marco and told himself he was being noble, that he was giving her a better life than he'd ever be able to offer. A better husband.

He sat there gazing into her dark eyes and feeling as if he'd been sucker punched. She meant something to him. Something more than he was prepared for.

And there was no way out, no denying it. He cared. A lot.

Her brows drew down as she watched him. "You okay, handsome?"

He cleared his throat. "Yeah, fine. I was just thinking."

"Must have been serious." She squeezed his hand and grinned, and he smiled back though it felt like it belonged on someone else's face.

"Everything about this trip is serious."

She sighed. "I know. I sometimes wish you'd never found me, but then I also know it's good you did. I'll just pretend for a moment like we really are tourists, okay?"

He wanted to reach out and touch her face, trace his fingers along her lips. But he didn't. "Whatever it takes."

The door opened then and a man came in. Kev stood but the guy motioned to Lucky to stay seated when she started to rise. He held out his hand and Kev shook it.

"David Capretti."

"Kevin MacDonald. This is my wife, Lucy MacDonald." God, that was strange to say.

"Hello, Mrs. MacDonald."

Lucky smiled serenely, as if she were accustomed to being called Mrs. MacDonald on a regular basis. "Mr. Capretti."

They'd agreed she would be Lucy on this mission because Al Ahmad knew that she was called Lucky. It was too unique a name to put out there, especially when they were this close to the Freedom Force's home base.

Capretti took a seat and flipped through some paperwork. Kev studied him for a long while, his mannerisms, the precise way he scanned the files. Capretti was former military for certain. Probably CIA, but since he wasn't their contact, he wasn't going to self-identify. Just as they'd not identified their affiliation with the military either.

After a few moments, he found what he wanted. "Ah, yes, we have an opening at the Prince Faisal School for Girls for an English teacher. Does that sound good to you folks?"

The Prince Faisal School was precisely the one they wanted. Lucky confirmed it while Kev sat silently and waited. Sometimes he hated these games they had to play between the services, but that was the way the government worked. At least they were cooperating these days, unlike in the past when one branch didn't want to share intel with another. They'd learned the error of their ways, but not before a whole lot of people died.

"It's very exclusive, Mrs. MacDonald. Only forty students in the whole school. They'll rotate through your class in groups of ten, so you'll need to spend four hours each day teaching. Is this acceptable?"

"Of course."

The man switched into Arabic then, and he and Lucky conversed for several moments that way. Kev wasn't precisely comfortable with it, but it was her job. What she was here for. And if he needed to know something that was said, she'd tell him.

The interview finished and David Capretti stood. The door behind them opened and the brown-haired woman walked in again. "Lisa will show you out. Mr. MacDonald. Mrs. MacDonald," he said, shaking each of their hands in turn. And then his face grew solemn before he added, "Good luck to you both."

They left the embassy and filed out onto the street to catch a taxi outside the perimeter of the embassy's security zone. Kev scanned the area out of habit, but he knew at least three of his team members were close by, watching and ready to leap into action if it was needed.

He found Knight Rider leaning against a wall. Iceman was down the street, playing with a dog. And Hawk—cool, lethal Hawk—strolled down the sidewalk like he didn't have a care in the world.

Lucky didn't see them, and Kev didn't point them out. "What did that guy say to you?" he asked as they waited for a taxi to pull up.

She glanced up at him. "He told me about protocol at the school, which echelon of society the students came from, and some general information. He was making sure I could understand the dialect."

"You must have passed."

She rolled her eyes. "I have no accent. He does. Of course I passed."

"Why don't you have an accent?" He'd never thought about that kind of thing before, but of course there were accents in other languages.

"Okay, it's not that I don't have an accent at all—I don't sound like a Qu'rimi, precisely, but more like a Saudi national. My father left my mother very early, when I was still a baby. Before she met and married my stepdad years later, she had to work a lot to take care of us. We lived in California then, and it was very expensive for a single woman with a child. The neighbors were Saudis, and I spent a lot of time with them." She shrugged. "That's where I learned Arabic. The Defense Language Institute perfected it. But that was the beginning. When we moved to Montana, I didn't forget, though of course I had no need to speak it there. I got rusty, but once you learn something as a child, you're much more likely to retain it."

He didn't want to think about the things he'd learned as a child. "Yeah, it's hard to unlearn what you learn growing up."

She shaded her eyes as she looked up at him. He knew she couldn't see his because he was wearing the reflective Ray-Bans. And he was glad of it because he didn't know why he'd said that.

"What did you learn that you want to unlearn?" she asked. She was too perceptive not to sense the undercurrents.

Kev held up his hand as a taxi approached. It began to slow and steer toward the curb, though the driver cut off everyone in his path to do it. Cars honked and people shouted curses in the air. A donkey brayed.

The taxi jerked to a stop and Kev reached for the door. Then he stopped. She was still waiting for an answer, and he found he wanted to give it to her.

"Evil," he said, his voice flat and emotionless. "I learned about evil."

Lucky reached out and put a hand on his arm. "Oh, Kev."

But whatever else she might have said was cut off when a blast of hot air knocked her against him. They fell to the pavement together, Kev rolling to shield Lucky with his body as the shockwave blew out windows and set off alarms in the street.

His heart pounded with fear as he waited for a second blast. But it didn't come and he pushed up to get a look at Lucky. Blood slid from a cut on her forehead, staining her cheek red. The windows of the taxi were gone, which is where she'd gotten the cut.

"Are you hurt?" he demanded, running his hands over her body.

"I don't think so." She pushed herself up to a sitting position.

Kev raised his head to look at the taxi driver. The man was slumped over the wheel, his body unmoving. Blood poured from a wound in his throat, and Kev realized that a piece of glass must have sliced his jugular. Poor bastard.

Hawk bounded up to them, his face creased with worry. Kev gave him a thumbs-up and he knelt beside them, his gaze bouncing from one to the next.

"We have to get out of here," he said.

"Definitely. Iceman and Knight Rider?"

Hawk looked fierce. "Waiting for the go signal."

Kev looked around at the scene. The destruction wasn't anything he hadn't seen before, but it rattled him in a different way now that he had Lucky to take care of. This wasn't the life she'd signed up for, and it pissed him off that she had to be exposed to it. That she was in danger because of it.

Sirens wailed in the distance, and people yelled and cried. He blocked it all out and focused on the woman in front of him.

"Then let's go," he said.

"We have to help." Lucky grabbed his arm when he started to stand.

"We have to go," Kev told her. "We have no idea if there are more bombs, and we need to get back to the hotel. You're the asset, and we have to protect you."

Panic was a bubble in the bottom of his throat, trying to claw its way up and out. And all because of her. Because she was in danger and he had to protect her.

She stuck her chin out and stared at him and Hawk both. "We can't leave these people here. Some are hurt, and the two of you have medical training. So do Garrett and Sam. You can't walk away. It's not right."

Hawk met his gaze and frowned. Kev knew that Hawk was on the same page with him, but she looked so hopeful and determined.

"It's too much of a risk." But Kev knew when he said it that she wasn't buying into it at all. This was the part of the job that was hard—knowing when you had to leave a situation, and knowing that people were suffering. Lucky wasn't accustomed to that, and she wasn't going to be anytime soon.

She grabbed his hands and held them hard. "What if it were Marco lying there? Or Jim? You guys wouldn't have left them, would you?"

Kev's jaw ached with how tightly he clenched it. *I will never leave a fallen comrade.* It was part of the warrior ethos and she knew it. "No."

Her gaze slid to Hawk, who looked equally uncomfortable. "We have to help," she said. "At least until the ambulances get here."

Kev closed his eyes and swore. *Goddammit.* "We'll stay as long as we can, but I can't promise you it will be long."

She shuddered with relief, and he wanted to yank her into his arms and hold her tight just because she was still breathing. Instead, he reached out and wiped the blood off her cheek. "Leave my side for an instant, fail to obey me, and we're going. No second chances, Lucky."

"Copy," she said, her eyes on his, sucking him in. *Goddamn.*

SEVENTEEN

LUCKY WAS HOT AND TIRED by the time they got back to the hotel. Her abaya was sweat- and blood-stained and torn, and her joints ached. She knew why Kev had thrown her to the ground, but that didn't change the fact it had hurt. She could still see the taxi driver slumped over the wheel, and tears threatened to spill down her cheeks.

She still didn't know how she'd managed to talk Kev into it, but they'd helped the people who had been hurt. The guys staunched wounds, splinted limbs, and managed to keep the area from disintegrating before the authorities arrived.

The blast site wasn't far from the embassy, and it went into lockdown right away. Lucky knew that Kev had been right to worry about a second device, or a third or fourth, but she'd heard the people's cries, the screams, the pleas for mercy from God, and she couldn't walk away from all that suffering.

She'd been lucky—*they'd* been lucky—to escape with scrapes and aches. Now, she went into the bathroom and stripped off the abaya. Her eyes were bloodshot, and her skin was streaked with dirt and blood. The silken hijab was ruined and she tore that off too. Her hair was matted to her head with sweat.

She turned on the water in the sink and splashed her face. Her hands were shaking when she turned it off again. She needed a shower. A long, hot, mind-melting shower.

And a surfboard, an ocean breeze, and no cares in the world. God what she wouldn't give for those days, which now seemed so far away.

It's not true about no cares in the world.

She glared at herself in the mirror. No, it wasn't true. She'd had plenty of cares in Hawaii. She'd thought about Marco, about all that had gone wrong in their marriage, about her mother and sisters, her stepdad, the Army, Al Ahmad—and Kev. Oh yes, she'd thought about him a lot. Wondered where he was and if he was still banging trashy waitresses or if maybe, just maybe, he missed her a little bit.

She'd thought he might since he'd called so often. She'd wanted to answer the phone, but she'd refused to do it. She'd worried about the flood of emotion it might open if she did. So she'd sat there and listened to his voice on the answering machine asking her if she was all right and telling her to call if she needed anything.

But how could she call him? How could she ever, ever call him? Her life had been a mess, and that wasn't something Kev really wanted to be a part of.

Lucky bit back a sob. She clenched her hands into fists and stared at herself in the mirror. What the fuck? Was she going to fall apart now? Was she going to melt down just because of a few destroyed cars, a few destroyed lives?

She dropped her head into her hands and let the tears flow. And then she felt hands on her, turning her, yanking her against the solid weight of a male body.

Kev.

His hand was on her hair, her nose was against his chest, and she clutched her fingers into his shirt and held on.

"It's okay, Lucky. It's all right. Cry if you want. No one will stop you. No one will blame you. Let it out." He rubbed her back. "Let it out."

She held on to him, because she could do nothing else, and sobbed her heart out. Her body shook like the last fall leaf clinging desperately to a branch, and her heart ached as if it were breaking anew with every tear she shed. Her throat hurt.

Kev held her close and didn't say a word, didn't try to stop her or tell her she was being silly. He just let her cry. And then, when she felt her tears subsiding a bit, when she thought she might survive this crying jag after all, he pulled her with him until he could reach the shower. He turned on the water. It took a few moments, but steam began to fill the cubicle.

"Think you can do this?" he asked her, still holding her close, his arms around her, buoying her up.

She swallowed, her throat aching. She didn't want to be alone with her thoughts and the images in her head. "Don't leave me. Please don't leave me."

He set her gently away from him until he could meet her gaze. The pain in his eyes sent a sharp ache plunging into her heart.

"I can't stay. If I stay…"

It was the first time since the night in his bed that

she'd gotten the idea he might not be unaffected after all. That he might, possibly, truly want her again. That he wasn't teasing her to make her laugh. Her heart thumped as she sucked in a breath and ran a shaky hand over his hard chest. "I want you to stay. I want to be with you."

He closed his eyes for a moment. "Mendez ordered me not to have sex with you. The night before we deployed."

Anger burned in her belly. So Mendez knew something about the two of them. Or suspected anyway. And he'd gone to Kev instead of her. Just like a man. She might be a part of this team, but she was still a woman. And women needed a man to make decisions for them. Or so a man like the colonel believed.

"Mendez doesn't run my life. He doesn't get to say who I care about or what I do." She cupped his jaw in her palm. Her fingers trembled. "He's not here, and I know why he said it, but Jesus, Kev, we could have died out there. We still could."

He kissed her palm. "You have no idea how that thought tears me up inside. How it gets inside my head and makes me crazy. When I think of anything happening to you…"

"You won't let it," she said softly. "I know you won't."

He looked so lost and fierce in that moment that she stepped into him and pulled his head down to hers. He didn't try to stop her. When their lips met, it was a soft, tentative kiss that quickly turned hot and intense.

"We shouldn't," he said, tearing his mouth from hers. Yet he slid his hands beneath her dress and yanked it up and over her head. "But damned if I'm capable of walking away."

Joy blossomed in her soul as their mouths fused again. They kissed hard and long, and then he divested her of her bra and panties while she fumbled with his belt buckle. Her fingers were clumsy, and she made a noise of frustration.

"Wait a minute," he said, setting her away from him and disappearing into the bedroom. She thought he might have changed his mind, and she wondered what she would do if so—but he was back a moment later with a condom package. Relief threatened to make her knees weak.

He gave her the package while he stripped off his shirt and pants. His body made her mouth water. It was hard and perfect, with rippling abs and tight muscle that flexed and bunched with every movement. She couldn't help but run her hands over him, learning his shape by touch.

He growled as he shoved his pants off, and she wrapped her hand around his hard cock.

"Lucky."

"I've dreamed of this for days now. Dreamed of you."

He backed her into the shower, his body in her personal space, his hands sliding over her hips, her waist. Hot water pummeled her back, plastered her hair to her head, and washed away the dirt and blood from the afternoon.

Kev reached for the shampoo at the same time she stroked him. His flesh was so hot it burned. His breath hitched.

"You seriously want to kill me, don't you?"

"I just want you." She felt achy and needy and so very alive when she was with him. It was as if she'd swallowed sunshine and it burned her from the inside out.

She didn't care about anything but getting him inside her. If he was inside her, he wouldn't spend much time looking at her skin, noticing her imperfections.

"First things first." He poured shampoo in his hand, and even though she ached with need, a surge of tenderness warmed the darkest reaches of her soul.

He turned her until her back was to him and lathered her hair. When she reached behind her and cupped his balls, he took her arms and put her hands over her head, palms against the wall.

"Move your hands again and I'll spank you," he growled in her ear.

A shiver tripped down her spine. "You wouldn't dare."

He nipped her earlobe, and an arrow of longing went straight to her clit and made it throb. Oh, she loved that he didn't treat her with kid gloves. Not this time.

"Try me."

She stood with her palms flat against the wall while he washed her hair. He used a cup sitting on a ledge to rinse her hair instead of letting her turn and duck under the spray again. Another bottle popped open and she wondered what he was doing—but then his soapy hands moved over her and she wanted to scream. His palms slid against her wet flesh so erotically, so teasingly. His fingers explored, dancing over her skin, and all her fears about her scars fled.

He pinched her nipples softly and repeatedly until her body was a bundle of nerve endings waiting to explode. She dropped her forehead against the wall and tried to breathe normally.

It didn't work.

"Kev, please…"

"Please what?"

She grabbed his hand and slid it between her legs. The slight stinging slap on her ass made her jerk, but in a good way. It was a shock, yes, but it was also erotic as hell. Especially when he touched her where she wanted. His fingers glided between her folds, found her clit. Lucky whimpered with the rightness of it.

"I told you I'd spank you." His voice was a sensual rasp in her ear.

"And I'll pay you back for it." She gasped. "Later."

"I'll look forward to it."

He made her part her legs a bit more, and then he began to roll her clit between his thumb and forefinger while she pressed her palms to the wall and thrust her hips back toward him.

"You're so hot," he said. "So beautiful. I want you to come, Lucky. Come hard. Scream my name."

His mouth was on her neck, her shoulder, his fingers working their magic as the tension built higher and higher. And then it was simply too much and she shattered with a sharp cry. Her orgasm ripped through her, scouring her body and soul with its power. With the power of all the things she felt for this man.

Confusing things. Hot, needy things. Forbidden things.

He turned her in his arms and pressed the condom package into her hand. She'd forgotten all about it, but he'd taken it from her and set it on the ledge when they'd entered the shower. Now she ripped it open and sheathed him with trembling fingers.

He was a hard male animal, completely focused as he

pushed her back against the wall and lifted her up high. He hesitated just a moment, their gazes tangling.

"Tell me you want me."

As if he didn't know. But she sensed it was important to him somehow, that it went deep and soothed something inside him that she didn't know existed. It made her long to know him, but she wasn't certain she ever would.

Kev had always been a closed book, a secret wrapped in mystery. A lonely man living a lonely life. Her heart ached and swelled with love.

"I want you, Kevin. Only you."

With a groan, he plunged into her.

Two bombs were nothing, but they were a start. Abdul Halim watched the news reports of the bombings on four different television screens set up in his personal sanctuary—his wife was not allowed in; Lana was, but only when invited. This evening, both his wife and Lana were visiting friends in another apartment, so he was completely alone.

He lifted the cigarette to his lips and took a long drag. The Qu'rimi reporters were nearly hysterical. CNN, the BBC, and Al Jazeera took it as a matter of course. There were security cameras in the vicinity of the embassy, and they'd captured the explosion. The footage was now looping on all the networks.

Of course he couldn't bomb the American embassy. It

was too difficult to get inside and almost impossible to bring in explosives even if he got someone through security. Besides, his target wasn't really the embassy so much as he wanted the Americans to think so. If they were focused on themselves, they wouldn't realize what was happening in the Ministry of Science until too late.

If he knew anything about Americans, he knew they were paranoid about being targets. They'd gotten so accustomed to fielding attacks from small-minded people with short-term goals that it had affected their strategic thinking.

His goals were much broader, of course. He wasn't hampered by the small thinking that had characterized so many other movements. No, he was able to think much bigger than anyone before him had done. And that was why he would succeed.

The Americans wouldn't see it coming. No one would.

The film of the bombing played again, and again he felt that visceral rush when the flash of light blazed from the car parked on the street. Glass shattered and people screamed. He enjoyed that bit. It wasn't quite as good as inflicting the pain himself, but it would have to do.

On CNN, footage played of a reporter talking to witnesses. The camera was set up on a sidewalk, and people crossed behind the man as he pulled in random bystanders. The camera zoomed in, just for a moment, on a woman in a torn abaya. Beside her was a tall man. Not a Qu'rimi, but a blue-eyed foreigner.

Yet it was the woman who caught his attention. He grabbed the remote and rewound the broadcast until that precise moment when her face was onscreen. And then he used the zoom function to get closer, to study her features. Her face wasn't as sharp at a higher power as it was in regular playback mode. But it was familiar in a way that made his blood beat.

Was she here? Was Lucky Reid in Baq instead of the United States? Was this why his people had not yet managed to find her? He leaned toward the television, studying the blurry face. Was it her? Or was he seeing a mirage because he wanted to find her?

He zoomed out and looked at her again. He could not be certain. Yet a cold, knife-sharp pressure bloomed in his gut. He did not ignore those feelings when they happened.

It was entirely possible the Americans were moving much faster than he'd thought they would.

He studied the man beside her. A pale-eyed foreigner who was not small in the least. A man with a grim expression and broad shoulders. Abdul Halim told himself to be calm, to be methodical. It could be nothing. But his heart pounded with excitement as he picked up his phone and dialed.

There was only one place foreigners tended to stay these days. And he had a man on the inside.

EIGHTEEN

BEING INSIDE LUCKY WAS HEAVEN. And hell, because he wasn't supposed to be doing this. But how could he stop?

Kev held her hard against the wall and rolled his hips into her, sliding into her slick heat again and again. Her legs wrapped high around his waist and her back arched, her nipples thrusting up toward him, so beautiful and tight that he bent his head and captured one in his mouth. He sucked hard and her fingers curled into his shoulders as she moaned.

Thank God for stone walls, he thought. Matt and Billy were across the hall, and if they had any idea what he was up to right now, they'd both be pretty pissed.

As if he gave a good goddamn right this second about anything but the way he felt being buried inside this woman who meant so much more than anyone had in a very long time.

His entire body was on fire. His skin sizzled and smoked, and he felt as if the top of his head would blow off at any second. The tingling at the base of his spine was pretty intense, but he did everything he could to hold back the orgasm building to a fever pitch inside him.

He had to make her come first.

He had to feel her shatter around him, her body milking him, squeezing him, until he could let go and burst deep inside her.

Her body glistened with the water pounding down on top of them. Her skin was golden and beautiful. Even her scars were beautiful because they were a part of her. He lifted his head and took her mouth again, and then he pulled back until he could see her face.

Her eyes opened, her dark irises fastening on him, widening with the coming storm rolling through her.

"Kev." She gasped as he thrust into her harder than before, again and again. "Yes, oh yes."

Her body tightened, her legs gripping him tight—and then she cried out, shuddering in his arms, quivering around his aching cock, squeezing him so tight it almost hurt.

He didn't ease up, kept up the pressure of his thrusts while she chanted his name—and then his own orgasm hit him and his back bowed with the strength of it. He couldn't contain the hoarse cry that escaped him, and he couldn't stop the buckling of his knees when it was over.

They sank to the hard tile floor together, their bodies separating as they sat beneath the spray, arms wrapped around one another, holding tight. He couldn't speak, couldn't get any words to form. So he sat back against the wall and tugged her against him, pressing her smooth flesh against his and tucking her head against his shoulder.

They sat that way until the water started to cool. Finally, Kev found the strength to stand and turn off the taps.

He grabbed towels and dried her off. Then he dried himself and scooped her into his arms like she couldn't walk on her own.

She didn't protest. She just wrapped her arms around his neck and let him carry her to the bed.

There was no doubt they'd spend the night together. He laid her down on cool cotton and followed, stretching out beside her. They didn't speak and he woke with a jerk sometime later, shocked that he'd fallen asleep so easily.

It was full dark out now, and the room was lit only by outside lights shining inside. He reached for his phone and checked it. He didn't expect he'd missed any calls, but who knew after the stress of the afternoon what he might have done. It wasn't like him to fall asleep so easily, and he'd done that with no problem.

But he hadn't missed anything, so he set the phone down and scraped a hand through his hair. Lucky stirred beside him, and his dick began to harden.

"What time is it?" she mumbled, turning into his body and putting an arm over his chest.

"Eight o'clock."

"Wow, I thought it must be midnight at least."

"You okay?"

She yawned and stretched, tilting her chin to gaze up at him. "Why wouldn't I be?"

He could feel the elephant in the room staring at him, but he decided not to go there. He wouldn't bring Marco between them right now. "It's been a rough afternoon."

"It has." She sighed softly. "All those people. They were innocent, going about their day as usual—and they had the misfortune to be in the wrong place at the wrong time."

"We were almost in the wrong place too."

She reached up and slid a finger along his lips. "I know. But you protected me. You threw me under you like it was as instinctual as breathing."

He grasped her fingers and kissed them. "It is. I would die for you."

She dragged in a breath. "I hate when you say things like that."

"And yet it's the truth."

She hesitated for a moment. "What you said right before the bomb exploded…"

"You remember that?" Fuck, he wished she didn't. He didn't know where his head had been at the moment, but he'd blurted the words out and now he couldn't call them back.

Her brows drew down. "Of course I do. I remember everything about you. And you said you saw evil growing up and you wanted to unlearn that. What did you mean?"

Fresh pain sliced into him. He could still see the scene as if it were yesterday, still feel the helplessness. He didn't talk about this with anyone. And yet he found himself wanting to tell her. Wanting to unburden himself, just once, with someone who might understand.

Hell, what did it matter anymore? His family was dead, and nothing he said or did would bring them back again. Maybe it would ease the tightness in his chest if he said the words for once.

"My father was a drunk. A mean, evil, hot-tempered drunk. He beat us when he had too much, which was often. Too often."

"Oh, Kev." She pressed her lips to his cheek and he put his hand on the back of her head and slid his fingers into her silky hair. "I'm sorry."

"I was bigger than him by the time I was fifteen. The beatings stopped, at least for me. Because I fought back. But he would still hit my mother when I wasn't home. And my sister too, though she denied it."

He could feel hot tears pressing against the back of his throat, threatening him in a way they had not since he was a teenager and realized what his father had done that day. What he'd stolen from Mom and Bethie.

"There's more," she said softly, and his heart throbbed.

"Yeah."

"You don't have to tell me. It's okay." She wrapped her arm around him and held on tight, burrowing her nose against his neck.

God, it felt so right to have her beside him. So perfect. And yet the guilt was still there, because she was Marco's widow. Because Marco had loved her when Kev hadn't been capable of it. Or capable of admitting it.

He should have fought for her, but he'd been a coward. The better man had won—and now he had her by default.

Fucking disgusting, and yet another thing that tore him up inside.

Still, he sucked in a breath and gritted his teeth. The least he could do was tell the truth.

"He killed them. Shot them both and then shot himself. I found them."

"Oh my God." She hugged him tighter than before, and then she was raining kisses on his cheek, his lips, his neck. "I'm so sorry. So sorry."

Comforting kisses. Sweet kisses. They weren't sexual, and yet he felt the sexual need beginning to pound in his veins again.

Urging him to take her. To lose himself inside her.

"Lucky, I—" He couldn't speak as the urge scoured through him. It was as if, looking at death, he had to do something that reminded him he was alive. Vibrant and alive.

"Take what you need, Kev. Take what you need."

Her words released him. He pushed her over, pushed her hands above her head, and thrust hard and deep. She gasped—and then she clutched him to her and let him use her body. The bed creaked and rocked with the power of his thrusts. Lucky moaned and said his name, arching her body up into his, taking his thrusts and meeting them eagerly.

Their bodies moved in a frenzy now, the bed rocking hard against the wall—and then she came with a sharp cry and he followed her over the edge, falling so hard and fast that he felt as if the breath had been knocked out of him.

Reality flooded him like someone had thrown a bucket of ice water on his head. He'd used her, fucked her as if she meant nothing to him—and he'd done it without a condom.

"Jesus," he said, his heart thrumming hard and fast, dizziness swimming in his brain, making spots appear in his vision. What the fuck had he done? Treating Lucky like she was nothing but a body? Forgetting to protect her?

"Hey, big man," she said, her voice soft and sweet as she rolled onto his chest. She cupped his face between her palms and held him in place while she gazed down at him. "I loved every moment of that. It was amazing. So don't you dare act like you did something terrible."

He'd behaved like an animal, and she told him it was wonderful. He loved her even more in that moment, if it were possible.

Love. Oh, Jesus. He was stunned at the way the word broke through the barriers he'd erected against it. It broke through and filled his heart—and terrified him at the same time.

"No condom." His voice was raspy.

Her smile lit him up inside. "I suppose I should be worried, considering your reputation. Care to tell me how many women you've gone commando with?"

His brain could hardly keep up. He'd just used her hard and she was smiling at him. Asking him about other women. And in the meantime his heart was about to burst.

"None but you. And I'm clean because we have to be tested for the job. But, Lucky..." He swallowed. He could hardly think of what he'd just done. Of the possible consequences of his actions. To love her was one thing. To bring a baby into the world was another. "What if you get pregnant?"

"Oh, Kev, you adorable man. Do you really think I'm so dazzled by your charms that I would forget something so vital?"

"I didn't give you a chance to say no."

She kissed him quickly. "Of course you did. And you always will, because you don't force women to have sex with you. My mouth works, and I could have said no. Plus I'm on the pill, so there's nothing to worry about there."

"Lucky—"

She put her hand over his mouth. "I told you to take what you needed, and I knew precisely what that meant."

He processed that for a moment. "But I used you. I

overpowered you. Why aren't you pissed?"

She sat up, straddling him, and his mouth went dry at the sight of her beautiful breasts thrusting outward, her curves teasing him, tantalizing him. If he hadn't just come so hard, he'd be ready to go again in a few seconds.

"You didn't overpower me. You wouldn't. How many times do I have to tell you? If I'd screamed, you would have stopped. If I'd cried or fought, you'd have stopped."

He let out a shaky sigh and put his hands on her thighs. "You're amazing."

She shook her head. "No, not really. But I'm learning to be me again. You've given me back something I thought I'd lost. Until you, until this… I didn't know if I'd ever be able to be with a man again. But I can… and I like it."

He didn't know if her doubt was because of Al Ahmad or Marco and he didn't want to know. He swallowed hard and willed his pounding heart to slow down. Willed his brain to engage.

She lowered herself toward him in slow motion. "I just want to spend the rest of the night with you. In your arms…"

Her lips touched his—until a sudden rap on the door made them spring apart like teenagers caught making out.

Kev found his voice first. "Who is it?"

"Billy. Open up."

Lucky rolled away as Kev swore softly. She was already on her way to the bathroom as he shot out of bed. She turned around and grabbed clothes out of a drawer before hurrying into the bathroom and locking the door behind her. Her heart pounded hard and her hands shook from the adrenaline coursing through her.

Her body—oh, her body—felt hot and melty and on edge all at the same time. She looked at herself in the mirror and blinked. She looked like a woman who'd been thoroughly bedded. Her hair had dried into a mass of curls and stuck up on one side. Her mouth was swollen from kissing, and she had beard burn on her cheek where he'd pressed his face against hers while pounding into her.

Her body ached, but in a good way. She was a bit sore between her legs, but that was to be expected after such ardent, ahem, exercise. Her heart simply turned over when she thought of how it felt to have Kev inside her, moving so powerfully and yet taking care of her needs too. Making sure she came before he did, even though he didn't have to.

That last time—God, that last time, he'd been so hurt and alone, and she'd wanted to soothe him. She'd known he was on the edge of control, and she'd known she was the only one in that moment who could help him. He'd needed her.

She could hear the rapping on the door again, and Billy's voice, sounding urgent. Shit, they'd really screwed up this time. And it was her fault. Kev told her he'd been ordered not to sleep with her on this mission, and she'd all but begged him.

No, she *had* begged him.

She ran a brush through her hair, yanked on her bra,

fresh panties, and a pair of jeans and a plain T-shirt. She thought about putting on a little mascara and some lipgloss, but how obvious would that be? Fresh makeup was more obvious than no makeup, so she left the cosmetics alone and waited until she heard voices.

She counted to one hundred and came out of the bathroom. Billy and Kev looked up at the same time. Kev, she noted, had managed to get on his clothes—except his T-shirt was inside out. She bit her lip to keep from groaning and pasted on a smile.

"Hey, Billy, what's up?"

"You tell me."

She shrugged. "I had a shower and a nap. I have no idea what Captain America was doing while I slept." She shot Kev a smile. "But thanks for letting me sleep. I needed it."

"No problem."

Billy gazed at them both for a long minute. Then he shook his head. "Look, I don't know what's going on with you two, but I'd like for all of us to get out of this fuckhole with our lives. This isn't the time to forget what we're here for."

Kev growled. "No one's forgetting anything."

For the first time since she'd come back to HOT, Billy looked pissed. "You sure about that?"

Kev took a step toward him and Billy rocked back as if he expected a fight. She didn't know if they would fight or not, but Lucky rushed between them and put her hands out. "Stop, both of you. Kev, he's got a right to say it. And Billy, considering what you've just been through with Olivia, I understand why you're concerned."

She knew he was worried about her ability to see this

mission through, and she understood why. Hell, she'd wondered it herself. But she was determined. She wasn't going to let any of them down.

"I don't care what you say about me," Kev said, "but lay off of Lucky. I think she understands better than any of us what's at stake here."

Billy shoved a hand through his hair and took a step back. "Yeah, you're right. Lucky, I'm sorry." He pointed at Kev. "Your shirt's inside out."

Kev blinked. Then he swore. "So fucking what? Since Lucky was asleep, I slept too. You woke us both up, ass-hole. I grabbed my fucking shirt and put it on inside out. So what?"

"Kev," Lucky said evenly, and he looked at her, eyes blazing. "Calm down. It's no big deal."

Billy's jaw tightened. "Look, I came over here be-cause Richie wants a meeting. He's had intel from HQ. Twenty minutes. Everyone's coming."

Kev still looked pissed as he moved away. "We ha-ven't eaten. Can you stay here with Lucky while I go downstairs and get something?"

Billy shoved his hands in his pockets. "Sure."

Kev grabbed his ankle holster and wrapped it around his leg. Then he sheathed his knife at his belt and, at the last minute, whipped his T-shirt off and turned it right side out. Lucky looked away, afraid there would be something on his skin, some dead giveaway, though she knew she hadn't bitten or scratched him.

When he was finished, he gave them both a hard look and then went out the door and shut it behind him. Lucky gave Billy a wan smile and went over to the bed to smooth the covers. She felt self-conscious, and she knew she shouldn't let it show.

Finally, she turned and sank down on the bed, pulling her legs up cross-legged. "How's Olivia doing?" she asked.

Billy flopped into a chair. "Good. All hell's breaking loose at Titan Technology now, but she'll find another job."

"Things moved kind of fast between you two, huh?"

Billy smiled. "Unfinished business, I guess. But yeah, it moved fast. She walked back into my life two days before Christmas. Now I'm thinking of picket fences and his-and-hers towels. It's crazy."

Lucky laughed. "That's great."

His smile faded a bit then. "I miss her and we've only been gone a couple of days. I know she's back home, scared and lonely, and I hate it."

Lucky threaded her fingers together. "She'll be all right. You get used to it." And numb, in a way, but she wasn't telling him that. Maybe it was just her, but numbness had been a big part of her routine when HOT went out on a mission.

"Yeah, I guess you do."

He didn't say anything else, and she knew he was thinking about what it had to be like when the Army came calling with bad news. She'd come home that day to find an unfamiliar car in the driveway. Two Army officers got out. When she'd seen their dress uniforms—and the chaplain's cross—she'd known. She hoped Olivia never had to go through that.

The door opened then and Kev came back in with a bag that smelled delicious. Lucky's stomach rumbled and she realized she hadn't eaten since breakfast.

"Chicken and rice," he said, setting it on a table. "And some other things. I didn't ask. If it looked good, I bought it."

She came over to the table and dished out some food on the paper plate he gave her. They ate quickly while Billy sat and talked to them about different things. The tension in the room eased somewhat as they talked normally. The other guys arrived soon after. Everyone looked grim.

Matt leaned against the desk and fixed them all with a look. "No one has claimed responsibility, but the bombings are coming from the Freedom Force. We've intercepted one of their communication channels, though we don't know how long that will last. Al Ahmad sent out the order the day we arrived. We know he's getting reports about new arrivals in country, but we don't think he knows who we are or why we're here. If he did, we think he'd have hit closer to the hotel."

"Maybe he's trying to confuse us," Kev pointed out.

"Yeah, but that bomb today was awfully fucking close," Hawk said. "It almost turned you and Lucky into jelly."

Lucky shivered. She'd been trying not to think of how close they'd come to being blown apart, and it had worked so long as she'd been focused on Kev. She didn't think that going over and sitting in his lap to distract herself would be a good idea right now though.

"If he'd wanted us specifically," she interrupted, "we'd be dead. We were in the wrong place at the wrong time."

The guys were all looking at her now and her heart thumped. She hoped the beard burn wasn't obvious as they studied her. But no one said anything about that. They just looked at her like she'd said something important to the conversation. Even Billy. It made her feel warm inside.

"I think you're right," Matt said. "And that's why we're moving."

Everyone looked at each other. And then a certain acceptance settled over their features as they processed what he'd said.

"Where to?" Kev asked. "A group of us moving out will be noticeable. What if we're followed?"

"There are more new arrivals every day with the situation escalating, and there's a lot of confusion right now. Our CIA contact has found a safe house for us. Besides, there *are* Americans living and working in Baq, so we won't stick out as badly as we might otherwise. Right now, the mission's success hinges on us going about our business, and that'll be easier to do if we aren't worried about the safety of this hotel."

No one argued. They just continued to look grim.

"This hotel is compromised," Matt said. "We're moving tonight. Pack your gear."

NINETEEN

THEY DIDN'T LEAVE THE HOTEL together. Matt had the team split into three groups, and then they used three different rendezvous points where they were met by a van that took them and their gear to the safe house. It was on a quiet street in a section of town that seemed to be a mixture of middle-class and poor dwellings. Their house was a solid white building that fronted the street as part of a row of houses and apartments. The front was stone, with three windows high up and a large double wooden door that opened to reveal a courtyard, which meant the house was actually at the rear of the structure and not the front.

The van drove through the doors, and Kev breathed a sigh of relief as they passed into a courtyard and the doors swung shut behind them. A much safer and more defensible option than a house on the street.

The back doors of the van opened, and Matt and Hawk were standing there, ready to help with the gear. Kev stepped out and purposely ignored Lucky, though he wanted to offer her a hand and then tug her close. Hawk did it instead—the hand, not tugging her close—and Kev pretended not to notice.

He shouldered his pack and camera gear and then grabbed one of her suitcases. Matt led the way into the house where the other guys were already ranging around the living area and setting up computer equipment and surveillance gear.

"Maybe we should have done this to start with," Kev said to Matt's back. Matt tossed a look over his shoulder.

"Not disagreeing with you, but the powers that be thought we'd be less conspicuous in the hotel."

Kev frowned. "Maybe we would have been, but this certainly feels more like a proper mission."

"Copy that."

Matt started up the stairs and led them to a small room that had two twin beds set up in it. Kev nearly sighed in relief. He'd thought when they moved that he and Lucky would be separated, but nine men and one woman in a house still necessitated bunking up. And since he was the designated bodyguard, he was bunking with Lucky.

Though it might not last long if Billy went to Matt with his concerns.

Not that Kev was going to have sex with Lucky in this room. He set the gear down and turned around. The room was small, and while the walls were stone, he didn't want to test their soundproofing qualities.

Lucky walked in behind Hawk and set down the small case she was carrying. Their eyes met across the room and he felt a jolt down to his toes. It was hell being with her and not being *with* her. He wanted to hold her close for the rest of the night, but that clearly wasn't happening.

"I'm sorry it's not as nice as the hotel," Matt said,

"but it's clean and safe. We gave you the room with the bathroom so you won't have to share with the guys."

Lucky pushed her hands into her jeans pockets. "It's fine."

Matt and Hawk left the room, and Kev closed the door once he heard their feet on the stairs. Then he turned back to Lucky. She was watching him closely, hands still in pockets, expression a little wary.

He walked over and pulled her into his arms. She wrapped hers around his waist and held on tight. He dropped his cheek against her hair and just stood there breathing her in.

"I'm sorry."

"For what," she mumbled against his chest.

"For losing control with you. For forgetting for even a second that this mission is the most important thing, and your safety is my sworn duty. For losing my temper with Billy—hell, you name it."

Her grip on him tightened. "It takes two, Kev. I couldn't have cared less about anything but being with you. I still want to be with you."

His chest ached. "We can't. Not here."

She pushed back and gazed up at him, her beautiful eyes so soft and tender. "I know. Billy's right, and we have to have our heads in the game. I don't want anyone in danger because of me."

He put his palm against her cheek, reveling in the silky feel of her flesh. "None of this should have happened. I should have been stronger…"

Her fingers curled into his T-shirt. "I'm glad it happened," she said fiercely. "And I'm glad you told me about your family. I'm so sorry for what happened to them. But it's not your fault. I didn't get to say that earlier, but it's not your fault."

He felt as if she'd reached inside his chest and squeezed his heart. "You don't know that." He moved away from her and went over to put a hand on the small desk sitting near the door. He gripped the edge hard for a moment. And then he turned back to her. She looked confused, and he felt an almost desperate need to protect her ripple through him.

But he had to confess his sins. It was only right to tell her.

"I fought with my dad that morning. He'd been drinking all night, and I fought with him even though I knew he was volatile. Then I walked out. He screamed at me, told me not to go or I'd regret it." He could still see his father's face twisted in helpless rage. Still smell the stale odor of cheap beer and bad breath as it blasted over him. His father had swayed on his feet, reaching for him, but Kev moved out of his way. And then he laughed when his father fell. Laughed and walked out while his mother looked terrified and his sister ran from the room.

That was the last time he'd seen any of them alive. *His fault.*

Lucky wrapped her arms around herself, but he didn't spare her. He found that he couldn't. That her pity and her sympathy turned on a flood inside him that he couldn't stop. She had to know what kind of man he was.

"He shot them sometime that morning. He didn't kill himself until later in the day. He must have sobered up and realized—"

He raked a shaky hand through his hair. "Maybe he realized what he'd done and couldn't live with it. Or maybe he was too much of a coward, and it took him a few hours to pull the trigger on himself. I'll never know which. But I know it wouldn't have happened if I hadn't left."

"Oh, Kevin," she said. She took a step toward him. Stopped, as if she were afraid he might not want her comfort. "It's still not your fault. He made the choice to kill them, and he made the choice to kill himself. If you'd stayed, he might have killed you too. Did you ever think of that?"

Tears rolled down her cheeks now, and he went over and put his arms around her. "Fuck. You don't need to hear this after the day you've had. I'm sorry."

"No." Her voice was harsh as she pushed him back and tilted her chin up to look him in the eye. "I want you to tell me. I want to know what made you you. I'm crying because this hurts you, not because I don't want to know."

His throat was tight. If he'd gone this far, he could go the rest of the way. "Maybe now you can understand why I wasn't right for you. When I said I couldn't be what you need, this is what I meant." He choked down a bitter laugh. "Billy's thinking of picket fences these days, Matt's planning a wedding, Sam can't take his eyes off Georgie Hayes whenever she's in a room—how do they *know* it's going to work? That they won't wake up someday and find out they've failed the people they love?"

Deep inside he always wondered if his past had damaged him so badly he could never be the kind of man any woman should take a chance on. He wasn't about to start drinking and kill his family—but he'd made such a fundamental mistake in judgment that day when he'd left his violent father alone with his mother and sister. His entire military career had been about rectifying that mistake, and yet it still haunted him. Thirteen years later, and he couldn't ever forget the fresh pain of that moment when he'd found them.

She put her hands on his jaw, held him gently and made him look at her. "None of us are perfect. You were a child, and you didn't fail anyone. Your father is the villain in this story, not you. But even then, relationships are never smooth. And sometimes it doesn't work out no matter how you try. That happens too."

His heart thumped. What she said made sense, and yet... It finally hit him what she wasn't saying. "You and Marco?"

She let him go and went over to sit on the bed. Her shoulders slumped as she studied her lap. "He asked me for a divorce."

Kev felt as if she'd punched him in the gut. He couldn't breathe, couldn't process it. He sank onto the opposite bed and stared at her. "Another thing he didn't tell me."

Marco had kept a lot from him, it seemed. Why?

"I'm sorry." She pulled in a breath, huffed it out again. "This isn't supposed to be about me. It's about you."

"You can't drop a bomb like that and not tell me what happened."

She looked sad for a long moment. And then her jaw tightened. "I don't know what happened. It's just, well, we weren't right for each other. We shouldn't have gotten married, but he was kind and I was messed up... and I said yes."

His gut churned. He didn't want to hear this... and he did. Guilt burned in his soul. "He fell for you the first moment he saw you. He told me you were the girl he was going to marry."

Her eyes flashed. "And you stayed out of the way because of that, right?"

His fingers rolled into fists. "I told you what I wanted from you. But Marco wanted to take care of you. I thought that was more important."

"Marco was a good man. But we both did him wrong. And I'm not talking about tonight. You were the one I was interested in back then, the one I wanted. I think Marco knew that on some level. I convinced myself I was in love with him though." She ran her fingers along her thigh in a quick back-and-forth motion, like she had to do something to keep her emotions in check. "No, I did love him. But it wasn't enough. He tried to stick it out, but I guess he got tired of my hang-ups. He wanted out, though he planned to let me be the one to file."

Kev stood up then. Sweat popped on his skin. He couldn't process this. Marco had wanted her, married her. Loved her. But it hadn't worked out.

Kev's gut churned. What part had he played in that, wanting her from afar? Had Marco known? Had he suffered because it was obvious his best friend wanted his wife? He remembered that Marco had stopped sharing things with him long before that final mission. Had he somehow known what Kev hadn't admitted to himself?

Lucky was looking at him sadly, knowingly, but he couldn't discuss this a moment longer. He had to get out, had to clear his head.

"I, uh, need to go see what the plan is for tomorrow." He strode to the door and opened it. "Don't wait up."

But he didn't go see the guys. He pounded down the

stairs and out into the night air.

TWENTY

LUCKY DIDN'T SLEEP WELL IN the too-soft bed with the creaky springs. Every time she turned, the creaking of the bed woke her up. She raised her head to look at Kev's empty bed each time. It was hours before he returned. She heard the door open, heard his footsteps across the floor and the whisper of his clothing as he shed it. His bed creaked when he lay down but she didn't open her eyes and let him know that she knew he was back.

What would she say if she did? He'd looked like a thundercloud when he'd left earlier and she had no idea what he was thinking now. Maybe she shouldn't have told him she'd wanted him before she'd married Marco, but it was the truth. On some level, he had to have known it too.

Guilt and fear nearly made her sick. She listened to him breathing, her heart hurting for him and her—and for Marco. She shouldn't have been a coward. She should have refused Marco's advances, and she should have refused to marry him until she knew what she really wanted.

But she hadn't, and she didn't know how she would ever get rid of the guilt of not being what he'd wanted in the end.

Kev had his own guilt to endure. He'd had a horrible childhood, and it was clear he'd been damaged from it. That was the secret he kept close, the reason he didn't commit to anyone. He was afraid of failing the ones he loved—hell, maybe he was afraid of loving anyone too. He'd loved his mother and sister, and he'd lost them so senselessly.

And then he'd lost Marco, and she knew he blamed himself for that as well, even if it wasn't his fault.

She wanted so desperately to crawl into bed with him and curl up in the warmth of his body, but that wasn't going to happen. Even if he would welcome her, she could hear the other guys beyond the door from time to time. The walls and doors weren't precisely soundproof.

No, there would be no more frantic sexual encounters before this mission was done.

Hell, maybe there'd be no more encounters at all. The way he'd looked at her when she'd told him about her and Marco. He'd been stunned. And maybe even a little horrified at her confession. Maybe he was wondering what was so wrong with her that Marco had wanted out.

She blinked back tears, her body rigid as her nerves stretched thin, and she tried to think of something to say to Kev. Something that would put everything right again. But it was useless. She didn't know what to say, and she didn't think he wanted to hear it anyway.

Lucky dozed throughout the night, never fully resting. Finally, when she was sinking into a dream of her mother baking cookies in the kitchen with the triplets while she stood outside the window and looked inside at the warm tableau they made, a hand settled over her shoulder and shook her awake.

She looked up into blue eyes, confusion fogging her brain for a moment. But then reality returned and she knew where she was and why. What she didn't know was if Kev would ever kiss her again. It was ironic that it was so important to her considering the gravity of what they were here to do.

"Time to get up. We have to get you to the Prince Faisal School in an hour so you can start classes."

Lucky pushed herself up, wincing as she did so. Kev frowned. "What's wrong?"

Warmth flooded her at that small sign of concern. "Bruises and sore muscles. I'll be fine after I stretch a bit."

"It's my fault. I'm sorry for throwing you on the ground."

She didn't bother to mention that her inner muscles were also sore. It was a lovely reminder of how hot and desperate the sex had been. "You had no choice. Besides, I'll be fine."

He held out a small round device that looked like a very thin watch battery on his palm. "Need you to put this in your bra."

She dragged her gaze to his. It was the first time she'd managed to look at him for more than a second. He gazed at her evenly, no sign of anger or hatred in his eyes. It was enough to make her want to melt in relief. "Why?"

"It's a tracking device. So's your phone, but this is just in case you were to get separated from it."

She swallowed. "Okay."

He dropped the device in her hand. "It's just a precaution. We won't let anyone take you."

"I know." She smiled as he got to his feet and stood

over her. She thought he might say something, but he turned away and went to the door.

"Come downstairs when you're ready."

Disappointment pierced her as she got out of bed and went into the bathroom for a quick shower. She tucked the device in her bra as instructed, against the cup, and then dressed in a pair of capri pants and a tank top before tugging on an abaya and covering her hair. She'd learned yesterday that it was a good idea to have on something a bit more flexible under the abaya just in case. When she was ready, she went downstairs and found five of the guys at a table, eating honeyed pastries and drinking coffee.

She sat next to Jack and grabbed a pastry while the guys talked. They joked and laughed as if they hadn't made a run for it in the middle of the night, as if their plans were still going smoothly and hadn't required a rethink. Then again, that's what they did. They changed plans on the fly.

When it was time to go, Kev rose and she followed his lead. The guys went silent as Kev grabbed his camera gear. Flash joined them with a laptop bag since he was the reporter to Kev's photographer.

"Y'all be careful out there," Matt said. "And Lucky, don't worry about a thing. You got this."

No one looked at her with an iota of doubt. If they felt it, they didn't let it show, and for that she was grateful. She'd spent weeks training with them and now, today, this was it. And they believed she could do it. She nodded. "Thanks."

She followed Kev and Flash through the door and out into the courtyard where the van from the night before waited. The driver rumbled through the city streets until they reached their destination. He let them out two streets over, and they walked the rest of the way. It seemed safe enough, though Kev and Flash were wound tight as they walked. The school was in an exclusive area surrounded by shops and cafes that weren't quite as busy as they might have been before the bombings rocked the city. Still, there were people out and about, and the school itself was heavily secured.

Kev and Flash went inside with her because they'd secured an interview with the headmaster. Something about life in Baq under the new king. Lucky couldn't imagine anyone mistaking these two tall, broad, warrior-like men for journalists, but people often believed what they were presented.

The headmaster met them and ushered them into his office. After a bit of talk, Lucky was shown to the classroom by another teacher. It was a small room, bright and cheery with student drawings of flowers on the wall, and she felt a pang for the woman who'd been shifted out of her job to make an opening. Lucky picked up the papers that were labeled with different parts of a house in English and Arabic and clutched them to her as she wondered what the previous teacher must be thinking today.

Hopefully, this assignment wouldn't last too long and everything would go back to normal.

But how normal would it be once they'd taken some little girl's father away? It was hard to imagine anyone as cold and cruel as Al Ahmad with a child, and yet it wouldn't be the first time a stone-cold killer had a family.

But she couldn't think about that, could she?

Lucky sat and sifted through the materials on her desk, organizing them for the day. And then the students arrived and her heart kicked even as butterflies swirled around inside her belly. This was it, the beginning of her task. The reason they were here. She had to find his daughter.

But that wasn't going to be easy. She studied the students in each class carefully, wondering which of them might be the one she sought. She tried to pick out his features, but how impossible was that when she didn't really know them well enough to do so?

She pored over the girls' names on the roster, hoping something might trigger a memory. Nothing did.

Four hours later, time was up and she was no closer to discovering who Al Ahmad's daughter was than she had been that morning. Disappointment tasted bitter and hard, like an unripened cherry.

Kev was waiting at the entrance when she walked out, and happiness filled her at the sight of him there. She tamped it down as she went up to him. He didn't say anything, just put his arm around her and ushered her down the street. She couldn't help but focus on the easy pressure of his arm on her shoulders, or how her heart fluttered at his nearness.

Was he still angry? Was this all for show?

She told herself she was supposed to be thinking about Al Ahmad and his daughter, but all she could think about was how good it felt to be wedged against Kev's body, walking down the street like a normal couple.

"How'd it go?" Kev finally asked.

"It's an impossible task." She sounded frustrated, but she couldn't hide it. "Nothing about those children seems familiar. There are forty of them, Kev. *Forty*. Unless the man himself shows up for a recital one day, I don't see how this is going to work."

"Maybe he will. In fact, I'm pretty certain of it."

She ground to a halt on the street, and he had to push her out of the way before someone plowed into her. Her back was against a building as she faced him. He was big and dark and lethal. And handsome. God, she could never forget handsome. The sun beat down on him and his eyes pierced hers, and all she could think about was lying beneath him with nothing between them but skin and sweat.

"That's an insane idea," she sputtered, dragging herself back to the conversation. "He'd never do it. Why would you think he would?"

He shrugged. "Maybe he won't. But there's an event coming up that the king is supposed to attend. The headmaster says all the parents are invited. Do you really think our guy will refuse an invitation that involves the king? Wouldn't it be suspicious if he's the only parent who doesn't go?"

She gaped at him, her brain whirling. "He can't possibly run his network while living a normal life, can he? Can he really go to school events and be so… *normal*?"

Even as she said it, she knew it had to be true. It was the secret of his success, the reason why he'd gone undetected for so long. Al Ahmad was only a code name. Behind that name was a man who *must* be connected in order to achieve the things he'd achieved. He'd escaped death and gone underground. He'd only been discovered when his lieutenant had outed him—and that had taken nearly two years to do. Jassar ibn Rashad had been afraid—and then he suddenly hadn't. Though perhaps he should have been, considering he hadn't been heard from again. They could all guess what the outcome of that betrayal had been.

Or maybe he'd just been stupid instead of brave. Whatever the case, he'd let the truth slip, and now almost every government in the world had an interest in finding Al Ahmad and putting a stop to his machinations. But Al Ahmad had to know that, so would he really go to public events where he might be identified?

Kev seemed to know what she was thinking. "If he thought we knew about his daughter, she wouldn't be in the school anymore. There've been no new enrollments or withdrawals in a year. She's there, which means he will most likely be there. It's something we have to consider."

She couldn't breathe for a moment. She thought back over all those faces, which had ranged in age from six to sixteen, and wished she could pick out his features in his child's.

"If he's living a normal life, and his child goes to that school, then he's wealthy and connected. So he might not be in town for this. That's certainly a legitimate excuse if he has a business, right? He could be anywhere for all we know."

Kev arched an eyebrow. "He could be. But what if he's not? What if he *wants* to go to this event? It's the king, Lucky. The fricking King of Qu'rim."

Her blood ran cold as she considered the implications. The King of Qu'rim and Al Ahmad in the same room. For all they knew, it had happened before. If he was a businessman of some description, it probably had. But now that the violence was escalating, could he be planning something against the king?

"When is it?" Her throat was tight.

Kev grinned. "Three days from now."

Abdul Halim was growing impatient. When he gave an order, he expected results. His contact at the hotel said there was some confusion about recent guests. Several had checked out after the bombings, and several new people had checked in. The hotel was swarming with media, and while there weren't a lot of women, there were a few. His contact wasn't quite certain how many because the bombing had upset the city and some of the staff were refusing to get on buses or take taxis to come to work.

Abdul Halim's phone rang and he snatched it up. Farouk was on the other end. "We have a report of some Americans leaving the hotel last night, but they didn't go to the airport."

"And where did they go?"

"We don't know. Two of our men were following them, but the Americans slipped past the perimeter and we were unable to pick up their trail again."

Abdul Halim's gut churned. "Incompetence, Farouk. I will not tolerate it. There is too much at stake."

"What does it matter?" Farouk blew out a breath. "We will have the king himself in just a few days, so why worry about disappearing Americans? When the king is ours, we will control Qu'rim. We'll shut the borders and hunt down all the foreigners."

Abdul Halim ground his teeth. "Because it is an anomaly. And because I saw the woman on camera."

"You saw a woman who *might* be Lucky Reid. And

what can she do, brother? Even if she's here with an army of Americans, they do not know where to find us. With the city in chaos, they'll have their hands full."

Abdul Halim stared at the golden domes of the palace in the distance. They were so close to achieving their goals now. The king's appearance at the school was a last-minute addition to his schedule, and it had the Freedom Force scrambling. They would not miss this opportunity, though capturing the king had never been on their agenda before now.

But the fighting in the desert was taking too long even though the forces guarding the mine were stretched thin. Yet they had not given up. With the king under the Freedom Force's control, the king's military would have to stand down. Taking the mine would be so simple.

And after they had the mine, their men at the Ministry of Science would open the doors and give them access to the enrichment program and the secret warheads the government had been building. Oh, yes, he knew about those, even if the IAEA did not.

Abdul Halim rubbed his temples. It was a delicate operation. He had access to the king in his real life, but forcing a kidnapping that way would reveal his identity. At an event where he was also scheduled to appear? Where he could orchestrate everything and yet not implicate himself in any way?

It was too good to pass up.

"Nothing can interfere with our plans, Farouk. This is the culmination of all we have worked for."

He punched the button to end the call and stood there for several more minutes, anger churning in his gut. A high-pitched giggle came from the direction of the apartment entrance, and he knew that his wife had picked up Lana from school. He walked out of his office and into the hallway.

Lana came running. "Guess what, Daddy!"

"What?" he asked, picking her up.

"I got perfect marks in math. And then Aija pulled my hair and Jada threw up her lunch. And we got a new English teacher. She's American."

Abdul Halim stilled. A new teacher? Now? Ordinarily he would not think twice about such a thing. But this was an unexpected change, and unwelcome.

"What happened to the old teacher?"

"Mrs. MacDonald said she got sick, and she might be gone a while."

A sick teacher was nothing to be suspicious about, and yet a change right before the king's visit did not sit quite right in Abdul Halim's mind. He hadn't gotten as far in life as he had by not being cautious. It might be nothing, but what if it was?

"Ah, I see. And do you like this Mrs. MacDonald?"

"I guess so. She's not as old as Mrs. Fortson. And she's pretty."

Abdul Halim set Lana down, though she pouted when he did so. "Go and play with your dolls. Daddy has phone calls to make."

She skipped off a second later, and he turned and went back to his office. He was simply too close to achieving everything he'd dreamed to allow anything to interfere.

He would learn who this Mrs. MacDonald was before they commenced with their plans. God help her if she wasn't what she claimed to be...

TWENTY-ONE

"THE KING OF QU'RIM. JESUS." Matt raked a hand through his hair.

Kev frowned. "We don't know that's Al Ahmad's plan, but it's a small event and the security detail will be small as well. If the Freedom Force wants to make a grab for the king, that would be the place to do it."

"They might be planning to assassinate him. We should consider that possibility." It was Hawk who'd spoken. Thinking like a sniper, naturally.

Kev shook his head. "I'm not disagreeing that we should consider it, but we also need to consider what grabbing him would mean for them. They'd have the fucking King of Qu'rim under their control. And even if they planned to kill him in the end, they'd surely milk the power that controlling him would give them first."

Matt chewed his lip. "It could be either one. If they kill him, they plunge Qu'rim into chaos. And that would certainly help their cause. But the king's brother would take the reins of government, so they wouldn't be without a king for long."

"Unless the brother is the one feeding information to the Freedom Force."

They all looked at each other. Anything was possible and they didn't trust anyone outside this room. There'd been fears of a leak in the king's inner circle, which was why they'd been very careful about the information they'd fed to the Qu'rimis. But they had no proof. No one did.

Billy Blake tapped on his computer like a madman. "I've got the schematics for the building. We can plan for an assault."

"Either way, we have to go in," Kev said. Several of the guys nodded.

Matt had that look that said he was concentrating. "I need to inform Mendez. But the NSA hasn't reported a damn thing about an attempt on the king."

"You said they'd broken one channel," Kev replied. "Maybe he hasn't let the plan filter down to the rank and file yet. That's obviously not his main channel if there's no word."

"Or he's not planning to do anything," Hawk said. "If he has a real life here, and a child in school, why would he jeopardize that for a risky operation to grab or kill the king?"

"Because he's a sociopath," Lucky interjected. As one, they swiveled their heads to look at her. She'd removed the Arab garments and sat there in her long-sleeved white shirt and pale blue pants. Her hair was curly today, and Kev thought of it wild and messy as she'd sat on top of him in bed with her beautiful curves within reach.

It seemed a lifetime ago now.

Lucky set down her bottle of water. "He thinks he's a god. Maybe not literally, but figuratively. He's smart and patient and arrogant. If he hasn't made an attempt on the king before now, it's because it hasn't suited his plans. But it might now. Because Qu'rim is falling apart and Baq is no longer safe, as we know from experience. It's not definitive proof he'll try to kidnap or kill the king, but I wouldn't bet my life on it. If he's going to act, it'll be now."

The guys all looked at her with respect. Not that they didn't respect her already after how hard she'd worked to be here, but the fact she was contributing to the discussion in such a vital and thoughtful manner went a long way toward making them more certain she wasn't a liability. Kev knew they'd worried about it, and it filled him with a strange kind of pride that they saw her as capable of contributing something useful besides a visual ID of their target.

Kev met Matt's gaze. "We have to be ready," he said. "If we aren't and Al Ahmad succeeds, the tide of the conflict will turn."

"Agreed," Matt replied. "I'm calling Mendez."

He went over to the table and picked up the satellite phone. Kev followed him outside as he popped up the antenna and made the call. A few seconds later, the phone connected and Matt hit the secure button. It was a direct link to Mendez, so there was no waiting for the colonel to get the phone. Matt laid out the situation while Kev listened. There was a long minute where Matt said nothing. He met Kev's gaze while they waited.

And then he nodded, a grin forming on his face. "Copy that, sir." He ended the call and huffed out a breath. "We've got a go order. Mendez will liaise with the NSA and CIA, but we're set to begin operations."

Relief and apprehension washed through Kev at once. He was relieved they had a target and apprehensive because it meant they had a definite date when Lucky would be in greater danger than she was now. Because she had to be at that event, and she had to be ready to ID Al Ahmad. He'd never relished putting her in the line of fire for this mission, but so long as she taught school children English and tried to figure out which child was their target's kid, it didn't seem as life-threatening a mission for her.

But now the hard work would begin. They had three days to get the plan in place. And three days before Lucky came face to face with the man who'd carved his marks into her flesh. Kev hoped she was strong enough to face it. And that he was strong enough to let her.

The next three days passed in a whirlwind of activity. The guys kept watch throughout each day and night while simultaneously planning to thwart a kidnapping—or assassination, since they couldn't be sure which way it would go—down to the last detail. The atmosphere in the house was tense, but there was an undercurrent of excitement. Lucky remembered it from when she'd been assigned interpreter duties with HOT. The energy surrounding a mission was always palpable.

But this was the closest she'd ever been to the actual execution of a critical op. Always before, she'd been on the periphery. Far on the periphery, smoothing the way in

Arabic-speaking countries where her language skills were needed. Here, she was a critical member of the team.

It was exciting and frightening all at once. She still dreamed about Al Ahmad, still woke in a cold sweat with the memory of his gleaming eyes and the glitter of his knife's edge as it descended toward her skin. But there was something else too—determination, fierce and icy. She wanted to stop him. She wanted him trussed up like a pig, and she wanted to slip a knife between his ribs.

She told herself that was carrying it a step too far, and yet he'd caused so much pain and suffering for so many people that she couldn't help but feel he deserved a measure of the same. It wasn't the plan, however. The plan was to thwart any kidnapping or assassination attempts on the king and sweep up Al Ahmad and transport him to the States to stand trial for the murder of innocent Americans.

It was a delicate operation. So delicate that they had not warned the king's government about their plans. They couldn't take any chances that the information would leak. Once Al Ahmad was in their control, the king would be notified. They had to do so in order to get clearance for an immediate military transport out of the country. Every step was delicate, and there were so many things that could go wrong, but she trusted that the team knew what they were doing. This wasn't their first rodeo, as her stepdad would have said.

The reception would take place in the grand hall of the Prince Faisal School where all the teachers, students, and parents would mingle as they celebrated the success of the school and solicited the continuing support of the community. Education for girls was a controversial topic in a nation like Qu'rim, but with the government behind it, the initiative was winning the hearts and minds of the people.

Many of the girls' parents were high-placed government officials, which was worrisome in its own way. Because they had to ask themselves if Al Ahmad was a government official. Or maybe he was just one of the wealthy businessmen who sent their daughters to the school for an exclusive education. Either way, the fact he had a daughter there was of concern.

Lucky turned her thoughts to the girls. She had spent the last three days studying them closely, talking with them, and trying so hard to figure out which one of them could be Al Ahmad's daughter. But she was no closer than she'd ever been. Some of the girls were gregarious. Others were shy. Which would his daughter be? How could anyone know?

The night of the party, Lucky put on a dark silk abaya and a cream hijab and then studied herself in the mirror for a long time. She wasn't the same person she'd been two years ago, but of course her features were the same. Her skin was darker and her hair was hidden, but that wasn't enough to hide her from Al Ahmad. They'd debated putting in false teeth to give her an overbite and contacts to change her eye color when they'd been planning this mission back at HOT HQ, but they'd dismissed the idea because the overbite would make talking a challenge and the contacts would only make her eyes stand out rather than recede. Her eyes were already dark—blue or green contacts would make them too different from the majority of Qu'rimis and therefore noticeable.

In the end, Mendez had accepted her reasons for not wanting the teeth or the contacts. Now she was almost wishing she'd gone for the teeth, no matter how difficult it would have been to speak to the girls and teach them proper English.

The door to the room opened and Kev walked in. He was wearing a tuxedo, and her heart skipped several beats. As her "husband," he was invited to the reception. As her protector, she was damned glad he'd be there.

She turned and let her gaze fall from his face to his broad shoulders, the crisp white shirt and black silk lapels of his jacket. She'd never seen him in a suit before, so a tuxedo was just this side of miraculous. And it was most certainly stunning.

His brows were drawn low. He looked dead serious. "Wow," she said, hoping to elicit a grin at least.

He didn't crack. But he glanced down at his tux and then back up at her.

"Give you a Lamborghini and a slinky blonde, and no one would think you were anything but a movie star," she teased.

He snorted softly.

"You ready for this?" His voice was filled with concern, and she knew it was all for her. Warmth glowed inside her.

"As ready as I can be." She stepped away from the mirror and went to join him. "Truthfully, I'm glad we're going to this thing. I want this over with, and if that's where he's going to be, that's where we'll get him."

He frowned. "This isn't what I anticipated. I thought we'd watch the school for a few weeks, and you'd figure out which kid was his. Or maybe we'd intercept a call, and you'd ID his voice. Anything but this."

She touched his arm. "I don't know what I thought,

but I always thought I'd have to see him again. Anything else would be too simple, right?"

He caught her hand in his and tugged her toward him. The door was still open and she glanced at it, but then she went into his arms anyway. They'd barely touched in days now, and it was almost too much to be next to his heat and hardness again. Emotion overwhelmed her and her eyes filled with tears that she didn't want him to see.

But somehow he knew. He cupped the back of her head and held her close.

"There are about a million things I want to say to you right now, but I don't know how." His voice was low and intense and she shivered.

She could feel his heart beating hard, and she closed her eyes and just let it pound against her ear. So long as he was alive. So long as he was alive...

"You don't have to say anything. This is enough for now."

He squeezed her to him—and then he tipped her chin up and fused his mouth to hers. She met him hungrily, greedily, kissing him as if it were the last time. Someone made a noise and they broke apart guiltily.

Hawk was standing in the doorway, his eyebrows a little higher than usual. But he didn't say anything other than, "We're ready to go whenever you are."

Kev put his hand on her back protectively. His eyes flashed, as if he dared Hawk to say anything else. Instead, he turned and disappeared, and she felt Kev's stance relax slightly.

"Busted," she said, and he laughed.

"Darlin', we've been busted for a while. They're all just pretending not to know."

She glanced up at him. They still hadn't talked about the night he'd walked out when she'd told him about the divorce. "Does it bother you that they know?"

His eyes were troubled. "Marco's gone and we're still here." His chest drew up tight as he sucked in a breath. "I'm working on it not bothering me."

She squeezed his hand as relief slid through her. If he could say that much, then maybe there was hope after all.

"It takes time." And then she drew in a breath for courage. "I won't let any of you down, I swear. I'm focused on this." She swallowed the lump in her throat. They'd been like family in their own way and she loved all these guys, even if she loved one in particular more than the rest.

If only she could tell him that.

"I'll be at your side the whole way, Lucky. When you ID him, we'll take it from there. In and out, clean and quick."

She nodded firmly. "Copy that."

She wanted to say more. She wanted to tell him she loved him, but she was afraid to do it when there was so much on the line. And yet some sixth sense insisted that she needed to say the words, no matter how difficult. That it was important to do it before they went out there tonight and the mission was the only thing on their minds. She took a deep breath.

"Kev, I—"

"Transport's here." Billy Blake stood in the door, and the words died in her throat. Kev took her hand and led her from the room. The moment was gone and the drumbeat of worry began its tattoo in her belly.

Tonight was the night. Abdul Halim waited for his wife to finish getting dressed as he walked to the window. The sun was sinking and Baq glowed in the golden light. Like a beacon. Like a new beginning.

Abdul Halim's chest swelled with pride and satisfaction. This was it. He'd worked hard and long for this moment. He'd suffered. He'd lost everything and started over more than once. He'd been dirt-poor, and he'd been wealthy, and he liked wealthy far better. But even better than wealth was power. The power to shift nations. The power to make the United States sink to their knees and beg for mercy.

The power to craft his own destiny. He had that now, and tonight he would have the power to craft the destinies of many.

He heard Fatima bustling around in their room, heard the rustle of silk and the soft feminine voice as she sang to herself. He glanced at his watch. There was time, if he wanted to have her. He could walk into the bath and, with a look, she would drop her gown and come to him on her knees. It was fitting on the night of his triumph that she should do so.

And yet he could not afford to wreck his concentration on the task at hand for even a moment. Tonight, when they had the king and the mine had fallen, when the Ministry of Science was theirs for the taking and the world trembled because the Freedom Force had pulled off a major coup, then he would indulge. And not only with Fatima.

Fatima was for sex and spending his lust. But tonight he also wanted pain. Not his, certainly not. Someone else's. Male or female, he did not care. Someone would pay for all the angst and drama he'd had to suffer to get to this moment.

He wished it could be Lucky Reid. He lifted his coffee cup and took a sip of the sweetly bitter brew. Ah, what a glorious night it would be if he could have her too.

His phone buzzed in his pocket. Not his personal phone, but the phone that mattered most to his life.

"Yes?"

It was Farouk. "All is in place for tonight."

"Excellent. And the teacher?"

"We have just obtained a photo of her and her husband from one of our contacts. I'm texting it to you now."

Abdul Halim waited impatiently for the ding. When it arrived, he pulled the phone from his ear and looked at the photo. The woman was wearing traditional garb, and her face was in profile as she looked up at the man. A shot of ice rocketed down his spine. It was the same tall man he'd seen in the news video from the bombing near the American embassy.

And the woman. His breath caught in his lungs, stopped utterly until he forced it out again. There was no doubt it was Lucky Reid. And she would be at the reception tonight, which meant this was no coincidence. The man at her side was most likely a military operative.

His fingers curled hard around his phone. The edges bit into his skin, and he eased his grip before he crushed the screen. Damn them! The Americans had somehow learned about the plan to take the king. Rage rolled through him in bright, blood-red waves. Someone would pay for this betrayal. Heads would roll.

"Abdul Halim?"

He realized that Farouk had been repeating his name for several moments. "It is her, Farouk. The Americans are here."

There was silence on the other end of the phone for a long moment. "We should call off the operation."

They should. It was prudent and logical.

But fury held him in its grip. He was too close to winning everything to let this chance go.

"No." His voice was a slash in the air. He stood bathed in the light from the setting sun and let his mind whirl through the possibilities. There *must* be a way. He would not accept defeat. Not this time.

"We're altering the plan, Farouk. But we are still going to take the king."

TWENTY-TWO

KEV SAT ACROSS FROM LUCKY in the van. Her head was turned so she was in profile, and he caught himself studying her endlessly. She was quietly beautiful. Elegant. Fierce and small. She was determined tonight. He could see it so clearly on her face.

And yet she was scared. He knew that too. No one else did, probably, but he knew it because he knew her. He thought back to the moment when he'd held her close. She'd trembled slightly and he'd never wanted to let her go.

He'd wanted to tell her he was sorry he'd reacted the way he had when she'd told him Marco had wanted a divorce. He'd felt blindsided by that news, and yeah, he'd felt guilty for whatever part he'd played. He'd pushed them together when it hadn't been right for either of them.

He also wanted to tell her the things he felt for her. But it was new and frightening, and he was completely out of his element when it came to matters of the heart.

But he hadn't said a word because the time wasn't right. Her focus had to be on tonight. Besides, he was still

233

dealing with the realization himself. It was frightening to care so much about someone else. The last time he'd loved people, he'd lost them senselessly and irrevocably. No matter what Lucky said, he still believed he could have changed it. But it was in the past now and there was no going back. That was what he had to live with.

And then there was Marco. He couldn't change that either, but it was still a knot in his heart that wouldn't go away. Was it wrong to love his best friend's widow, even when he knew that their relationship had been over? Maybe it was, but there was nothing he could do about it. He'd tried to hold back the tide, tried to hide it and keep it contained, but at a certain point it swelled over the barriers and there was no containing it.

It was frightening and amazing all at once.

Lucky turned her head and caught his gaze. She gave him a soft smile and his heart thumped. He winked at her and she dropped her gaze to her lap for a long moment. He wondered what she was thinking, but there was no opportunity to ask.

It was dark out when the van halted on the corner to let them out so they could walk the rest of the distance to the school. They would have taken a taxi, but with the bombings in the city and the uncertainty hanging like a miasma over everything, it was safer to stick with the team as far as they could.

Kev popped in his earpiece and the hidden mic and then nodded firmly before stepping from the van and offering his hand to Lucky. She scooted to the edge of her seat and then stepped down to the street. Kev caught her against him, not because it was necessary, but because he wanted to.

"I got you," he said as her hands went up and flattened against his chest. She tilted her head back and met his gaze.

"I know."

"We'll be in position in a few moments," Matt said from the open door. "The minute you spot him, give Kev the signal. We'll move in."

"Copy," Lucky said firmly.

The door closed and the van rolled away. Kev checked his watch, and then they started walking the two blocks to the school. The street wasn't as crowded as it had been during the day. There were people near the shops and cafes, but they weren't as numerous as before the two bombs had struck the city. Kev kept Lucky's hand firmly in his as they walked. He wished they could just keep on strolling, but the school loomed in the distance and danger soured the air the closer they got to it.

Kev stopped when they were still a block away, though the timing was synchronized to the minute and he shouldn't stop at all, and Lucky turned with a question on her brow.

"What's wrong?"

"Nothing." He scanned the area and then looked at her again. "Everything." He pulled in a breath and squeezed her hand. "Lucky, before we go in there, I want you to know that—"

A van screeched around the corner and jerked to a stop beside them as the doors blasted open. Men with dark keffiyehs, wrapped to cover their faces and leave only their eyes showing, burst from the interior. AK-47s jammed in Kev and Lucky's faces as a stream of Arabic burst from one of the men.

Kev's body coiled tight as he forced himself to study the men around him instead of the terrified look on Lucky's face. "Got a problem here," he said softly, hoping his team heard him. "Six men. Assault rifles. Dark Mercedes van. Can't see the tag."

"Jesus Christ." Matt's voice in his ear. "Hang tight, Big Mac. We're coming."

Someone jabbed Kev in the side with a gun and Lucky grabbed his arm, her fingers digging into muscle.

"We have to go with them. They say they'll shoot us here on the street if we don't."

"They'll shoot us anyway," Kev ground out. He lifted his hands skyward, trying to appear as clueless and harmless as an average guy might be in this situation. "But we're going. Tell them we're going."

He wanted to buy time for his team to get back, but everything was happening too fast. If he resisted, he might gain some time for Lucky because they would surely shoot him. But maybe they'd shoot her too, and that was a risk he simply couldn't take.

The man closest to him jabbed him in the side with the rifle barrel again, and Kev moved toward the opening of the van. Someone shoved Lucky and she stumbled. Kev ground his teeth together until he thought his jaw might crack. Trying to defend her wasn't wise in this moment. He had to get his head off of her and on the job.

Someone yanked Lucky into the van and threw a sack over her head. And then they did the same to him. They shoved him down on the floor, and he hit something soft. The intake of breath told him it was Lucky. Before he could reach for her, someone grabbed his arms and zip-tied his hands in front of his body. Then they relieved him of the guns he had in the shoulder and ankle holsters he wore.

The van screeched away from the curb, and they were thrown against each other as it careened around corners. His hopes for immediate rescue dwindled by the minute as nothing impeded their progress.

The men were silent, and Kev tried to concentrate on the feel of the ride. When they stopped or turned, he tried to pay attention to it. Not that it would help much since he didn't know their actual speed, but he knew the van had been headed north when it stopped. They hadn't made any U-turns, only a right and a left. And then they picked up speed, and he knew they must have reached the highway that ran along the outskirts of the city.

He drew his knees up and put his head down and prayed the road noise would prevent anyone from hearing him talking.

"On the highway. Think we're heading north."

The earpiece crackled. "Copy," came through, but it sounded weak.

Kev concentrated on the sounds around him. He was afraid for Lucky, but not for himself. This is what he did, and he had confidence in his ability and his team. He was wearing a tracking device, and so was she. His team was already mobile and following the GPS to wherever the tangos took them.

He had to focus on staying alive long enough for HOT to get here. And he had to keep Lucky alive at all costs.

He could feel her beside him, trembling, and he wanted to put an arm around her and hold her close. Instead, he leaned into her as much as he could, hoping to impart strength. She leaned back, and warmth flowed through him. And frustration.

He'd told her he would protect her, and he damn well would. She trusted him. Believed in him. And he believed in her.

The van started to slow, and he knew they'd taken an exit ramp. Finally, they turned right and drove for several minutes before they swung hard right again. And then they stopped and the doors burst open. Kev and Lucky were hustled out of the van and pushed, stumbling and tripping, until a door clanged shut. He waited a few moments, listening hard for noise.

But there was nothing and he reached up and ripped the hood off. Kev spun around to take in their surroundings. The room wasn't very big, but it wasn't the size of a single cell either. There was no furniture. No windows. Nothing but the door with a tiny barred window and the sound of men outside, shouting to each other.

"We're alone," he said, reaching for Lucky's hood and lifting it off.

Her eyes were wide, her skin pale. He wanted to kill those men for the way they'd handled her.

"What are they saying?" he asked gently, lifting his bound hands and running a finger over her cheek.

She fixed her gaze on him and licked her lips. "The order is not to harm us. Al Ahmad wants us alive... for now."

"Please tell me they're coming for us," Lucky said softly. Kev's gaze was busy gliding over the walls of their prison, but he jerked his eyes back to her.

"Yes. But this is an opportunity. Don't forget that."

She flexed her hands against the restraints. These were cheap plastic zip ties, not the steel-reinforced ones they should be. Stupid bastards.

She knew how to break out of them and so did Kev, but he hadn't yet done so. Since she figured it might be necessary for them to appear incapacitated, she didn't bust them.

God, she'd been grabbed from a public street. Like last time. Only this time she had an operator with her and it still happened. Lucky shivered. She didn't want to be scared, but she couldn't quite help it. Yes, she had her HOT training to fall back on, and she was damn well determined to do so. But waiting in this room for Al Ahmad to arrive would drive her insane.

"I wonder how he found us."

"Contacts at the school, probably. It was always a risk."

Sharp anger flooded her at the way Kev spoke. So matter-of-fact. So cool. Like he was reciting facts for a quiz instead of being held captive by an insane terrorist.

"How can you be so calm? He's a madman, and he's going to kill us both if we don't get out of here."

Kev strode over and stopped inches away. He was crowding her, but she didn't really care as his big body radiated heat. It took her a second to realize that he was utterly furious. Behind all that calm, cool demeanor was a tiger on a leash.

His tuxedo was rumpled, his tie askew. And the white

zip ties stood out in stark contrast to the darkness of his suit. "We have to be calm. He wants us scared, but calm is what we need. HOT won't leave us."

"But the king…" Tears pressed against the backs of her eyes. They were the only ones who knew there was a plot against the king. If HOT had to choose rescuing her and Kev or rescuing a king whose survival could dictate the balance of power in the region, which would they choose?

She knew the answer and it wasn't them.

His eyes flashed hot. "Don't think about that. Concentrate on us."

She wanted to do that so much, but it wasn't easy when her body bore the marks of that madman's knife. And he was coming. She felt his impending arrival like a malevolent cloud hanging over them, squeezing the life from their tortured bodies. Because he would torture them. She had no doubt.

And she would rather die than ever be at his mercy again.

"You won't let him take me, Kev. Promise you won't."

His brows slashed down. "I said I wouldn't."

She reached out and gripped his fingers with her own. "No, I mean it. Whatever it takes, don't let him take me away from here. Away from you."

His eyes searched hers, widening when he realized what she meant. "No," he said hoarsely. "Fuck, no. We aren't going there. You aren't going to die, you understand me? I won't let it happen."

She squeezed his fingers. "I only meant it as a last resort. If all is lost."

"All is not lost," he said fiercely. "They're out there."

"Are they communicating with you?"

"No."

Her heart squeezed. "Maybe they've lost the signal. This room is completely closed in."

"Or maybe they've gone into radio silence because they had to. This isn't our first mission, for chrissakes. HOT knows what they're doing."

She didn't mention Marco and Jim because she knew that wouldn't help the situation. Instead, she pulled in a deep breath and turned to study the walls too. Maybe there was something they were missing. A weakness, a secret entrance, something.

"These things have got to go," Kev growled. She turned back to see him ram his elbows against his hip bones—and the zip ties broke, falling uselessly to the floor.

Keeping his eye on the door, he bent and picked up the useless plastic and stuffed it in his pockets.

Then he produced a small knife from somewhere and sliced her restraints. Lucky rubbed her wrists where the plastic had cut grooves into her skin.

"I could have broken out on my own."

"I know. But it's nicer on your skin this way."

"I thought you wanted us to stay bound."

"I did. And then I didn't." He shrugged. "Change in plan."

There was shouting somewhere outside their cell, and they both stiffened, listening. But no one came to the door.

Kev slid the knife back inside his cuff and she shook her head. "They should have searched you a little more thoroughly."

He shot her a grin. "They should have. Thank God they didn't."

"So what's the plan, Captain America?"

She had to have something to concentrate on other than the fact Al Ahmad was coming. This time, he wouldn't spend days torturing her. This time, he'd make sure she suffered hard and fast. And then he'd kill her in the most painful way he could devise.

She ground her teeth together. At the very least, she'd take a chunk out of him before she died.

"We wait." Kev shrugged. "If the plan is to take the king, Al Ahmad will be tied up for a bit. And when they open this door again, we'll take them out. If we're lucky, that'll be before he gets here."

"We don't know how many of them there are."

"No." He smiled. "But we have something they don't."

She knew he meant the hand-to-hand-combat skills she'd spent week after week learning. Her heart thumped up a few degrees.

"You sure are sexy when you're determined, you know that?"

He lifted an eyebrow. "You know someone's listening to what we say, right?"

"I don't care anymore." She walked over and put her arms around his neck before pulling his head down and pressing her lips to his. He took her mouth passionately, their tongues rolling and sliding together as desire set up a drumbeat in her belly. She couldn't hold it in any longer, and she didn't want to. Whatever happened, happened. But not without her telling him how she felt.

"I love you, Kevin MacDonald. And I don't care who

knows it."

He squeezed her tight against him. "Jesus, Lucky, you rip me inside out, you know that? You always have."

Her heart thumped for a different reason now. "Does that mean you love me too?"

He hesitated for a long moment, and her blood pulsed slow and sticky in her veins as she waited. It was as if time slowed too.

"Yeah, that's exactly what it means." He tilted his head back and looked up at the ceiling. "Forgive me, Marco. And while you're at it, can you help us out of this mess?"

She tilted her head back too, her throat tight with emotion as she gazed at the peeling plaster on the ceiling. "I hope he's listening."

If she expected a sign, she didn't get one. It was eerily quiet in their prison as they stood there together and just held each other. She never wanted it to end—and yet it had to if they were going to have more than a few stolen moments together. This was a moment in which she should be elated. But instead, she felt a heavy sense of dread.

"I wish they'd get here already," Lucky said.

"Have faith, sweetheart."

There was a shout in the distance that rang down the metal corridors. Answering shouts sounded, and then it went quiet again. Lucky's heart throbbed.

"Could you understand that?"

"It was too garbled."

Kev kissed her again, a brief touch of his mouth that had her wishing she could lean into him and let herself go. "We're getting out of here, Lucky," he said firmly. "Never doubt it. This doesn't end here."

She nodded, even though she wasn't as confident as he was. What if the team didn't come? What if Al Ahmad had found them too? They could be blown to bits even now, their van overtaken and obliterated with a rocket launcher or an IED. Al Ahmad had to know they were coming, or he wouldn't have been able to grab her and Kev off the street the way he had. He'd been expecting them.

The mission was compromised. And they were in grave danger.

Booted feet sounded in the corridor, running toward the cell. Kev pulled her over to the wall beside the door. "Stay back when the door opens."

"What are you going to do?" she whispered.

His eyes looked hard. "Whatever it takes."

Panic threaded through her then. She reached up and curled her hand around the back of his neck, pulling him down for a kiss. "I love you."

He grinned. "Ditto, babe."

Someone banged on the door and she jumped as it reverberated through the wall. A man's voice shouted, "Move where I can see you. Do it now or I will kill you when I enter."

She knew Kev didn't understand a word the man was saying, but he also didn't look concerned. He put a finger to his lips and she kept her mouth shut. The lock on the door clanged—and then the door slid back on the track, and the barrel of an AK-47 poked through.

Kev lashed out and grabbed the barrel, jerking the gun forward. The terrorist on the other end came with it, pulling the trigger as he did so. Automatic gunfire erupted, the muzzle flashing repeatedly as the sound echoed like a sonic boom in the empty space. Lucky put her hands over her ears instinctively.

Kev had the man partially through the door, and he still had a firm grip on the gun. "The door," he yelled at her. "Shove it closed as hard as you can."

Somehow she heard him. And she obeyed. The heavy iron door didn't slide easily, but it picked up momentum the harder she pushed—and it slammed into the terrorist's arm. He screamed and let go of the gun. Kev jerked it the rest of the way through and flipped it. Then he shoved the door open again and shot the man on the other side.

His face was grim as he looked over his shoulder at her. "Come on, we're getting out of here."

More shots rang out and he ducked back into the room. "Goddammit," he breathed. He waited a few seconds, listening hard at the door. And then he sprang into action, rolling out the open door and over the body that lay there, firing the entire time. When he stopped firing, the echoes died away. Kev jumped to his feet and motioned to her.

Lucky hopped over the man in the door. At the end of the corridor, two men lay still, blood pooling on the floor beneath them. Kev took her hand and they ran down the corridor in the opposite direction. Each time they came to an opening, he stopped and listened before sweeping across it with the gun at the ready.

They finally came up to a massive door that was rolled down over what must be a loading dock. Off to the side, there was a smaller door, and he headed for it, pulling her up short when he reached it. There was no window to look out of but they both knew this had to be a door to the outside.

"No telling what's on the other side," he said. "You ready to do this anyway?"

"Anything's better than waiting for Al Ahmad."

Kev eased the door open softly. There was no noise outside it. He went through it with the gun to his shoulder. "Nothing," he called back to her.

Lucky joined him. They stood against the wall, surveying the area. They were in shadows here, but the light on the lot in front of the warehouse wasn't strong. It was quiet and empty.

"That was too easy," Kev said. "It shouldn't have been so simple to get out of there."

Lucky's heart thumped. "There were three bodies. I didn't see all the men when they grabbed us, but there were three on the street and at least two in the back of the van—and one driving. So where are the other three? And were there more?"

"Good question."

"It's not his style to let us go after having us captured. But maybe it was just a diversion. Maybe the real trouble is still to come."

"That's what I'm afraid of." Kev tapped his ear. "Hey, Richie, you copy? Y'all out there?"

Lucky bit her lip. "No communication?"

Kev frowned. "It's possible the unit was damaged when they threw us in the van. But I'm getting nothing on this end. Doesn't mean they can't hear us though."

In the distance, they could hear a car engine approaching. Tires squealed against pavement, and a pair of headlights grew larger as the vehicle raced toward the warehouse. Kev hunkered down behind a stack of pallets, braced the rifle against the wood, and aimed.

TWENTY-THREE

THE AK-47 DIDN'T HAVE A scope, but he didn't need a scope to spread rapid fire across the vehicle's surface. Kev kept his eye on the target as his finger hovered over the trigger. The car slowed as it passed into the yard. The headlights were still aiming toward him, so he couldn't see what kind of car it was. But the closer it got, he realized the silhouette was taller than a car. Didn't mean it was HOT, but it could be. His finger slid to the side as he waited.

And then the van stopped about twenty yards away, and a door opened. A man stepped out and a light flashed. Morse code. Kev breathed a sigh of relief as he unfolded himself from behind the pallets. He stepped out into the meager light and waved. The man hurried toward them.

It was Hawk. "You two okay?"

Kev helped Lucky jump down from the loading dock. "Yeah, we're fine. Three dead tangos in there. No idea how many there were or where the rest are."

The van pulled up and the door slid open. "Hey," Iceman said, "didn't anyone ever teach you not to accept rides from strangers?"

Kev laughed as he let Lucky go in front of him. Iceman tugged her into the van, and Kev and Hawk followed. "Yeah, well, they made me an offer I couldn't refuse."

Kev put an arm around Lucky as soon as he sat down and tucked her into his side. He didn't care if the guys had heard them or not, but now that they were safe—for the moment—he wasn't wasting the opportunity to be close to her. This night wasn't over, and there was still a job to do—and he had no idea what would happen next. If he had his way, he'd put Lucky on a plane out of here right now.

It wasn't up to him though.

"We got caught behind a pileup in the city," Matt said. "Your comm link went out but we still had the GPS. We had no idea what we'd find when we got here."

"It's all right. We held our own."

"Tell us what happened."

Nick Brandon shoved the van in gear and tore out of the parking lot while Kev repeated everything they'd been through, with input from Lucky.

"Jesus," Iceman said. "Those are some incompetent fucks. Dude actually stuck the rifle in first? Amateurs."

"Al Ahmad probably figured he'd finish the job at the school and then deal with you two later. Here," Hawk said, handing Kev new pistols. Thankfully HOT traveled with extras. Kev tucked them into his holsters and breathed a sigh. It felt good to be armed again. Billy gave him a new earpiece and mic, and Kev dropped the old ones into Billy's hand.

"Thanks for coming to get us," Lucky said softly.

"Told you we'd have your back," Hawk chimed in. "Though you only needed us for a ride out, it seems."

"He might have planned it this way," Lucky said. "Divert us, divert you—and complete his plans before we can react."

Billy's fingers were flying across his computer screen. He looked up and grinned. "Yeah, well, he didn't count on the king being late. He's running almost an hour behind schedule."

"Copy that," Matt said. "We're still going in."

"If he knows we escaped, he'll call off his plans," Lucky said.

Matt looked grim. "It's a chance we have to take."

"If he sees us there," Kev added, "he's going to know the game is up."

Matt shrugged. "Either way, it's our best chance. We have to take it." He looked directly at Lucky. "Can you still do it?"

She pulled in a breath. "Yes. Hell, yes. He has to be stopped."

Kev's heart swelled with pride. She'd been through hell and back with that monster, and yet she still wanted to go after him. Tough and determined, that was his Lucky.

She pulled away from his embrace and reached for his tie. "If we're still going in, we have to fix this."

Her scent drove him crazy, but now wasn't the time to do anything about it. He let her fuss over his tie, his throat feeling tight as he looked down at the top of her head. She was his now, and that thought filled him with quiet joy. *His.*

He was still getting used to what that meant. She smoothed his lapels and then ran her fingers through his hair. It was a sensual shock to his system. Another second and he'd grab her wrists to halt the torture, but she leaned back and studied him with a critical eye.

"There. At least you don't look like you were in a cat fight anymore."

She reached up and fixed her hijab a little tighter before smoothing the silk of her abaya. It was wrinkled, but there was nothing they could do about it now. He glanced at his team, saw that most of them were busy looking anywhere but at the two of them.

It didn't matter whether they approved or not, but it bothered him that maybe they were thinking of Marco and wondering what would be happening if he were still alive. Hell, he wondered that too. But that wasn't the hand they'd been dealt.

"There's not going to be a lot of time," Matt said. "We're inserting together, and then you can make your way to the ballroom through the maintenance corridor."

Kev nodded. It's what he'd have chosen to do too, given the circumstances. Soon they rolled to a stop and shoved open the van doors. Billy and Flash stayed in the van to monitor the comm links while the rest of the team piled out at the rear of the school. It was dark now and there was activity near the rear entrance, but the team didn't go that way. Instead, Matt led them to a fire escape on the side of the building. Iceman scaled it first and reported the all clear.

One by one, the rest of them went up. Kev sent Lucky ahead of him. When they hit the roof, they ran for the entrance. Iceman popped it open, and then they were inside, heading down the stairwell that came out into the school's maintenance area.

Matt gave a signal and everyone stopped. "Everyone in position in three minutes."

They checked their watches to make sure they were still synchronized, and then Kev drew his MK23 with the suppressor and led Lucky toward the ballroom. There was a chance they'd run into someone on lookout, but he'd deal with them effectively and swiftly if so.

Lucky clutched the tail of his jacket as they crept through the darkened corridor. They could hear voices coming from inside the ballroom and the tinkle of plates and glasses from the kitchen where the caterers had set up. There was a bright light shining from the kitchen up ahead, and men rotated in and out of the doors with trays as they went from the kitchen to the ballroom and back. Kev stopped as they got closer and pulled Lucky into the shadows.

As soon as it was clear, they hurried to another door that opened onto the ballroom, and Kev holstered his weapon.

"You ready?"

"Yes."

He kissed her swiftly and then opened the door and they slid through. A lady looked up as they walked in, but she only smiled and went back to her conversation. Kev took Lucky's hand and walked casually around the perimeter, studying the crowd. People milled in clusters while a string quartet played in one corner. The men and women glittered in their evening clothes. Most wore native dress adorned with shiny embroidery, but there were a few tuxedos and modest evening gowns. The school girls gathered into small groups where they talked and laughed together while their parents chatted with school officials and teachers.

A photographer circulated, snapping photos. Kev

grabbed two glasses of something fizzy from a passing waiter—not champagne, since alcohol was forbidden in Qu'rim—and handed one to Lucky.

"Don't drink it," he said under his breath. He didn't think there was anything wrong with the stuff, but why take that chance? They didn't know what Al Ahmad had planned and had no idea how he would execute it. Drugging a crowd with poisoned drinks was definitely within his capability.

She nodded, her gaze straying over the crowd. He knew she was searching, hoping like hell to find Al Ahmad, but the truth was they didn't even know if he would be here or not.

He took her hand again and they started to circulate. The headmaster came up to them and chatted about the upcoming article that he and Flash were supposedly doing. Kev was beginning to feel on edge the longer they stood in one place, but finally the man's cell phone rang and he excused himself to take the call.

"King's car just pulled up." It was Matt's voice in his ear. "Showtime, Big Mac."

"Copy that."

Lucky's gaze collided with his. "What?"

They hadn't given her an earpiece or a mic, so she didn't have access to the reports coming through.

"King's here. If our boy's going to make a move, it'll have to be soon."

She searched the crowd, desperation and frustration clouding her expression. "There are too many people. He could be anyone. He could have changed his face…"

The main doors burst open a few seconds later as the king and his party strode inside. The entire ballroom sank into curtsies and bows, and a hush passed over the group. Even the quartet stopped playing.

"Six men," Kev said softly. "Only two appear to be bodyguards."

"Copy."

He bowed even as Lucky curtsied. Her head was still up, studying the men, searching. And then her grip on his hand tightened as she sucked in a breath. "I think maybe… it could be… Dammit, I can't tell."

Kev looked at the knot of people she was watching, but he didn't know what he was looking for. The men wore traditional robes, and they had all bent forward in deep bows. But one glanced up, his eyes glittering as he watched the king's party. It didn't mean anything, and yet there was a certain coldness in his gaze. Whether or not he was Al Ahmad, he definitely wasn't a fan of the current king.

There was a hush and a murmur, and Kev realized that the waiters had set down their trays. That shouldn't be odd, and yet…

"Something's happening," he said, alarm churning through him.

One of the waiters stood tall as the king passed. He cried out in sharp Arabic, opening his robes as he did so. The two bodyguards drew their weapons, but the man said something else and they dropped the guns to the floor and kicked them away. Two of the other waiters grabbed the guns.

"What the fuck is happening?" Matt said over the comm.

Kev couldn't see the waiter's face, only his back, but he didn't like the way the man stood there so confident and sure. Dread crawled up Kev's spine and settled at the base of his brain. "Not sure."

But Lucky's face had drained of all color. Her voice was barely a whisper. "He's wearing a bomb."

Fear ricocheted around Lucky's belly, making her nauseous. The waiter—suicide bomber—stood there so erect and proud and fearless. Willing to die.

A murmur rippled across the crowd. A woman screamed and then dropped in a faint. Many of the girls started to cry while others screamed and ran to their parents' sides.

Lucky focused again on the man she'd spotted right before the suicide bomber revealed himself. He stood with his arms around a woman and a girl—Lana, she was called. Lucky remembered because she'd been so gregarious. Not at all the sort of child you'd expect to belong to a madman.

Lucky searched her brain for a name. She couldn't think of the girl's surname because Arab surnames were long and she'd been working on memorizing the girls' given names first.

The man's face was hidden now as he stood with his arms around the woman and girl. He didn't seem like a crazed terrorist. He seemed like a frightened spectator, same as the rest of the people in this room.

Her heart thumped. She was wrong, and this man

wasn't the one. So where was he? Why couldn't she find the man who'd tortured her, the man whose face should be seared into her brain no matter how briefly she'd seen it?

Kev's hand tightened on hers. He stood upright now, as did everyone else in the room. Another man in a waiter's uniform spoke to the crowd, and Lucky whispered the words, hoping Kev—and the team—would hear them.

"In the name of Allah the most mighty, the Freedom Force promises you will not be harmed if His Most Revered Highness, King Tariq bin Abdullah, accedes to our demands. If he does not, you will be executed one by one."

The king's chin went up. He was resplendent in a dark thobe with ornate embroidery in golden thread running down the edges. He was also young, perhaps thirty or so, and handsome. His cheeks were slashed with red as he spoke.

"My government does not bargain with terrorists," he said in a clear voice.

"As you wish."

A shot rang out and everyone jumped. A few people screamed. And then a man sank to the tiles, a bullet hole in the center of his forehead. A different waiter lowered a gun as a woman began to sob.

"Jesus," Kev said under his breath.

"Your Excellency?" the first waiter asked again. The bomber stood by with a serene expression on his face, awaiting orders from the apparent leader.

Lucky had no doubt he'd detonate the weapon if told to do so. Footage of the suicide bombings carried out by the Freedom Force played in her head, as well as her memories from the other day. So many people hurt. So many lives torn apart without remorse. And for what?

She glanced at the man with Lana again. His head was still down, his face partly obscured. Dammit! She had to find him, or what was the use of her being here?

"What do you want?" the king snapped.

"You will come with us. Never fear. You are too valuable to be harmed." The waiter let his gaze slide across the gathering. "These people, however, are not. Choose wisely, Your Excellency."

"I've got the shot," Jack Hunter said softly from his hiding place in the dome that rose over the ballroom. There was a small gallery that ringed the dome, and he'd scaled the stairs double quick to make it up here after the team had split earlier. He didn't have his spotter, but he didn't need him for this close-proximity shot. "I can take the bomber out and the leader next."

"Negative, Hawk," Matt said. "We have no idea how many of them there are. Or if there's more than one bomb."

"We can't let them take the king," he ground out.

"I know. But we still have no idea who Al Ahmad is, and if we blow this, we may never get another chance."

"Can you see Lucky and Big Mac?" Iceman's voice.

"Yeah," Jack said. "They're behind the bomber."

"Kev, you got anything?" Matt said. "If you can't speak, signal."

Kev shook his head slightly.

"That's a negative," Jack reported.

"Sonofabitch."

Jack didn't know who swore, but it was pretty much what they were all thinking. The fucking King of Qu'rim was about to be kidnapped by terrorists, and they still had no idea who Al Ahmad was. He had to be in the room—unless they'd been wrong about his daughter. What if it was all a smokescreen? What if they'd been led on a wild goose chase?

He could be anywhere, laughing his ass off and planning what he was going to do with those weapons once he had them.

Jack scanned the room. The man who'd been shot was definitely dead. A woman sobbed over his body, and a girl sat and rocked back and forth as if she were in her own world. Old sorrows threatened to break loose and overwhelm him, but he forced them down again. He had a job to do. He did not get emotional. Ever. He'd left emotion behind the day the Red Cross had called his commander and said they needed to speak with him.

Loss. Jesus Christ.

He sighted down the scope and watched the man who'd spoken to the king. He didn't have any emotions either. The suicide bomber stood placidly by, also devoid of emotion.

Jack couldn't understand what was being said, but the king held up a hand to the men on either side of him and walked toward the terrorist leader.

"Something's happening," Jack said.

"Copy," Matt replied.

Jack knew he wasn't the only one who could see what

was happening in the ballroom, but he had the bird's-eye view.

The terrorist smiled at the king and said something. Then the two of them turned and walked toward a side door. Another terrorist went with them, but the bomber stayed behind. Jack counted eight men with weapons. Fucking waiters. It was the perfect way into the school. Obviously, the screening process for the caterer had been shit.

Jack's finger hovered over his trigger. He didn't know what these assholes were going to do, but if they started shooting, he'd have a hell of a time getting them all before they took out at least a dozen innocent people. And that's only if there were no other bombers in the group.

Definitely a fucking nightmare.

The gunmen barked orders at the crowd, and they all began to move toward the center, clustering together. The littlest girls cried and Jack gritted his teeth. Goddamn. He wanted to put a bullet in that asshole's brain, but he couldn't.

Lucky and Kev moved into the crowd, but Jack was able to keep sight of them because Kev was one of the tallest men in the room. There was movement at the edge of the crowd, but Jack's attention shifted because one of the gunmen said something that made Lucky stop and turn. Kev turned with her. The gunman motioned at them, separating them out. Jack wasn't sure why, but then they were so clearly foreign in that crowd that it should be no surprise they were being singled out.

And yet it made Jack's gut tighten. The Freedom Force didn't love foreigners. And they loved Americans least of all. Jack's trigger finger itched, but he had too much training to let it tighten before it was time.

"They're pulling Kev and Lucky aside," he said.

"I know. Jesus. We need that fucking ID, Big Mac," Matt said. Kev shook his head again and Jack's stomach sank.

"She doesn't know. We're fucked."

There was silence for half a second. "Shit." Matt huffed out a breath into the mic. "We aren't losing our teammates while we wait for a fucking terrorist. We're going in on my count…"

Lucky stumbled at that moment and Kev righted her. She leaned into him, and then she was on her feet again while the gunman shouted and waved his weapon. But Kev looked up and nodded once, sharply.

"She's got him," Jack said. "He's there."

"Halle-fucking-lujah."

Jack's heart pumped adrenaline into his veins. So fucking close now. "That's all I've got." He sighted the crowd, looking for an anomaly, a signal. This shit was getting out of hand. "I don't know which one he is."

"Holy fuck," Billy said. "I think I do."

TWENTY-FOUR

LUCKY'S STOMACH TIGHTENED INTO A knot. There was no doubt it was him. Lana's father, the man who'd hugged a woman and child to comfort them when he knew damn well what was happening, was Al Ahmad.

This was the man who'd tortured her. Who'd made her believe she was a piece of garbage and that she was going to die. The man who'd carved her flesh because it had amused him to do so.

He stared at her across the open space between them. She wondered that he didn't make a move since he had to be surprised to see them, but then she realized that whoever he was in his formal robes, that was his real persona. And he couldn't appear as anyone different in front of the families whose daughters went to the same school as his child. Even if he planned to kill them all, he would not break his cover to do it.

The man who'd separated Kev and Lucky called an order to one of his men. That man went over and put a gun to Al Ahmad's head. His eyes glittered, but they did not leave her face. He wasn't frightened.

Nor should he be. This was all part of the plan.

The terrorists took some of the other men aside too, no doubt to demand ransoms from their families. These were the wealthiest and most connected of Baq society, and it would be a wasted opportunity not to use them to enrich the Freedom Force's purse.

Not that any of it mattered now that they had the king. He'd departed through a side door with two of the terrorists, and God only knew where he was now. They would use him, and they would kill him. That much she knew.

Lucky's heart hammered as Al Ahmad crossed the room under his guard's direction. Those eyes filled her with terror. And rage. He'd kept her captive, poisoned her mind, cut her skin again and again—tiny, painful cuts that had bled and scarred—and threatened her with sexual violence.

She hated him.

And if she was going to die anyway, she was determined she wasn't going to die alone. She would take him with her one way or the other.

He came closer and she tensed. Beside her, Kev kept a firm grip on her hand. She'd said she'd found their man but she hadn't been able to point him out.

Yet Kev knew. How could he not? The way Al Ahmad stared at her, that unholy gleam in his gaze, his steps measured and sure as he strode toward her.

"Lucky," Kev growled under his breath. A warning, and yet she no longer cared.

"We meet again, Lucky Reid," Al Ahmad said quietly as he stopped in front of her. The man behind him held a gun on him, but it was only for show. His gaze flicked to Kev, and her heart rate notched up. "And this is the famous Mr. MacDonald, I assume? When Lana told me there was a new teacher in school, I admit I was curious. Especially since I'd seen someone who looked remarkably like you on news footage of the bombing near the embassy."

Lucky's insides turned liquid. But then anger scorched through her as she thought of what he'd done to those people. Of how evil and unfeeling he was.

"You aren't going to get away with this," she spat.

One eyebrow arched. "Am I not? I have the King of Qu'rim. Even now, he is issuing the order for the army to stand down at the mine. The uranium will belong to us in precisely fifteen minutes." His gaze flicked to Kev again, who had yet to say a word. He spoke in English. "There is an American military team waiting for the order to kill me, I assume? I would advise that this is not a good idea."

One of the men put a gun to Kev's head then, and Lucky couldn't stop the gasp that burst from her. *Please God, no. Don't let this happen. Don't let them kill him too.*

"If you think killing me will stop them, you're mistaken." Kev's voice was full of menace, and Lucky almost recoiled from the barely leashed violence in his tone. But that's what he did. What they all did. You couldn't deal with a man like Al Ahmad by being soft. You couldn't plead. It wouldn't do you any good.

"I don't think that at all," Al Ahmad said. "But I think so long as I threaten to kill you, it will give them pause."

"Don't bet on it."

Al Ahmad snapped his fingers then. The suicide bomber was still in the room, and he walked over to the crowd of women and children, who'd been made to stand with their faces to the wall. The men had been taken from the room, and only the women were left. No one could see that this man was in control.

"But you Americans don't like it when women and children die, do you?"

Horror crawled up Lucky's spine. "Your daughter's in that crowd. If you kill them, you kill her too."

His black gaze flickered with a real regret that almost made her feel sorry for him. But then it was gone and the monster stood there once more. Maybe he was bluffing, but she sensed he would do whatever it took to achieve his aims in the end. "We must all make sacrifices for the greater good."

Kev's jaw ground together. "They're standing down. There's no need to kill anyone."

Al Ahmad lifted an eyebrow. "Ah, yes, you are communicating with them. I admit I was quite angry to see the two of you here when you should have been waiting for me at the warehouse. But one cannot always count on the help to be as thorough as one would like. Perhaps I should have sent more men to deal with you." He sighed as if he were discussing a party gone awry rather than a kidnapping. "You will hand over all devices—and your weapons—before we leave this building, or I will give the order for the bomb to be detonated. Once more, it is your choice."

Kev slowly slid the guns from their holsters and handed them over. Then he removed the tiny earpiece that was nearly undetectable and the microphone from beneath his lapel. He dropped them into the gunman's hand.

"And the tracking device."

Kev reached into his pocket and took out the small disc that was just like the one she had in her bra, as well as his phone. The gunman snatched it all away and then dropped everything on the floor and stomped on them. The weapons he tucked into his robes.

"And you, Lucky Reid."

She lifted her chin. She thought about lying but she wouldn't take that chance. The Freedom Force wasn't completely unsophisticated, and they might have scanners that would detect the GPS device if she lied. She would not be responsible for this madman blowing up a roomful of women and children that included his daughter and wife. "I only have a phone and a tracking device. It's in my undergarments."

"Then you will remove it."

"Not with your men watching."

"I care not about your modesty. The device."

Lucky growled as she reached into the neckline of the abaya and fished downward toward her bra. Somehow, she got her fingers on the disc and worked it free. Then she dropped it on the ground rather than hand it to the man whose hand was outstretched. Al Ahmad lifted his expensively shod foot and stomped on it.

"And the phone?"

She fished it from the pocket in her abaya and dropped it. He stomped on that too.

His smile made the hair on the back of her neck prickle. "And now we are leaving."

They'd only taken three steps toward the same exit the king had left from when an explosion rocked the building. Plaster fell from the ceiling, and the light fixtures rattled and clinked. Lucky jerked her head around to see if the suicide bomber had detonated his bomb, but he wasn't where he'd been.

He was on the ground, a pool of blood forming around his body. Before she could puzzle out what was happening, a shot rang out and Kev dropped to the ground. Lucky screamed.

Abdul Halim wrapped an arm around Lucky Reid's neck. He wanted to squeeze the life from her body then and there, but that would not be prudent. Instead, he drew his knife and jabbed it into her ribs. The sharp point just penetrated the silk of her abaya, and she stiffened as the cool metal met her soft flesh. Her lush body pressed up against his, reminding him of his sexual needs earlier tonight.

Perhaps now he could indulge both desires at once: sex and pain. Even better.

He shoved her through the exit and into a corridor. One of his men was waiting.

"We're under attack," Abdul Halim barked. "Go!"

The man led the way outside and into the waiting car. Abdul Halim shoved Lucky inside and climbed in after her. She'd turned her body and met him with a swift kick to his thigh. He yowled in pain and lunged for her. She kicked again and again, but he managed to wrap a hand in her hijab and catch her hair as well. Then he shoved the knife against her throat and lay on top of her in the back seat of the car as it sped away from the school, his body hardening with excitement and exhilaration.

"I will kill you."

"I don't care!" she screamed. "You killed Kevin! You killed all those people! You would have murdered your own daughter!"

He felt no remorse at that accusation. He would have sacrificed Lana and Fatima if necessary. But there was no need.

It had not quite gone as he'd intended. His people were supposed to capture Lucky and her military watchdog. They were supposed to draw the Americans away from the school. The last report he'd had, they had taken their target.

But here she was. And she'd brought an American military team with her. They'd attacked, but he had escaped.

Better yet, the Freedom Force had the king. Abdul Halim's identity was compromised, but it no longer mattered. He would be a hero to the people after this night. After his triumph.

"Silence, woman!" he roared. He wanted to slice her open from stem to stern, but he would not do it yet. He pressed the knife into her throat and watched blood well up from the tiny cut he made. Her eyes went wide. Her throat worked as she swallowed.

Abdul Halim laughed.

She would pay for her crimes against him, most certainly. He would have immense fun extracting his price. All in good time, of course.

He withdrew the knife and sat up and she scrambled away, huddling against the door. She reached for the handle, though they were going around eighty, but he did not fear she would escape. The doors were controlled by the driver, and he wasn't about to let her open it.

Her eyes flashed hotly as she glared at him. He nearly laughed. She wasn't ready to die, no matter what she said. She would fight him to the end. He loved it when they fought. And when they realized it didn't matter, and they were going to die anyway…

Too delicious.

Kev slapped Iceman's hand away as he ripped open Kev's tuxedo shirt and pressed his fingers to the bullet wound oozing blood like a motherfucker.

"He's got her," Kev said. "Have to save her."

Matt hovered over him. There was Hawk and Billy too, their faces looming overhead. Brandy and Flash wouldn't be far away. Nor would Knight Rider or Whisky.

But he didn't care about any of them. He only cared about Lucky. Al Ahmad had her. He'd taken her, and Kev had sworn he would die before he let that happen.

He'd lied.

"You still might," Iceman snapped, and Kev realized he'd been babbling. He had to get it together, had to stop fucking falling apart and concentrate so he could go rescue his woman. He closed his eyes and winced as Iceman used a new experimental plunger device packed with tiny sterile sponges to fill the bullet hole and stop the bleeding.

"We're going after her just as soon as we've got you patched up," Matt said.

"Going with you."

"Yeah, I know it."

"What the fuck did you guys do?" Kev managed after a few moments of sucking in his breath and working past the pain. The sponges worked fast to stop the bleeding, but pain was another story.

"Wasn't us. They had another bomb tucked away. Someone detonated it, probably by accident since it happened when it did. Hawk used the opportunity to take out the suicide bomber."

Hawk was as cool as ever. "He was surprised by the explosion and let go of the detonator on his device. I dropped him before he could remember it."

"Thank God," Kev said. And someone had shot him in the ensuing panic. He could still hear Lucky screaming. The sound of her terror had sunk into his bones. He'd tried to get up, but he couldn't. He'd watched her and Al Ahmad disappear out the door. He'd been crawling toward it when Iceman got to him.

And then he'd tried to make Iceman go after her, but his teammate wouldn't listen.

"The women and children are terrified," Matt continued. "But no one is hurt."

"You know which one is Al Ahmad yet?" Kev asked.

"Working on it. Knight Rider and Whisky are reuniting the husbands with the wives. Whoever is missing has to be him."

"Jesus," Kev said as Iceman taped the wound. "Hurts like a motherfucker."

"Yeah, crybaby, it does," Matt said. Then he squeezed Kev's shoulder. "It's gonna be fine, yeah? We'll get your girl, *mon ami*."

Kev closed his eyes again and concentrated on overcoming the pain. If Matt was lapsing into Cajun, then things weren't quite as rosy as he wanted them to seem. If Kev knew anything about his team CO, he knew that much.

Iceman gave him a shot of painkiller, and then they were helping him up. Kev stood and swayed for a second before he got his head on straight and the room stopped spinning. He started for the door, but several pairs of hands stopped him. He spun on them—or he tried. It wasn't a spin so much as a stumble.

"What are we waiting for? We got to go."

"There's nothing we can do until we hear from him." Matt's voice again, soft and firm. "She's not wearing a tracking device, and there's nowhere to go. We have to wait for intel."

Kev shoved at their hands. "Fuck that. We're going."

"There's nowhere to go, Big Mac. Stand down."

Kev blinked at them all, his brain working hard to process what they were saying to him. Lucky was with that madman, and they had no idea where he would take her. Or even if he would keep her alive.

His knees gave out again and he sank onto the tiles. Goddamn. He'd done it again. He'd failed to protect someone he loved, and he was going to lose her...

"Abdul Halim bin Khalid al-Faizan!" It was Knight Rider. He skidded to a halt, waving his hands excitedly. "He's a fucking defense contractor. He sells guns to the Qu'rimi army, for fuck's sake."

Iceman and Billy pulled Kev upright and steadied him. "You hear that, Big Mac. We got a name. We're going after the bastard."

Lucky huddled against the door, dividing her gaze between the city rolling by and Al Ahmad. She didn't trust that he wouldn't kill her right away, though part of her was banking on his sick fascination with torture. She'd escaped once before, and he would want to make her pay. Especially now that HOT had interfered with his plans.

She didn't know what had happened back there at the school, but the fact there was an explosion and the suicide bomber lay dead—not blown apart—told her that the explosion hadn't been his doing and that someone in HOT—Jack, probably—had dropped him before he could detonate.

Her heart felt as if someone had pierced it with a hot needle when she remembered what else had happened. The team attacked and the gunman watching Kev had shot him. She could still hear the explosion, still feel the concussion of the gun. And she could hear Kev's body dropping onto the tile.

She wanted to put her hands to her head and squeeze the sound out of it, but she couldn't. She had to think. Had to stay focused and use whatever opportunity she got to stop this evil man. She didn't care if she had to sacrifice herself to do it. Because why would she want to live in a world without the man she loved?

Kev was dead and she was too. But not without taking this bastard with her.

The guys weren't coming for her. She wasn't wearing

a tracking device, and there was no way they could find her. Maybe they'd figure out who Al Ahmad was, but she couldn't count on that because she didn't know what the situation was back at the school. If HOT hadn't set the explosion, someone else had—which meant they could have killed the men who'd been taken from the room. It would take a long time to identify the bodies, and the woman and girl with Al Ahmad wouldn't know he wasn't among them for days. By the time the team figured that out, it would be too late.

Her captor seemed agitated. He'd made several calls, but not all of them appeared to connect. His terse demands for information were met with various answers he didn't seem to appreciate. She hoped that something was going very wrong for him. Perhaps the king was being uncooperative after all, or perhaps he'd been rescued at the last moment.

The car slowed and turned into a parking garage. When it came to a stop after navigating several levels, Lucky jerked at the door, but it didn't open. And then it did, and she tumbled out and hit the concrete. The driver stood over her with a gun pointed at her heart.

Al Ahmad walked around the car and kicked her. His booted foot connected with her hip, and she winced as pain exploded in her body. But she refused to make a sound. She wouldn't give him the satisfaction, not this time.

A hot breeze blew through the garage, ruffling Al Ahmad's robes and the keffiyeh on his head. "Get up, woman. We're going on a journey."

Lucky pushed herself to her feet, though her hip ached and she'd scraped her hands falling onto the concrete. Her hijab had come loose when he'd grabbed her earlier. She'd tried to fix it but apparently not too success-fully since it whipped violently in the wind. A moment later, it tore free and blew across the empty garage. Her hair whipped into her face and she dragged it back so she could see the man she needed to kill.

The driver grabbed her arm and shoved her toward a stairwell. She went up first, stumbling and trying to keep her feet beneath her. The wind grew stronger as she got to the top. That's when she realized they were on a roof and a helicopter sat on a pad, rotors spinning.

Her heart sank as the driver shoved her forward. The helicopter door swung open as they ducked beneath the rotor. The man picked her up and tossed her into the craft, and then he and Al Ahmad got inside and slammed the door.

The helicopter lifted off the pad and rose into the night-darkened sky. Below them, the city sparkled bright. Lucky's eyes filled with tears as she gazed at the lights. She'd been happy for a few hours in Baq. She'd been in love and she'd been hopeful for the future, even while she'd been terrified it wouldn't work out.

Well, she'd been right to be terrified, hadn't she? Kev was dead and she was alone. And Al Ahmad wasn't fin-ished with her yet.

TWENTY-FIVE

WHEN KEV WOKE, HIS HEAD was pounding and his throat was dry. He sat up abruptly and clutched his head as pain shot through it.

"Man, don't do that," Iceman said, coming over and handing him a bottle of cold water. "You got shot, dude."

"Lucky." His voice came out as a croak, and he twisted off the cap and slugged down some water.

Iceman gripped his shoulder. "Calm down. We've got a vector on her and we're on the way."

Kev blinked. And then he realized that his surroundings rattled and hummed; he turned his head and tried to focus. It was dark and the environment was tinny. Hollow.

That's when it hit him they were in a military transport and the turboprop engines were turned full bore. They were going somewhere as fast as possible in a C-130 Hercules.

He shook his head and focused until the other guys came into view. They were suited up and getting ready to jump. He lurched to his feet.

"I'm going with you."

"No. Fuck no." It was Matt. His CO stood and ranged over to him, looking like six foot two of pure pissed-off Cajun. "You got shot, Kev. The bullet passed through and we've patched you up, but you're out of commission until this op is over."

"Do I have a fever?"

Matt glanced at Iceman. Iceman shook his head.

"Then I'm going."

"The landing could make you start bleeding again."

"I'll take that chance."

Matt's eyes flashed. "How helpful do you think you'll be to her if you're bleeding out in the fucking desert?"

"I'm not going to bleed out from a bullet wound that missed an artery, and you know it. It's packed tight and it's got clotting powder on it. I can feel the fucking burn." He sucked in a breath, his lungs filling. He ached, but he could function. "What if it was Evie out there, huh? Then what?"

He ground his teeth together when Matt didn't reply. "If you don't let me go, you'd better leave at least two people behind to watch me or I'm following you out that door."

"Jesus Christ." Matt blew out a breath. He looked utterly furious. And then he deflated like a popped balloon— but only for a second. "Suit up, asshole. If you fucking die, Lucky will kill me. And then I'll follow your ass around in the hereafter, saying *I told you so, motherfucker.* You got that?"

"Yeah, I got it."

Matt waved a hand. "Fine. Knight Rider, give this eager volunteer his gear, would you?"

"Copy that," Sam said, coming over with a shit-eating

grin on his face. "Knew you'd be going with us. Never doubted it for a moment."

"Care to tell me where we're going?" Kev said as he started peeling out of the remnants of the tuxedo.

"Abdul Halim al-Faizan took a company helicopter out of the city an hour ago. Turns out the government has been tracking his movements for some time now, for various reasons. They've shared the information with us, thanks to Mendez leaning heavily on somebody in the Qu'rimi government. We have satellite coordinates for his destination."

"What about the king?"

Sam snorted. "That's the bitch of it. The king we saw was a body double." He shrugged. "Don't know if they always intended to send a double, or if it was a last minute switch, but the King of Qu'rim is safely tucked away in his royal palace."

Kev's heart fell to his toes. *Sonofabitch.* Not that Kev wasn't glad Al Ahmad didn't have the real king, but the moment he discovered the truth, he would take it out on those around him. And Lucky, if she was still alive, would be a perfect target for his anger. Kev's gut clenched hard.

"Does Al Ahmad know yet?"

Sam's eyes clouded, as if he knew what Kev was thinking. "We don't know. The fake king ordered the stand-down the Freedom Force asked for at the mine, but it's taking some time to happen. It's a trap, obviously, and they need time to get assets in place. But the longer it takes, the more suspicious it looks."

"Fifteen minutes to the DZ," someone called, and Kev finished buckling into his parachute. Sam inspected Kev's gear, though the jumpmaster would do it again before they fell out of the plane and into the dark sky below.

"Let's go get our teammate," Sam said with a grin. "No man or woman left behind, right?"

They'd flown for close to two hours before the chopper set down on a rooftop pad on what turned out to be a fortified compound in the desert. Lucky had been shoved into a room with barred windows, and then the door had slammed shut with a resounding clang.

The room was empty of furniture other than a bed, a night table, and a chair. There was an adjoining room with a toilet and sink. Lucky gave up trying to find something to defend herself with after a few minutes and went over to look out the windows. She could see nothing but concrete walls.

She hugged herself tight and turned again, eyes blurry. Goddammit, she just wanted this over with. If Al Ahmad was going to kill her, she wanted him to do it.

Not that she wanted to die, but she didn't want to think about it for hours or days either. The last time he'd captured her, he'd kept her in a room like this one and she'd nearly gone mad. She rubbed her hands up and down her arms, generating warmth.

She didn't want to be at his mercy ever again. Didn't want to beg and plead for her life while he carved his marks into her flesh. Or worse.

She didn't want to think about *worse*.

"Stop it," she hissed. "Just stop and think, dammit."

He wanted her scared, there was no doubt about it, and he wanted to torture her. He wanted to break her and make her beg for death. But he was preoccupied with his coup at the moment. She'd listened to his conversations during the flight since he hadn't gone to any lengths to keep her from hearing. Why would he when he was planning to kill her?

The king had ordered the army to stand down at the mine, but it was taking time. Apparently, whoever the commander in the desert was, he wasn't just laying down arms and walking away. Smart man.

She had no idea where they'd taken the king, but she suspected they'd spirited him out of the city as well. Was he here in this compound too? Perhaps that's why Al Ahmad had come here.

If so, maybe a rescue force was on the way. Maybe there was still a chance.

She took a deep breath and forced herself to search the room again. She might be going down, but not without a fight. And not without doing some damage on the way. It's funny what you were willing to do when you had nothing left to lose.

She thought about using the night table as a weapon, but it was bolted to the floor. She stopped tugging on it and yanked open the drawers. They were empty.

Lucky tore the bedding off the mattress and upended it. The mattress sat on wooden slats, and she tested each one. They were solid. She nearly gave up, but she was determined to tug on them all to see if one came free... and one did.

Or, it didn't come free, but it wriggled when she

tugged. Upon closer inspection, she spotted a hairline crack running along the top half of the slat.

She stood on the slat and bounced—and it came free with a loud crack. Triumph surged in her veins as she worked the broken slat back and forth until she had two jagged pieces. The wood was solid and the edges were sharp. They'd do some damage if she managed to stab somebody with them. She quickly remade the bed and tucked both the broken pieces beneath the pillows where she could reach them easily.

And then she sat on the edge of the bed near the headboard and waited for someone to come for her.

The room was quiet, but she could occasionally hear voices filtering into her prison. At one point there were booted feet on the concrete over her head, and she guessed she was on the top floor.

She reached under the pillow and put her hand around the slat for comfort. It wasn't much, but it was something. She was not going to take whatever happened without fighting back.

She thought about Kev and about how he'd admitted that he loved her tonight. Was it just a few hours ago now they'd been held captive in another room and she'd thought their lives were over? She scrubbed an angry hand over her face. It came away wet.

They'd had so little time together. And it had been fraught with so much tension and unresolved feelings. Even if they'd made it out of Qu'rim alive, they would've had a lot to work through if they wanted to be together. And maybe it wouldn't have worked out, just like with her and Marco. Maybe the past was simply too much to over-come.

Lucky tightened her fingers on the slat. She would never know, would she? Kev had been shot in Baq and she was once more locked up and awaiting a madman.

Her head snapped up as she heard someone coming down the hallway toward her room. And then the door swung inward and her heart pounded with fear and adrenaline. It was now or never.

She jerked the slat from under the pillow and lunged.

The man coming through the door didn't know what hit him as she jammed the broken slat into his throat. A look of utter surprise crossed his face and she couldn't help but mutter an apology. Taking a life wasn't an easy thing to do, even when it was your only choice.

But it wasn't Al Ahmad she'd stabbed through the throat. It was the same man who'd shoved her up the stairs and into this room earlier. He clutched the slat, making gurgling noises as he stumbled into the room. She jammed the wood harder, and then she grabbed the other broken end from under the pillow when he toppled forward.

Lucky groped around his still-twitching body, searching for a weapon. There wasn't one. If he had a gun, it was in the front. She thought about rolling him over, but what if he wasn't dead? What if he grabbed her?

She didn't look back as she jumped over his body and ran out the door. She remembered the way they'd brought her in because they hadn't thought they needed to blindfold her this time. She slipped down the stairs, her brain whirling. If she could find another weapon, find a phone, something. Maybe she could get out of this alive. Maybe she could go home and see her mom and stepdad and the triplets again. She missed them, even if she felt like an alien in their presence.

They were the only home she had left. Despair threatened to choke her as she thought about a life without Kev in it. She pushed those thoughts away and tried to listen past the pounding of blood in her ears. The compound was strangely silent...

And then it wasn't. There was an explosion somewhere and gunfire, and Lucky's heart rocketed into overdrive. Maybe the king's forces had come for him, or maybe HOT had come for her.

She didn't care which, but for the first time all evening, she could taste freedom again.

She crept down the hall a bit slower now, listening hard for movement. The truth was she didn't know who was out there or which way they were coming from, and she needed to be smart and careful. She stopped at a door and listened. There was no movement inside, so she turned the knob carefully and stepped inside.

It was an office and there was a phone on the desk. She ran over and snatched it off the cradle.

But there was no dial tone. She set it down with a sob and clutched the broken slat against her chest.

"Going somewhere, Lucky Reid?"

She spun to find Al Ahmad standing in another entryway, a gun pointed at her. He'd removed his keffiyeh, and she was struck by the beauty of his face once more. He was a classically handsome man, dark and chiseled. But he was also evil, and it was his evil that made her stomach churn.

"You aren't going to win this time." The gunfire continued somewhere in the distance. "They're coming for you."

He strolled into the room, lowering the gun to his side

as he did so. She calculated whether or not she could rush him and jab the jagged slat into his throat before he could shoot her.

The odds were not in her favor, so she stood and held her weapon close, waiting.

His dark glittering eyes traveled down her form, fixing on the slat. Then he met her eyes again. "I could shoot you right now," he said softly. "In a place that won't kill you right away. That *weapon* will do nothing to save you."

The wood bit into her fingers as she squeezed. "Maybe not, but I'm not letting it go. Shoot me if you want, but if there's any strength left in my body when you approach me, I *will* stab you."

Because there was no doubt he would approach her. Killing her quickly or easily was not his style. Torturing her was. It was what he wanted, what he needed.

And they both knew it.

"You have grown tougher since the last time we met." He grinned and lifted the gun. "This only makes it more fun, you realize."

"Go ahead," she shot back. "But what will you use for leverage once they break in here? I'm your bargaining chip."

"What makes you think they will succeed? This compound is well defended." He snorted. "You and your pitiful military. Never able to see the bigger picture. A country like yours should rule the world, and yet you do not. You are weak, unable to do what needs to be done."

"And that's a good thing for you, isn't it? Because if we believed in indiscriminate killing, we would have eradicated the Freedom Force a long time ago—along with a lot of innocent people who would have been nothing more than collateral damage. But we aren't like you. We don't believe in killing innocent people to achieve our goals."

She felt the shot before she heard it. A sharp stinging pain radiated down her arm, up into her shoulder and collarbone. Her fingers opened of their own accord and the slat fell to the floor. Instinctively, she clutched her arm with her other hand and tried not to pass out from the pain.

Al Ahmad was still grinning like the madman he was. "A flesh wound, nothing more. But oh so painful, I'm afraid."

He closed the distance between them and punched her in the gut before she could react. And then he slapped her across the face. Her ears rang, and the metallic taste of blood flooded her mouth. Lucky tried to stay upright, but she fell to her knees, her head aching and her arm throbbing. Tears sprang to her eyes and made everything blurry. She let them fall because blinking them back only made it worse.

She groped on the floor for the slat, but he sent it flying with a kick. And then he grabbed her hair and yanked her head back, baring her throat. She felt the bite of his knife in her skin before she saw the glint of the blade.

"Just a little more pressure and your throat will open like a dam," he whispered in her ear. "What then, Lucky Reid? No one can save you when it happens. Your precious Americans will go home and forget you."

Lucky swallowed and the blade cut into her a little bit more. Fear swirled in her belly until she wanted to vomit. But there was something else too.

Anger. Pure, blazing anger.

She was not going to die without inflicting some kind of pain on him.

He was kneeling beside her now, his mouth at her ear, his knife wedged against her throat, biting into her. She flexed the fingers of her wounded arm. It hurt like a bitch, but they still worked. If she was fast enough, she could grab his balls and squeeze them tight.

He would cut her throat, of course, and that would be the end of that.

But it would be worth it, by God. And she would die much sooner than he planned.

He dragged the knife down a bit, slicing a vertical line in her skin, alongside her artery.

"Ah, but that would be too easy for you," he whispered. "Much too easy…"

He laughed and Lucky drew herself up tight, preparing to strike. A second later, as if in answer to her prayers, the lights went out. Al Ahmad stiffened, his knife slipping away from her skin for the barest of moments.

It was just the opportunity she needed.

His side hurt like a sonofabitch, but Kev pushed past the pain and kept going. They'd HALOed in and then started humping for the compound. The place was defended, but those defenses weren't much against a team like his. The tangos were no match, though of course there was always the danger one of them would get a lucky shot.

Hawk took out the rooftop defenders, then Knight Rider and Brandy set a charge and they all burst into the compound. They were met with gunfire, but they fought their way inward, taking out as many men as they could along the way. Iceman and Flash found the generator and the lights blinked out, leaving the team in the dark.

Just the way they liked it.

They systematically worked their way from room to room, shooting whoever got in the way and searching for signs of Lucky. Kev focused on the mission, but that didn't stop his heart from thumping extra hard, his side from aching, or pain from radiating throughout his body.

He gritted his teeth and kept on going. He wasn't stopping until he found her.

God, please let her still be alive.

Because he knew it was perfectly possible Al Ahmad had already killed her. He could have thrown her from the helicopter just for the fun of it, or he might have killed her and left her body behind in Baq. There was no telling, but this had been their best option for finding her.

"Anything?" Iceman's voice on the headset.

"Nothing." That was Knight Rider.

"Keep going, ladies." Matt ranged along beside Kev while the other guys swept the compound in pairs, search-ing every corner and closet. "We aren't leaving here with-out Lucky."

Kev swallowed against the lump in his throat. The guys knew as well as he did that she could already be dead, but none of them acted like it. And they wouldn't until they knew it for a fact. He was more grateful for that than he could say.

They turned and started down a hallway, helmet lights sweeping the area for signs of life. They hadn't run into a tango in minutes now and Kev was beginning to get worried. What if they weren't here? What if it was all a ruse?

Yeah, the helicopter was on the pad—disabled now that they'd arrived—but that didn't mean Al Ahmad had even been onboard when it left Baq.

A scream shattered the night, stopping them in their tracks. Kev's blood ran cold as he bolted forward. A woman's voice screamed Arabic words that pelted the air with their vehemence. Kev identified the room the sound came from and surged toward the door. Matt was on his six as the two of them burst through, assault rifles notched into their shoulders and ready to fire.

Two bodies tangled on the ground, writhing and twisting in a heap of fabric. Long tawny hair glinted in the light from his helmet. A knife flashed upward and then disappeared and Kev's heart leapt into his throat.

He wanted to shoot, but it was impossible to separate the two people twisting together on the floor.

"Jesus," Matt said. "I can't get a target."

Kev lurched forward just as the two bodies on the floor separated. Lucky sat up then and did something that made the man beneath her scream like a little girl.

"Goddamn," Matt breathed. And then he gave an order to the rest of the team while Kev went over and shoved the barrel of his rifle in Al Ahmad's open mouth.

Lucky blinked then, as if she'd just realized she was no longer alone with a terrorist shitbag.

"Get up, Lucky," Kev ordered. "It's over."

"Kev?" Her voice broke. And then she was clambering to her feet and backing away from the monster on the floor. He groaned as best he could with a rifle in his mouth. He brought his knees up slowly and tears flowed down his cheeks.

Kev wanted to take Lucky in his arms, but he couldn't turn his attention from their target.

"You were shot," she said. "I saw you fall."

"Down but not out," he told her, his voice gruff.

Two of his teammates came into the room then. While Matt fed orders to Billy Blake through the comm feed, Hawk and Iceman came over and jerked Al Ahmad from the floor. He didn't seem to be able to stand, but that didn't stop them from trussing him up like a goose and putting a sack over his head.

Kev turned and stared at Lucky. She blinked back at him, her arms wrapped around her body. He told himself he should grab her and hug her tight, but he was frozen in place. He'd let Al Ahmad take her when he'd sworn he wouldn't. She'd been in danger because he'd failed to protect her. He'd broken his promise to her and he didn't know how to say he was sorry for that.

His gaze swept over her torn abaya and back up to her wide-eyed face. That's when he realized that a small river of blood seeped from a wound in her throat. Worse, blood dripped down her arm and puddled on the floor. He hadn't seen that at first. Now that he had, his rage went nuclear.

It was the only explanation for what happened inside him then. Rage and fear and adrenaline coalesced into a tight ball in his gut until he thought he would explode with it.

"Gonna fucking kill him," he growled, turning toward the huddled and sobbing form of the world's most wanted terrorist.

"Kev, no, please." Lucky grabbed him then, her arms wrapping around him from behind. He winced as she put pressure on his side, but the rage didn't clear. He brought the rifle up and jammed it against Al Ahmad's head while Iceman and Hawk jumped back.

"Stand down," Matt ordered sharply. "Don't fucking make me shoot you."

"He needs to die," Kev snarled without taking his gaze off the man kneeling on the floor. "If he doesn't die, she'll never be safe."

"Kev, please." Lucky said. She didn't let go, didn't back away. "Please. I thought I lost you tonight, but you're here. After everything, you're here." She drew in a breath that sounded like a sob. "If you do this, I'll lose you again. Please, please don't."

There was a buzzing in his ears. "He will never stop hunting you. He'll do it from behind bars. You won't be safe."

She sucked in another breath. "This isn't what we do to people. It's what *he* does. And Mendez is going to bury him behind walls so thick he'll never get out. He won't piss without permission, and he damn sure won't talk to anyone. I'm not scared, Kev. I'm not scared."

Her hand moved to his arm, slid down the length of it until she could grasp the barrel of his rifle. Slowly, she pushed it down, away from Al Ahmad's head.

Kev blinked. And then he took a step back and sucked in a sharp breath. The buzzing in his ears intensified. His head was light, his vision spotty. The edges were black, the tunnel closing in. Relief, he told himself. Relief that she was alive. He turned to finally take her in his arms the way he should have.

But the blackness rushed over him and everything faded.

TWENTY-SIX

"SHE HAD HIM BY THE fucking balls!" Iceman howled with laughter. The other guys snorted and giggled. A couple of them clutched their crotches and winced.

Lucky couldn't help but laugh too. Here were these badass military men, tall and muscled and dangerous as hell, and they were snorting and giggling like a group of high school girls over the fact Lucky had taken down the world's most wanted man by the balls.

Another HOT unit ranged around the ready room, listening to the tale. One of them shook his head as his gaze drifted over to where she sat. He looked a little surprised and a little in awe all at once.

Lucky dropped her head and studied her lap. It had been a long couple of days. After HOT broke in and captured Al Ahmad, they'd bugged out pretty quick. They'd had to carry Kev to the extraction point, but they'd made it. The C-130 had set down in the desert and was waiting for them to arrive. Soon as they were onboard, it took off in utter darkness and climbed into the sky.

Iceman and Flash had started tending to Kev the minute they were onboard. He wasn't bleeding, thank God, but his body had been through a lot and he'd been pushing it hard. Iceman had given him painkillers and something to keep him asleep during the ride. Then they'd turned their attention to her.

The cut on her neck wasn't deep, but they'd cleaned it and bandaged it. She'd probably have a scar, but what was new about that? As for the flesh wound he'd given her in the arm, she'd have another beauty of a scar. These weren't the first scars Al Ahmad had given her, but they were certainly the last.

He'd been chained up at the rear of the plane under heavy guard, and it had taken everything she had not to go over and kick the hell out of him. Instead, after she was patched up, she'd sat at Kev's side for the rest of the flight, her fingers threaded through his. Matt had come over to tell her that the mine was safe and the Freedom Force had been rolled up with the Opposition. They were all going to prison for a long time. She'd thanked him and then laid her head on Kev's gurney to rest.

A few hours later, they'd set down at an undisclosed air base and transferred to a C-5 that had been fitted with a personal jail cell just for Al Ahmad. Hours of flying later, they'd arrived back in DC. Al Ahmad was currently being held somewhere so secret that she wasn't even sure Mendez knew the location.

Then again, knowing Mendez, he wasn't out of the loop on something like that. Hell, the president of the United States would be out of the loop before Mendez would.

Hawk came and sat down beside her. "You okay, babe?"

She ran her hands up and down her arms and nodded. "Yeah, I am."

And it was true. She'd been so terrified when Al Ahmad—Abdul Halim al-Faizan—had a knife at her throat, but the second the lights went out, she'd reacted without thinking. She'd grabbed his wrist and wrested control of the knife away. They'd fallen to the floor together, a tangle of arms and legs and lethal determination.

And then she'd gotten her hand on his balls. Since she wasn't an idiot, she'd twisted for all she was worth. She'd continued twisting until someone jammed a gun in Al Ahmad's mouth.

When she'd realized it was Kev, her heart had nearly burst.

But then everything had gotten weird. It was as if someone had put up a barrier between them that neither could cross. In the instant when they should have been wrapping their arms around each other, they'd simply stared.

Then all hell broke loose, and she'd not had a moment alone with Kev since. When they'd gotten back to DC, they'd been hustled to HOT HQ and put up in the dorms until they could be debriefed. There'd never been a moment to talk to Kev alone. She'd seen him in a group setting, and she'd watched him carefully.

He did not look at her, and her heart slowly cracked open as she realized he wasn't going to. Something had changed for him out there. She didn't know what it was, but she knew it affected his feelings for her.

All she wanted now was to escape, but escape wasn't happening quickly enough.

The door opened and Mendez came in, followed by

Matt and Kev. The guys quieted. Lucky tried to keep her attention on Mendez, but her gaze kept straying to Kev. He looked like a block of stone standing there. No emotion crossed his face whatsoever and her heart cracked a little more.

"Sergeant San Ramos," Mendez barked, and Lucky scraped to attention. All the guys snapped to as well.

"Sir, yes, sir," she replied.

"The world owes you a huge debt of gratitude. You found him and you stopped him. But no one's going to acknowledge that publicly, so we're acknowledging it here."

He lifted his hand in a salute. All the other guys did the same—but to her, not to the bird colonel in their midst. Her eyes felt gritty and misty, but she returned the salute sharply, swallowing the lump in her throat.

"As promised, you are relieved of duty," Mendez said. The guys shuffled and cleared their throats. Kev looked over the top of her head, his eyes carefully blank.

"Thank you, sir."

"As you were," he said to the group at large. Then he turned to go. But he stopped and turned back. "But I should tell you, Sergeant, if you wanted to stay, HOT could use an operator like you. Think about it."

He spun sharply on his heel and disappeared through the door. The guys all blinked at her. And then Hawk slapped her on the back. It was startling, but she didn't want to shrink from his touch the way she usually did when anyone but Kev touched her. No, it kind of filled her with warmth. Like she belonged.

These guys were family. She got all misty when that realization hit her, but Hawk just grinned.

"Helluva mission, huh? Just think of all the fun we could have if you hung around."

Then he filed out the door. The other guys followed.

Except for Kev. He was still standing there like a stone pillar when the last man walked out. The door closed and it was just the two of them.

He wouldn't look at her.

"Just say it, Kev," she said. "I can take it."

For the first time in days, his gaze collided with hers. His eyes were no longer blank. Her heart skipped a beat. No, they weren't blank—but she didn't know what emotion that was staring back at her.

"I'm sorry. I let you down. I promised I wouldn't let him take you, but I did just that. I failed to protect you, and I won't ever forgive myself."

Her chest felt oddly hollow at that moment. Because her heart was his, and it hurt to think he was torturing himself over a promise he never should have made in the first place.

But she knew why he had, and she knew why he was beating himself up so badly over it.

"Oh, Kev," she said, and her voice broke just a little. "I don't care about that. I only care whether or not you still love me."

It was his turn to blink. His jaw hung open and then he swallowed hard. "Of course I do."

Her laugh was rusty. "Well, I've spent the last couple of days thinking you didn't, so forgive me if that's what I care most about. Because I don't care that you didn't keep your promise. How the fuck were you ever going to be able to guarantee such a thing anyway? You did your best, and that's all you were ever going to be able to do."

His gaze fell to the bandage on her throat. "He cut you again. He nearly killed you. If that had happened…"

"Well, he didn't," she said fiercely. "And I took care of myself, thank you very much. So you see, you *did* keep your promise, because you trained me to defend myself. You were there with me, even when you thought you weren't."

His head dropped. He clutched the back of one of the chairs and stood there for a long moment, just breathing. "I can't stop thinking about it. About what could have happened. That cut on your neck…"

She got angry then. They'd come through so much, and no way was she going to let his past dictate the future for them both. To hell with standing back and waiting for the right moment to touch him again.

The right moment was *now*. She surged forward and put her palms on his jaw, turning his head toward her. He shuddered and she knew he felt the same heat and need that she did. Just touching him like this was enough to make her skin itch.

"You have to stop," she said, her voice tight with emotion. "It's not your fault what your father did to your mother and sister, and it's not your fault what Al Ahmad did to me. You can't spend your life blaming yourself for the actions of others. And not only that, but dammit, I'm getting really pissed here because who says I need rescuing, huh? You taught me to rescue myself, and I did it, so be proud of me, okay?"

He turned then, the full force of his gaze hitting her, making her breath catch. So handsome. So lonely and broken. So hers, dammit.

"I am proud of you. You did it, Lucky. You got him. I

293

only hate that you had to do it alone."

She sucked in a breath. "Well, I don't."

Hell, yes, she'd been scared. But now she was pretty stoked that she'd survived. She hadn't just taken whatever Al Ahmad dished out. She hadn't been broken and helpless and needing rescue. And she wasn't going to withdraw from the world now that she was free.

Hell, no, she was embracing it.

"I'm strong," she said. "Stronger than I ever believed possible, and that's thanks to you. If you'd been there to take care of him for me, I might not know what I could do. I'm glad I know. I'm glad I don't have to run away and hide ever again. I can face myself in the mirror every day, knowing I was strong. You did that, Kev. So if you want to wallow in self-pity, you go right ahead. But I'm not doing it with you."

Her heart thumped hard as she waited for him to say something.

"Jesus," he finally breathed. And then he grinned. "You really are a ballbuster, aren't you?"

Lucky laughed and blushed at the same time. Then she held up a fist. "Never piss off the hand of doom. Capable of taking down terrorists with a single twist."

Kev winced. "Kinda glad I didn't realize what you were doing at the time."

"Fear me, Kev. Fear me."

He laughed then. "I definitely fear you. I fear you'll wake up one day and decide you really shouldn't love a loser like me. And then what am I going to do?"

She frowned. "You aren't a loser. Stop it."

He reached out and ran a finger over her lips. "So fierce. It was just a figure of speech, darlin'. I know I'm a mighty fine catch."

Her breath hitched. "Turning up the drawl, are you? I know what that means."

"What's it mean?"

She arched an eyebrow. "It means you want to get into my panties."

"Is it working?"

"Oh, yeah. Definitely."

Finally, after what seemed like a year, he tugged her into his arms. Lucky sighed as she wrapped her arms around his waist—carefully avoiding his bullet wound. This was home. Right here, in his arms.

"Better hang on," he said, tilting her chin up with a finger. "Because I'm about to demonstrate my patented panty-melting kiss."

"Stop teasing and just do it."

He did.

Kev woke from a deep sleep to the sound of the ocean washing the shore. It took him half a minute to remember why he was hearing the ocean, and then he pushed himself up and grinned. Had to love R&R. He turned to look at Lucky's side of the bed. It was empty.

But that didn't worry him. He yawned and stretched and got out of bed. Then he walked out onto the lanai and found her wearing one of his shirts, standing at the railing and sipping coffee. She looked up when she heard him move, her eyes bugging out as she did so.

"Kev, you're naked! What if someone sees you?"

He shrugged and peered at the beach. "I don't see anyone out there."

"There are neighbors and they could walk by, you know. Beaches in Hawaii are public."

He shrugged again. "So they get an eyeful."

He turned to look at the breakers rolling in. In the distance, he could see Kaena Point, the northernmost point on the island of Oahu. Before him, there was nothing but beach and palm trees. It was January, but it was warm and heavenly.

"I could get used to this," he said.

She shook her head as she came over to his side. Wordlessly, she handed him her coffee cup. He took a sip and leaned against the railing.

"It's peaceful, isn't it? I missed Hawaii."

"There's a lot to miss." They hadn't talked about the future, not really, and he didn't know what she wanted. Oh, he was pretty sure she wanted him, but what if she wanted to live here more?

Then he'd come with her. Leave HOT when his enlistment was up and become a beach bum. It could work.

She laughed softly and he turned to look down at her. "What's so funny?"

"You. You're thinking about what you're going to do if I want to live in Hawaii."

He blinked. "How did you know that?"

"Because I know you. Because I love you."

He set the coffee down and wrapped his arms around her. "Yeah, you do, don't you?"

She knew him better than anyone. He'd always been

so alone, since he was sixteen and lost his family, and he'd closed in on himself in many ways. He'd never thought anyone would know him, really know him, the way a family was supposed to.

He loved that someone did. That Lucky did. He squeezed her. She squeezed back. He put his cheek on the top of her head and just stood there, watching the waves.

He was happy. And sad too.

"I wish Marco was still alive. I don't know how that would affect us, but I still wish he were here."

"Me too." She sighed. "Marco and I would have always been friends. I'm positive of that, because there was no animosity between us. I think he was just ready to move on, you know?"

"Maybe he was," Kev said. They'd never know, of course, but he no longer felt guilty about loving Lucky. He'd stayed away when she was Marco's wife. He had never done anything inappropriate, and he never would have. But after they'd divorced, who knows what would have happened? Maybe he'd have gotten the courage to ask Marco if he minded.

She pushed back a little bit until she could see his face. Her eyes were dark and filled with emotion, and it made his heart twist. He was growing used to that feeling, even if it still scared him sometimes. To need someone so much... God.

"I've been thinking about something, and I want to know what you think."

Her fingers smoothed over his skin, setting up an ache deep down.

"Keep doing that and you'll know what I think in about three seconds."

She smirked. "Always thinking with your dick. I like that about you."

"Hell, yes, you do. Especially when I use it for such naughty things…"

"Hold off on the naughty train for a few minutes, okay?" She sucked in a breath and fixed him with a steady look. "I want to come back. To HOT. I want to be a part of the organization, and I want to get the bad guys."

His mouth went dry. For a variety of reasons, not all of them positive. On the one hand, she'd be with him a lot. On the other, it was dangerous. Could he handle knowing she was in danger?

"You aren't saying anything," she said, frowning.

"I'm shocked. And, yeah, worried."

"Mendez isn't going to throw me into operations like the one we just went on. But I have a skill that's pretty useful to you guys and I want to use it."

"Honey, I hate to break it to you, but any one of us can twist the balls off some guy."

She sputtered. And laughed. Then she smacked him. "You son of a bitch, I'm talking about my language skills!"

He grinned. Damn she was tough. And his. So very his. "All right, so you can talk pretty in another language. I guess that's useful."

She said something in that language that he was kind of sure was a curse. It was, however, pretty.

"I can think of some other things you can do with that tongue if you're running out of ideas," he told her.

She arched an eyebrow. "Who said I was running out of ideas?"

"No one. But a man has to try."

"Oh, baby, I'm happy to use my tongue on you in just a few minutes. But first I want to know what you think. What you *really* think."

She was looking at him with a mixture of hopefulness and wariness. And he knew then that all he wanted was for her to be happy. If being a part of HOT did it for her, then he'd have to deal with it. Because she was strong and beautiful and perfectly capable of taking care of herself.

"I think so long as you keep going to bed with me each night and waking up with me each morning that I'll follow you wherever the hell you want to go. Come back to duty and join HOT. I'll be right beside you. Or stay here and surf all day, and I'll still be beside you." He frowned then, remembering how she looked on the surfboard when she was shooting back to the beach. He wasn't stupid enough to think it was an easy thing to do. "On the other hand, I'll wait on the beach for you. But whatever you decide, I'm there."

Her eyes got glassy. "That's pretty much the sweetest thing you could have said."

"That's me, babe. Sweet."

She laughed even as a tear spilled down her cheek. "Never stop making me laugh, okay?"

"Deal." He reached down and swept his arm behind her knees, pulling her up and into his arms.

She gasped. "What are you doing? You have to be careful with the wound on your side."

He silenced her with a kiss as he carried her into the bedroom. Then he laid her on the bed and tugged the shirt up and over her head, baring her naked skin for his pleasure. The thin line on her neck was healing fine, but it was the angry red scar of her gunshot wound that made him want to kill Al Ahmad all over again. Yeah, he'd stopped because she'd asked him too—and she was right, because if he'd killed the target, he'd be spending his time in a military prison instead of with her.

But damn if he didn't wish he'd blown the fucker's brains out.

Kev closed his lips over one tight nipple and sucked. Her fingers threaded into his hair as her back arched.

"You still want to know what I'm doing?" he asked a few moments later.

"Stop talking," she said on a moan.

He chuckled softly as he moved down her body. And then he spread her open and licked into the heart of her while her moans grew louder. When she came, he made it last, loving the way her body shuddered and clenched.

Then he moved up her body and slid home, right where he wanted to be. He groaned with the rightness of it. Instead of moving, he just held himself there, feeling her surrounding him. It was the sweetest kind of torture.

Her eyes opened, tangling with his. "Kev?"

"I kind of liked it when you were Mrs. MacDonald," he said.

She blinked. "Is that a marriage proposal?"

He flexed his hips and she sucked in a breath. "Yeah, I think it is."

"Oh," she said as he rocked into her again. Her legs came up and gripped his waist. "Ask me again. And again. And again…"

He withdrew and then surged forward. "Marry me, Lucky." He began to move, harder now, deeper and more sure, driving her toward the peak. "Marry me, marry me…"

"Oh, yes, Kev, yes..." She closed her eyes and arched her back. "Yes, definitely, I will... I will... I will..."

Her climax was exquisite. She gripped him hard, her body clenching around his, pulling him toward his own peak. He drove her up the bed, pushing them both as far as he could—and then the tension snapped and he came, pouring himself into her with a rough cry.

When it was over, they lay tangled together on top of the sheets. A soft, plumeria-scented breeze filtered into the room and blew across their bodies.

"I love you," he said softly, feeling happy and content and shaken to his core all at once.

She lifted her head from his chest and kissed him. "I know."

He pushed her tangled hair over her shoulder. "I was worried about saving you, but it turns out I was the one who needed saving."

"I think we both did."

"Now you're stuck with me. You agreed to marry me, and I'm not letting you back out, even if I did ask while using sexual satisfaction as leverage."

"Evil man." She pulled him over until he was settled in the cradle of her hips again. Her eyes sparkled as she gazed up at him. "I can't think of anywhere else I'd rather be than stuck with you. Stuck to you, stuck under you, over you..."

He was already growing hard again. "I like the way you think..."

ACKNOWLEDGMENTS

MANY THANKS TO MY AWESOME former-military husband for all his contributions to this series! I do take liberties. I'll just admit that to y'all up front. It's not because Mr. Harris doesn't know his stuff. It's because I make decisions based on story considerations and how I think it will be the most exciting for your enjoyment. A real military Special Operations team would probably have a bit less freedom than the HOT guys have. But what fun would that be, right?

I also want to thank Gretchen Stull for the time she took to beta-read for me. Her suggestions were invaluable! This book wouldn't be as good as it is without her and Mr. Harris.

Or without Alicia Hunter Pace, aka Jean Hovey and Stephanie Jones, who were there to brainstorm with me last year when I talked about finishing this story. It started as a chapter back in 2007 at my first-ever Romance Writers of America conference. It was Friday night, I was still unpublished, and my roommates were at the Harlequin party. But inspiration struck, and I wrote the first thirty pages or so that evening. Then I tucked it away and wrote twenty books for Harlequin.

Thanks as always to Anne Victory and her amazing team at Victory Editing. She is the Comma Queen, y'all. If there are any out of place, it's most likely because I failed to make a correction she pointed out.

Finally, thanks so much to YOU, the readers who are embracing HOT. I'll keep writing them if you keep reading them. Deal? ;)

ABOUT THE AUTHOR

USA Today bestselling author Lynn Raye Harris lives in Alabama with her handsome former-military husband and two crazy cats. Lynn has written nearly twenty novels for Harlequin and been nominated for several awards, including the Romance Writers of America's Golden Heart award and the National Readers Choice award. Lynn loves hearing from her readers..

Connect with Lynn online:
Facebook: https://www.facebook.com/AuthorLynnRayeHarris
Twitter: https://twitter.com/LynnRayeHarris
Website: http://www.LynnRayeHarris.com
Newsletter: http://eepurl.com/c5QFY

3972374R00184

Printed in Germany
by Amazon Distribution
GmbH, Leipzig